Highlander Deceived

Stolen Highland
Hearts
Book One

Jayne Castel

WINTER MIST
PRESS

A lie this bold will not stay hidden. He thought he was marrying a chieftain's daughter—but his young wife isn't who she seems. Deception and passion collide in Medieval Scotland.

When Keira Gunn agrees to swap places with her best friend and wed a man in her stead, she knows life is about to get complicated.

She's also risking her own future.

But Keira never wanted to be a nun and longs for a life outside the nunnery where she's about to take her vows. Her friend is desperate—and this could be Keira's only chance to forge a new path for herself.

The Mackays of Farr have a new chieftain. Connor Mackay is a reluctant husband, yet he's been betrothed for years.

Now he needs to honor his promise.

The woman he collects from the nunnery is a surprise. She isn't the great beauty Connor expects, yet her quick wit and passionate nature soon enthrall him.

But his bride keeps a secret that risks more than both their hearts.

Historical Romances by Jayne Castel

DARK AGES BRITAIN

The Kingdom of the East Angles series
Night Shadows (prequel novella)
Dark Under the Cover of Night (Book One)
Nightfall till Daybreak (Book Two)
The Deepening Night (Book Three)
The Kingdom of the East Angles: The Complete Series

The Kingdom of Mercia series
The Breaking Dawn (Book One)
Darkest before Dawn (Book Two)
Dawn of Wolves (Book Three)
The Kingdom of Mercia: The Complete Series

The Kingdom of Northumbria series
The Whispering Wind (Book One)
Wind Song (Book Two)
Lord of the North Wind (Book Three)
The Kingdom of Northumbria: The Complete Series

DARK AGES SCOTLAND

The Warrior Brothers of Skye series
Blood Feud (Book One)
Barbarian Slave (Book Two)
Battle Eagle (Book Three)
The Warrior Brothers of Skye: The Complete Series

The Pict Wars series
Warrior's Heart (Book One)
Warrior's Secret (Book Two)
Warrior's Wrath (Book Three)
The Pict Wars: The Complete Series

Novellas
Winter's Promise

MEDIEVAL SCOTLAND

The Brides of Skye series
The Beast's Bride (Book One)
The Outlaw's Bride (Book Two)
The Rogue's Bride (Book Three)
The Brides of Skye: The Complete Series

The Sisters of Kilbride series
Unforgotten (Book One)
Awoken (Book Two)
Fallen (Book Three)
Claimed (Epilogue novella)

The Immortal Highland Centurions series
Maximus (Book One)
Cassian (Book Two)
Draco (Book Three)
The Laird's Return (Epilogue festive novella)

Stolen Highland Hearts series
Highlander Deceived (Book One)

Epic Fantasy Romances by Jayne Castel

Light and Darkness series
Ruled by Shadows (Book One)
The Lost Swallow (Book Two)
Path of the Dark (Book Three)
Light and Darkness: The Complete Series

Highlander Deceived, by Jayne Castel

Published by Winter Mist Press

ISBN: 978-0-473-58887-8 (hardback)

Edited by Tim Burton
Cover design by Winter Mist Press
Cover photography courtesy of www.shutterstock.com
Brooch image courtesy of www.pixabay.com

Visit Jayne's website: www.jaynecastel.com

***

For Tim—we make such a good team, my love.

***

No legacy is so rich as honesty.
—William Shakespeare

1

AN OUTRAGEOUS LIE

Iona Nunnery
The Isle of Iona, Scotland

Early autumn, 1426

RHIANNA WEPT AS though her heart were breaking. Head buried in her hands, her shoulders shaking from the force of her sobs, the young woman appeared oblivious to her surroundings. Similarly, the apple tree she huddled beneath, laden with rosy-cheeked fruit, paid no attention to her suffering.

Keira approached her friend slowly, a frown creasing her forehead. She'd never seen Rhianna like this before. The lass was usually such lively, bright company. Keira couldn't imagine what had reduced her to tears. Despite that the two of them had become close friends in the months since Keira had come to the nunnery, she felt as if she was intruding.

Keira's step faltered. Rhianna had clearly sought out solitude for a reason.

And yet the muffled sound of her crying, which filtered across the walled garden behind the low-slung complex of stone buildings, rent at Keira's breast like a dirk-blade.

"Rhianna." Keira stopped before the spreading apple tree. She carried a basket under one arm, as she had come into the garden this afternoon intending to pick fruit. "What is the matter?"

Rhianna's sobbing stilled, and she raised her flushed, tear-streaked face, her watery gaze fixing upon her friend. Then, to Keira's surprise, she gasped, "My life is over!"

Keira's pulse quickened in alarm, and she hunkered down before her friend so that their gazes were level. Like her, Rhianna wore a black habit, girded around the waist with a narrow plaited-leather belt. However, despite the drab attire, the young woman's beauty shone like the afternoon sun above them. She had fine, aristocratic features and sea-blue eyes. Unlike the nuns here, Rhianna didn't wear a wimple. Instead, her thick mane of golden-brown hair was tamed into a long braid down her back. Even bereft, her face mottled from crying, she was still lovely. Keira knew *she* didn't look like that after she'd been weeping. Her eyes usually became puffy and raw, and her nose ran.

She'd wept much since coming to live at Iona nunnery, had soaked her pillow through many a night. Only her friendship with Rhianna had eased her sadness. As such, it pained Keira to see her best and only friend so upset.

"Whatever do ye mean?" she pressed. "Has something happened?"

Rhianna's throat bobbed. "I've just come from seeing Mother Jean," she replied, her voice raspy. "The day has come … my betrothed is traveling here to collect me … I will be wed."

Keira stilled. She and Rhianna had spoken little about the future over the past months. Of course, Keira knew that her friend wasn't a novice like her, a young woman destined for a future as a nun. Instead, Rhianna Ross was an oblate, given to the nunnery by her family to watch over her and ensure her chastity until her wedding day.

"I thought yer betrothed wasn't ready to be wed?" Keira asked weakly, disappointment a stone in her belly. Rhianna was the only good thing about this place, and now she was going to be taken from her.

More tears spilled down Rhianna's cheeks, but she knuckled them away. "My uncle has just sent me a missive. Apparently, there was a great battle between the Gunns and the Mackays over the summer ... a terrible slaughter on both sides." Keira inhaled sharply at this. *She* was a Gunn and knew nothing of this battle. However, oblivious to her reaction, Rhianna continued, "The Mackays of Farr lost their chieftain ... which means my *betrothed* is now laird. He's expected to take a wife."

It was hard to miss the bitter inflection on the word 'betrothed'.

Keira had always been bemused at the rancor Rhianna bore a man she'd never met. It had always been *her* dream to marry—a dream her parents had denied her. She would have given anything to be in Rhianna's place right now.

If only *her* betrothed was traveling to this isle to sweep her away from this life.

Swallowing down her own sadness that soon they'd be parted, and her bitterness that she wasn't in her friend's place, Keira reached out and took Rhianna's hand, squeezing gently. "Ye knew this day would come," she murmured, forcing what she hoped was an encouraging smile. "A new life at Farr Castle in the north will be far better than being stuck here. What do ye know of yer husband-to-be?"

Rhianna's beautiful features tightened, and she slowly withdrew her hand from Keira's. "Connor Mackay is reputed to be brave and handsome ... but it's not *him* I want."

Keira leaned back from the vehemence on her friend's face.

Seeing her confusion, Rhianna made a soft choking sound, her blue eyes filling with fresh tears. "My uncle had a specific reason for putting me in here," she said finally, her gaze spearing Keira's. "I'd grown close to one of his warriors ... a man named Callum. Fearing that I'd run away with him and not honor my betrothal to Connor Mackay, uncle sent me here."

Keira gave a soft gasp. "Why haven't ye told me this before?" Hurt twisted under her breastbone. She thought they told each other everything. Hadn't *she* done so? Rhianna knew everything about Keira's past, of how she was the youngest of six daughters—the plain one with no dowry. All Keira had ever wanted since entering womanhood was to find a kind-hearted husband to settle down and have a family with. But her parents had denied her that. Her father, Maddoc Gunn, was a wealthy sheep farmer and wool merchant, yet marrying off his first five daughters had emptied his coffers—or so he said.

There's nothing left for ye, Keira, he'd once sneered. *Not that any man would want ye.*

Rhianna looked away, her slender shoulders trembling as the grief that had consumed her threatened to resurge. "It was too painful," she whispered.

Her voice was so broken that Keira reached once more for her hand and squeezed tightly. "I'm so sorry," she said. And she was. The pain on her friend's face was difficult to look upon. "But perhaps this is for the best ... ye and Callum are separated now, and yer husband-to-be will arrive soon to collect ye."

Rhianna's gaze snapped up, her blue eyes filled with desperation. "Callum is *here,* Keira. He is hiding in a cove just south of the nunnery ... and I have been to see him."

Keira's jaw dropped at this revelation. She actually rocked back on her heels and gaped at her friend. Suddenly, she felt as if she didn't know Rhianna Ross at all.

"He wants me to go away with him," Rhianna continued, her voice low and fierce as teardrops sparkled off her long eyelashes. "But I am afraid to. My uncle's wrath will be terrible."

"Oh, Rhianna," Keira whispered, pity crushing her ribcage. "How tragic for ye both ... I so wish I could help ye."

The two women stared at each other, the moment drawing out. Warm sunlight bathed them, dappling through the sheltering boughs of the apple tree, while beyond, the rumble of the surf against Iona's rocky shoreline intruded.

And as their stare drew out, Rhianna's face altered slightly. The desperation faded, and in its place, Keira caught a gleam in her wide eyes. "Perhaps ye can," she murmured.

Keira inclined her head, confused by the comment. "Excuse me?"

Rhianna's fingers clenched around hers. "I know how unhappy ye are here, Keira. No one will ever rescue ye from this nunnery. Ye will be doomed to spend the rest of yer life here."

Rhianna's words were a punch to the belly; Keira knew that was to be her fate, and yet the words spoken aloud like this were cruel indeed. She hated a nun's life—the austerity of it, the endless prayers. She felt as if she were slowly being buried alive here. And Rhianna knew it.

"But we could change all that," Rhianna continued, leaning toward her. "Ye and I could swap places when Connor Mackay arrives to collect me … and then we could both go our separate ways … we could both have the lives we've dreamed of."

Keira knew she was now gaping at her friend like a dead carp, yet she couldn't help herself. Were her ears deceiving her, or was Rhianna suggesting they weave an outrageous lie?

"We can't do that," she finally gasped. "It's wrong … and far too risky. Connor Mackay will know he's been tricked."

Rhianna shook her head, vehement. "No, he won't … he's never seen me."

"But he would have heard ye are a great beauty … and I am not!"

Rhianna snorted and released Keira's hand, batting the comment away. "Ye speak as if ye are foul to look upon."

"Maybe not, but I am no beauty."

Rhianna shook her head, negating her words. "Ye have yer own charms, Keira ... and many men would find yer looks appealing."

Keira shifted back from her friend and rose to her feet. "None till now have," she pointed out, coldness seeping into her voice. She didn't appreciate being flattered. Rhianna was desperate; she'd say anything to get her to agree to this folly.

"That's because men are fools," Rhianna countered. She scrambled to her feet, dusting off her skirts. "Listen to me. This is yer chance to have the life ye have always hoped for. Ye could be a laird's wife. Ye could have a family of yer own."

"And all the while, I'd be pretending to be someone I'm not," Keira shot back. "I'd be living a lie."

"Would ye prefer that ... or to live here, cloistered for the rest of yer life," Rhianna hit back, gesturing to the surrounding walls. "Think hard before ye say 'no' ... for an opportunity like this will never come yer way again."

Momentarily rendered speechless, Keira stared back at her friend. They were both tall women and now stood eye-to-eye. Keira should have been collecting apples, but suddenly the chore was the furthest thing from her mind. Instead, Rhianna's cutting words rang through her head.

An opportunity like this will never come yer way again.

"If ye won't do it for yerself, then do it for me," Rhianna finally broke the silence between them. Her voice had lost its force now; instead, there was a brittleness to the tone. Desperation flickered to life in her sea-blue eyes once more. "Ye said ye wished to help me ... and this is the only way."

Keira swallowed hard. Her mouth had gone dry, and her heart was racing. She couldn't believe Rhianna was stooping to outright manipulation now. And yet, the fear she saw in her friend's eyes was real.

This wasn't just Keira's last chance. It was Rhianna's too.

Connor Mackay was on his way here, and once he took Rhianna away, the opportunity would be gone.

Keira wet her lips. "But my parents," she began weakly, "the prioress will send word to them ... will tell them I've run off."

Rhianna favored her with a sharp smile. "Aye, but they'll never suspect that ye have taken my place. The Gunns and the Mackays have nothing to do with each other these days ... except for when they're sinking their dirks into each other's bellies."

"And what about the Ross clan?" Keira couldn't believe she was even discussing this. It was utter madness. And yet, she couldn't help herself. "Surely, some of them will attend the wedding ... or pay ye a visit?"

Rhianna shook her head, folding her arms over her chest. "My parents are dead, and my uncle has only ever seen me and my elder sister as things to be bartered and traded. He won't attend the wedding ... and nor will he make the trip to Farr Castle."

"But ye can't be sure of that," Keira replied, shaking her head. Her heart was beating so hard now, she was starting to feel a bit light-headed and queasy. "If he ever—"

"I told ye he won't," Rhianna cut her off, taking a step closer. "That's the thing ye and I have always had in common. Our families don't want us ... that's why they locked us away in this place. Out of sight, out of mind. None of them care what happens to us ... and that's why it's up to us to fight for our own future ... our own happiness."

A bell started to toll then, intruding upon their exchange. Vespers. Heaviness descended upon Keira. From Lauds before dawn, till Compline after supper—the bell dominated her life. And so it would remain.

Unless she agreed to this mad plan.

"It will never work," she said finally, as the bell continued to toll. They would have to go now, or Mother Jean would reprimand them both for tardiness ... again. And yet, Keira's feet felt rooted to the spot.

Sensing her indecision, her conflict, Rhianna favored her friend with a slow smile. "Aye, it will ... if we do it right."

2

HE'S WAITING FOR YE

IT WAS AS good a day as any to meet the woman he was
going to wed.

Connor Mackay stood before his tent, stretching out
his long limbs and back, as he raised his face to the
sunrise. A pink blush stained the pale sky to the east, and
a salty breeze feathered through his hair.

Nonetheless, the pretty dawn did little to ease the
nerves in his belly. His neck and shoulders were as hard
as planks of wood, and his mood was shadowed this
morning, as it had been for weeks now. He'd had to force
himself to make this trip.

"Ready to collect yer betrothed, Connor?" Kennan
Mackay approached him, cup of steaming broth in hand.
Behind his cousin, a fire smoldered upon the wide strand
where they'd camped overnight, while their birlinn
bobbed with the tide, moored to the narrow jetty. They'd
arrived at dusk the evening before, and rather than go up
to the nunnery and meet his betrothed then, Connor had
put the meeting off—making the excuse that such a late
arrival would be rude.

He would do it at daybreak instead.

Connor pulled a face. Dawn had come too swiftly.
"Aye." He took the cup from his cousin, ignoring
Kennan's grin. It was fine for him: Kennan was happily
wed to Cait, the spirited blacksmith's daughter at Farr
Castle. Not only that, he'd actually chosen his wife.
Instead, Connor had been pledged to Rhianna Ross
when he was eight years old and had never even met the
woman.

"Och, stop looking like ye are going to the gallows, man," Kennan admonished him. He then flashed Connor a grin. "Word has it that Rhianna Ross is a rare beauty ... the 'Jewel of the Highlands'."

This comment brought a snort from Domhnall Mackay. Connor's uncle drew near, his boots crunching on pebbles. "Aye, a bonny face is always appreciated," he rumbled.

Connor's mouth twisted. A beautiful woman wasn't that hard to find. The Highlands were full of comely lasses. His uncle and cousin were ignoring the other rumors—the ones whispering that his bride-to-be had a rather inflated opinion of herself.

It didn't matter though if his wife was bonny or haughty; after the turmoil of the past year, wooing and marriage were the last things on his mind. Irritation simmered in his gut at how little control he had over his fate.

But at twenty-six winters, the time had come for Connor to wed.

Raising the cup of steaming broth to his lips, Connor took a sip. It was made with the bones of the fish they'd caught and eaten for supper the night before.

"Here." Kennan handed him a wedge of oaten bannock. "It's a bit stale, but good if ye soak it in the broth a little."

Connor nodded and did as bid, even if his appetite was off this morning.

Funny thing really. He'd faced down claidheamh-mòr-wielding warriors in battle but was skittish about meeting his future bride.

Pull yerself together, Mackay.

If Morgan were here right now, he'd be ribbing him mercilessly. Just as well then that he'd left his brother in charge back at Farr Castle.

Connor lacked a sense of humor this morning.

Thinking of his home, far to the north, made a heavy mantle settle upon him. It reminded him of all he'd lost of late. Their beloved mother had sickened and died the year before, and then that summer, he'd witnessed his father, Rory Mackay, cut down in battle. Now, just over two months later, Connor was the new chieftain of the Mackays of Farr—a position that he'd once thought was still many years away.

His gaze shifted then, to the grey stone walls behind him. The Augustinian nunnery sat a few furlongs south of Iona Abbey, where an order of monks resided. At the heart of the nunnery, the slate tiles upon the steep roof of the kirk gleamed in the morning sun.

Feeling someone's gaze upon him, Connor looked away from the complex to meet his uncle's eye. Domhnall was starting to look old these days, his dark-blond hair and beard now threaded with grey. However, it was his expression more than anything that aged him; his mouth was downturned, a frown permanently etched into his forehead.

Connor stiffened. He didn't altogether trust his uncle. These days, Domhnall was a bitter husk of the man he'd once been. Losing his beloved wife and their bairn during childbirth many years earlier had changed him. He'd never remarried. Instead, he devoted all his energy to protecting his clan and fighting their enemies.

His own brow furrowing, Connor glanced away. He sometimes wondered if his uncle resented him—for if Rory Mackay hadn't had any sons, Domhnall would now be laird of Farr Castle.

Connor took another gulp of broth, wincing as the hot liquid scalded his tongue.

His uncle's dour presence was an unwelcome distraction. At present, Connor needed to focus on what had to be done. Nonetheless, heaviness dogged his steps. Grief and self-doubt continued to haunt him.

Handing the cup and half-eaten wedge of bannock back to his cousin, he squared his shoulders. "Right then, let's get this over with."

"Rhianna is a willful lass," the prioress sniffed as she eyed the man standing before her, "but no doubt a husband will settle her down."

Meeting the woman's eye, Connor bit back a smile. Mother Jean made his betrothed sound like a temperamental filly. They stood in the prioress's hall, a sparsely-furnished space warmed by a tiny hearth. The prioress was a small, birdlike woman. Her face, surrounded by a white wimple and black veil, was gaunt, her grey eyes sharp.

Her disapproval of the oblate she'd taken in nearly three years earlier was clear.

"I appreciate ye sheltering my betrothed for so long," Connor replied after a pause.

The prioress continued to run an assessing gaze over him, before her mouth thinned. "I was wondering when ye would finally come for her. This union is well overdue."

Connor favored her with a cool smile, although irritation feathered through him. He didn't appreciate the tone the prioress was using. This woman needed to mind her own business.

"Ready Rhianna to leave immediately," he ordered, not bothering to respond to her comment. "I'd like to be away with the morning tide."

Mother Jean gave a brisk nod. "I will call her to me now. It will take little time for her to ready herself."

"Good. I will wait by the gates then."

The prioress nodded.

Giving a bow, Connor turned on his heel and left the prioress's hall. Stepping back into the autumnal sunlight, he walked across the wide yard toward the oaken gates. His exchange with the prioress had been brief and brusque, but the woman had vexed him. Who was she to question his decisions?

Even so, she'd gotten under his skin. The prioress had highlighted the fact that he'd been shirking his responsibilities.

Connor dragged a hand over his face. He suddenly felt bone-weary, old beyond his years.

Honoring his betrothal wasn't going to bring his father back. *If only it could.*

Heaving in a deep breath, Connor cast his gaze around him. The nunnery was a peaceful spot, a sanctuary from the outside world. A grey-stone kirk sat in the center of it with three wings—to the south, east, and west—stretching out around it. From where he stood, he could see the entrance to a large garden and the tops of apple and pear trees. However, this place set Connor's nerves on edge, and when he saw a flock of black-robbed figures enter the yard, gliding in pairs like swans across a loch, he shifted uneasily.

I'm intruding here.

The nuns glanced his way as they passed, many of their faces alive with curiosity.

Connor shifted his gaze from them.

He hoped the prioress would hurry Rhianna up. It was a three-day journey by birlinn back to Mackay lands, and he was suddenly anxious to make a start on it.

Keira stood before her sleeping pallet and gazed down at the dark cloak spread out upon it. It was a nun's winter cloak; the garment she would soon swap for Rhianna's blue mantle. Her friend had gone to bid the prioress farewell. After that, the pair would change places, and Keira would go to meet her husband-to-be, while Rhianna made for the nunnery's southern gate and freedom.

Swallowing hard, in an effort to ease the tightness in her throat, Keira picked up the cloak and slung it about her shoulders. Rhianna made this whole enterprise sound so easy—and yet it wasn't easy at all.

Two days earlier, when she'd agreed to take Rhianna's place. Her friend had been overjoyed. Rhianna had wept with relief and hadn't cared when the prioress punished both of them with extra chores for being late for Vespers.

In the days since, Rhianna had barely been able to contain her excitement. The nuns all thought she was merely happy to become a wife, but Keira knew differently. And unlike her friend, Keira felt steadily worse as the dawn of her departure neared.

Fastening the cloak around her throat and pulling up her hood, Keira swallowed once more. This time, it was to ease the nausea that pitched within her.

This is a terrible idea.

And yet she'd gone along with it. At any time in the past days, she could have changed her mind, could have gone to Rhianna and told her that she wouldn't go in her stead. But she hadn't—and now the time to swap places had come.

Slipping out of the dormitory, which was deserted at this hour of the morning, Keira made her way toward the gates. She kept close to the stone walls of the building, hugging the shadows. She was supposed to be working in the gardens, and shortly she would likely be missed. But hopefully, Rhianna would not spend long with the prioress. They'd agreed on a meeting point in a secluded spot next to the kirk, where they could trade places without anyone noticing.

Even so, nerves danced in Keira's belly, making the queasiness there worsen. It was a cool morning, but she found herself sweating heavily under her robes.

Keira halted under the lee of the kirk, partially hidden from view by a huge rosemary bush, and waited.

Lord forgive me for what I'm about to do.

Keira hadn't taken to religious life; she wasn't of a pious bent. But right now, guilt dug in its claws, making her breathing quicken and her limbs tremble. This deception was a sin. Surely, she'd burn in the pits of hell if she went through with it?

The way she felt right now, it would take little for her to give up on this whole escapade. She could turn and sneak away, hide in the infirmary until the Mackay chieftain left. Or she could go to the prioress, while Rhianna was bidding her farewell, and expose the whole ruse.

But her feet felt as if they were weighed down with rocks.

And moments later, when she heard the scuff of sandaled feet on the path that ran around the edge of the kirk, she knew it was too late.

Rhianna had come to find her.

A figure swathed in a blue cloak appeared, squeezing into the gap between the rosemary bush and the wall.

Pushing back her cowl, Rhianna's gaze speared Keira's. Her blue eyes were alive with excitement, her cheeks flushed. Wordlessly, the two women slipped off their cloaks and exchanged them. Underneath, they both wore their usual black habits.

"He's waiting for ye by the gates," Rhianna whispered, fastening Keira's cloak about her neck and stepping closer still. "Go to him."

Keira stared back at her friend, a lump rising in her throat. "This isn't going to work, Rhianna," she whispered back, her voice hoarse with nerves. "He'll know he's been tricked. We don't look alike at all."

Rhianna waved her objections away with a slender hand. "Nonsense … we're both tall, brown-haired, and blue-eyed. Most men don't have the wits to notice much else."

Aye, but ye are as slender as a reed and beautiful enough to lure ships onto the rocks.

The words bubbled up within Keira, yet she choked them back. Unlike her friend, she was strongly built with broad hips and heavy breasts, and a face that one of her pretty elder sisters had once described as 'horsey'.

The Mackay chieftain would know he'd been tricked the instant he looked upon her.

Sensing her turmoil, Rhianna stepped closer before reaching out and taking Keira's hands. "Men love women with flesh on their bones," she insisted.

Keira winced. Rhianna was only trying to help, but she was making her feel worse. Now she felt like a fattened sow about to be carted off to market.

I can't do this.

Rhianna's blue eyes filled with tears then, and she hauled Keira into her arms for a brief, hard hug. "I will never forget this, Keira," she whispered, her voice choked. "Never. Ye are a true friend indeed."

And that was it. Keira's urge to call this entire farce off crumbled. She couldn't let Rhianna down. Her man was waiting for her in a cove south of the nunnery; this was their only chance to escape together.

Keira wouldn't be the one to ruin it.

"Remember, ye aren't just doing this for me." Rhianna drew back, her gaze snaring Keira's once more. She then pressed a small leather pack, which held Rhianna's possessions, into her hands. "This is yer only chance to be free of this place. Soon ye will be a laird's wife ... and Keira Gunn will be but a memory."

3

IN DEEP TROUBLE

HOOD PULLED UP to obscure her face, head bent low, Keira emerged from the shadow of the kirk and rounded the east wing, which housed the dormitory. Then, increasing her speed, she stepped out into the open.

Glancing up briefly, she spied a tall, broad-shouldered figure standing before the gates. Golden hair glinted in the morning light.

Keira's belly flip-flopped. *Mother Mary, he's actually real.*

Till now, there had been a dreamlike quality about this whole undertaking. But now a man in flesh and blood stood just a few yards away.

And as she crossed the yard toward her future husband, Keira felt his gaze tracking her.

The closer she got, the worse Keira started to feel. Suddenly, she was wading through thick porridge, and her ears started to ring.

Lord, no ... I can't faint.

Keira clenched her jaw and drew in a deep, shuddering breath, as she realized she'd been so nervous she'd forgotten to breathe.

This wouldn't do at all.

She couldn't let Rhianna down—or herself for that matter.

She decided to chance another glance at her 'betrothed' then. She wouldn't be able to look at him when they stood face-to-face, not yet anyway. But curiosity got the better of her.

Her gaze shifted up and focused on the man awaiting her, and when it did, her step faltered.

God's bones ... he's beautiful.

'Beautiful' wasn't a word one used to describe men, but it was her first reaction to him.

Clad in leather with a fur mantle about his shoulders, his long blond hair stirring in the breeze, the Mackay chieftain was a sight to behold.

He looked like a Viking warrior, sent to plunder the Scottish coast; indeed, Keira would wager this man's ancestors were the Norsemen who'd made this land their home.

Even at this distance, she could see that he had penetrating dark-green eyes—the color of a pine thicket—a strong jaw, chiseled features, and a sensual mouth that made her already pitching belly do a full somersault.

The Lord preserve her—she was in deep trouble. This godlike creature was expecting a beauty to match his own.

He was about to be bitterly disappointed.

Heart hammering, Keira dropped her gaze. Moments later, she drew up before him and found herself staring down at his dusty boots.

"Lady Ross?" A deep male voice inquired.

"Aye," she murmured, her heart fluttering like the wings of a trapped bird.

"Is that bag yer only belongings?"

"Aye." Keira swallowed, forcing herself on. However, her voice sounded strangled. "I did not come here with much."

"Very well." There was a note of impatience in his voice. "My men have readied the birlinn. We shall leave now. Follow me."

Still staring at the ground, Keira nodded.

Meekly, she followed him, glancing up at his broad back as they passed through the gates and onto the narrow, pebbled path that led down to the shore.

As he'd told her, a boat sat moored against the narrow wooden jetty. She could see a few men moving about, readying the craft for departure.

Bile surged up Keira's throat then, even as she followed her betrothed down to the waiting birlinn. She'd done it, she'd swapped places with her friend and was now pretending to be someone she wasn't. Only, Keira wasn't feeling any victory right now.

Instead, she knew she was in deep trouble.

Rhianna Ross crept around the edge of the walled vegetable garden and entered the orchard. Pausing for a heartbeat, she listened to the soft sounds of the nuns' conversation on the other side of the wall as they worked.

Fortunately, a six-foot wall separated the vegetable garden and the orchard. Nonetheless, Rhianna was being cautious. She'd pulled up the hood of Keira's cloak, and carried a basket. If anyone saw her, Rhianna would pretend she'd come into the orchard to pick some apples. However, the other nuns would likely already be wondering why Keira hadn't joined them in the vegetable beds, and would soon start searching for her.

It was a flimsy disguise, and one that wouldn't bear up under scrutiny—which was why she needed to slip away now.

Rhianna firmed her jaw, gaze scanning left and right, while her right hand palmed a short knife she'd stolen from the kitchens the day before.

No one would prevent her from leaving today. No one.

She'd feared that Keira was going to let her down earlier. Her friend, usually so stoic and calm, had been trembling like a frightened doe, and Rhianna had seen the trepidation in her eyes. She'd been about to back out of their agreement, but Rhianna had stopped her.

Once again, she'd used their friendship to bend Keira to her will.

Guilt wreathed up through Rhianna then, clutching at her chest, although she shoved the sensation aside. She knew she'd taken advantage of her friend's good nature, but it had been necessary.

All her life, others had walked over her to get what they wanted. Now, it was Rhianna's turn to be selfish.

I'm doing Keira a favor, she assured herself as she approached the small gate on the southern wall encircling the nunnery. *She'll thank me one day.*

But would she?

Rhianna hadn't been entirely honest with her.

It was true that Rhianna's uncle wasn't likely to attend the wedding—but he *would* make a trip from his holding, Caisteal Nan Corr, to Farr Castle, to see his niece had settled in. And it would likely be soon.

It'll be long enough for Keira to be wedded and bedded, Rhianna assured herself. *And it'll be long enough for Callum and me to get away.*

She reached the gate, lifted the iron bar, and carefully pulled the heavy oaken door toward her. It creaked, and Rhianna whispered a curse. She had sneaked up here the day before and spread pork dripping all over the hinges to prevent this; nonetheless, this door wasn't used often and the hinges had rusted up.

Opening the gate wide enough to squeeze through, Rhianna pushed her way out. Then, gathering her cloak close about her, she took off at a run up the hill behind the nunnery.

Callum would be waiting. She had to reach him.

As she ran, Rhianna chanced a glance east, to where two figures walked along the wooden jetty to the birlinn moored there.

Keira and her husband-to-be.

No, she hadn't been honest with her friend at all. Instead, in pushing Keira out the door, she'd lit a tall candle—and was now slowly letting it burn. Sooner or later though, it would burn down to the quick, and when it did, Keira Gunn would be exposed as an imposter.

Tearing her gaze from the shore, Rhianna lengthened her stride. She flew over the crest of the hill, and out of sight of the nunnery now, she let her hood blow back.

She was sorry about Keira, but in desperate times like these, she'd do all she could to free herself of a betrothal she'd never wanted. There was only one man she desired, that she needed like air. And she wouldn't be kept from him.

Rhianna's breathing was coming in ragged gasps, and a stitch stabbed her side, as she finally reached the sheltered cove south of the nunnery. Relief slammed into her when she saw the small rowboat pulled up onto the rocks and the figure seated beside it.

"Callum!"

Her beloved leaped to his feet in an instant, swiveling to her.

"It's done!" she cried, rushing to him. "I'm free!"

Callum's rugged face split into a wide grin. "Canny lass!" He swept her up into his arms and spun her around. "I knew ye'd manage it." He kissed her then, his mouth slanting hard across hers. However, when he drew back, his expression grew serious. "Come, mo ghràdh ... we must get away from this rock before anyone notices yer friend missing."

Connor wasn't sure what to make of the woman he'd just collected from the nunnery.

For one thing, he hadn't even had a proper look at her face.

She sat now, perched like a condemned woman awaiting a trip to the chopping block, at the stern of the boat. His men were rowing the birlinn out into open water. Once they did, they would raise the sail and strike out north.

He could see that she was tall, something he'd expected, for he'd heard she was statuesque, but his betrothed seemed intent on shrouding her face from him.

The boat inched away from the shore, sunlight sparkling across the water. Spindrift coated Connor's skin, and a brisk breeze blew in from the south, catching his hair as he tied it back at his nape with a leather thong. Autumn was indeed upon them now, and it was likely they wouldn't get many more warm days like this.

A few yards away, Kennan was untying the craft's single sail, while Domhnall shouted instructions to the rowers. Kennan caught Connor's eye then and jerked his chin toward the silent, cloaked figure behind them. The message was clear: *Talk to her.*

Connor clenched his jaw. He really didn't want to.

Kennan inclined his head, his auburn brows rising in challenge.

Damn his cousin. He thought Connor was scared of her.

Casting Kennan a dark look, Connor moved to the stern and took a seat next to his silent bride-to-be.

"I think it's time we introduced ourselves to each other, lass," he said gruffly.

She gave a soft, nervous laugh that was barely audible against the splashing of the oars. "I thought we already did that, back at the gates?"

"Hardly," Connor replied with a snort. "Ye haven't even looked at me for one thing ... would ye mind pushing back yer hood?"

She hesitated, before a pale hand lifted to the deep cowl shadowing her face. Connor saw the faint tremble in her hand. She was clearly nervous, even more than he was about all of this. He felt a pang of sympathy for the lass then; it wasn't easy being a chieftain's son or daughter. Unlike lower-born folk, neither of them got a choice in whom they wed.

A moment later, she pushed back the hood, revealing her face at last.

Connor met her gaze, his breathing slowing.

Rhianna Ross wasn't what he expected. Not at all.

He'd heard she was a tall, willowy beauty with sea-blue eyes and lustrous golden-brown hair. And indeed, the woman before him had dark-blue eyes, milky skin, and oak-brown hair coiled around her crown in a severe braid. Yet her face was too long to be called classically beautiful. She had a sharp nose and a mouth that, although full and sensual, was slightly crooked.

She possessed high cheekbones, and her eyes were full of vulnerability and intelligence.

It was a face that caught his attention.

A slow smile curved Connor's mouth in response, a little of the tension he'd been carrying ever since setting off for Iona to collect his betrothed unknotting. "Pleased to meet ye, Lady Ross," he murmured.

4

OLD HABITS

THE MAN HAD a voice that made her pulse quicken: honey and gravel blended together.

And that smile. Her belly tightened involuntarily at how it slowly transformed his face from handsome to breathtaking.

It was a masculine expression, a sensual one.

An expression that took Keira by surprise.

She'd seen the surprise in his eyes when she'd drawn back her hood. She'd then braced herself for the disappointment, the anger that would surely follow.

But instead, Connor Mackay had gone still, his gaze roaming over her face, drinking her in.

And then he'd smiled, and she was undone.

"Pleased to meet ye too, Laird," Keira murmured, clearing her throat as her voice caught. "This day has been a long time coming."

Those sensual lips curved further. "Aye ... I've made ye wait longer than ye probably wanted."

"I was beginning to think ye'd forgotten me," Keira replied. It shocked her how easily she now transitioned into her new role. The lies slid off her tongue like butter. "I feared I'd remain at the nunnery for good."

That was the truth, at least. She had.

He inclined his head. "Ye didn't enjoy living there, I take it?"

Keira huffed a laugh. "Is it that evident?"

"Aye."

She glanced away. "The life of a nun suits some women ... but I'm not one of them."

"But ye were only there for safekeeping ... ye didn't need to take any vows."

"No ... but I lived as a nun nonetheless." Keira glanced back at Connor then, drinking in the handsome planes of his face. Although he'd tied back his golden mane of hair, the wind had whipped strands free.

Rhianna made a mistake running from this man, she thought. Not only was he a joy to look upon, but even their short exchange was enough for her to warm to him. She liked the easy way he spoke to her, his kind manner, and how he gazed upon her.

Excitement fluttered in the base of her belly.

Maybe this isn't going to be a disaster after all. Perhaps, despite all her fears, things would work out.

A few feet away, the sail unfurled before billowing. The birlinn shuddered, pitched to one side, and then bore north, away from the nunnery. Keira twisted her head west, her gaze taking in the stone walls and pitched roof of the kirk for the last time.

She'd barely been there a year but was just a month away from making the transition from novice to nun. Her rescue had come just in time.

Butterflies danced in her belly. Soon the prioress would discover that she was missing. They would then search the isle, but they would never find her.

They would never suspect the ruse that Keira and Rhianna had just worked together. They all thought Rhianna Ross was sailing away with her betrothed. And they would surmise that Keira's looming vows had compelled her to run away—not entirely a surprise as everyone at the nunnery knew she didn't want to be there.

Keira turned away from Iona then, her attention shifting back to Connor Mackay.

Her breathing caught when she discovered him watching her.

His green eyes were narrowed slightly, a pensive expression upon his face. "Ye aren't what I expected," he admitted softly.

Heat flushed through Keira, her nervousness returning in an instant. "I'm afraid tales of my beauty have been exaggerated," she replied, her tone brittle now. "I was a prettier child than I am a woman, I'm afraid." That was the truth. Her mother had often told her how she'd been the bonniest of all her sisters as a bairn. However, once she grew into a young woman, her comeliness faded.

Connor Mackay's gaze sparkled. He then shook his head. "I wasn't complaining about yer looks, Rhianna. I find yer face ... arresting."

Keira stifled a gasp.

Arresting.

Was the man half-blind?

Keira hadn't ever been complimented thus, and she certainly never expected a man like this one to find her attractive. Connor Mackay was the sort to have lasses falling at his feet.

"Ye are too kind," she murmured. The heat that rose to her cheeks then wasn't feigned. She wasn't sure how to respond.

"I speak what is on my mind," he replied, still smiling. "And I am glad to see that ye too have a frank tongue. Hopefully, we are well-matched after all."

After all.

So he'd worried about meeting her? It suddenly made sense—why he'd left it so long before coming to fetch his betrothed from the nunnery.

The revelation made Keira relax just a little. It was a relief to know that even a powerful, attractive man like this one could suffer from pre-wedding nerves.

It's a pity then that yer union will be nothing but a lie.

The thought rose unbidden and cast a shadow over Keira's brightening mood. Her belly clenched in response. It didn't matter that she was about to marry the man of her dreams, that he actually seemed to like her.

Keira's conscience wasn't about to let her forget what she'd done.

"It'll take us another day and a half of travel before we reach Farr Castle," Connor explained as he helped Keira down from the birlinn. They stood on the edge of a wide bay, fringed by a vast shingle beach. "Fortunately, the Frasers of Talasgair have always been happy to host the Mackays."

Intrigued, Keira glanced around her. They stood upon the Isle of Skye. It was getting late in the day, and dusk wasn't far off. The nights were drawing in. Despite that the warm days of summer were now behind them, they'd had a sunny day of travel, with a brisk wind pushing them north.

On Keira's journey to the nunnery a year earlier, the merchant's birlinn had passed Skye. She'd been awed then by the harsh, sculpted beauty of the coastline.

She was again now. To the south rose a rocky headland, carved into great stone terraces. Behind it reared a great mountain, its smooth slopes burnished gold in the late afternoon sun. Keira's attention shifted north, to where a fortress perched upon a crag, a cluster of sod-roofed sheilings—huts—beneath it.

"I've always wanted to visit Skye," she murmured, voicing her thoughts aloud.

"Well then, ye shall enjoy this," Connor replied with a grin. "Talasgair is an interesting place, with a long history." He pointed then to the fortress above them. "See there … it is formed of an ancient broch and a newer watchtower."

Keira nodded, her fingers now closing around Connor's as he helped her through the shallows to the shore. Sandaled feet crunching up the soft shingle, she was keenly aware of the heat and strength of his hand and was loath to release it. However, Connor left her there, above the tide-line, while he returned to help his men bring the birlinn up onto the beach. Unlike Iona, there was no jetty here; they would need to beach the boat and then push it back out tomorrow at high tide.

Observing the men work, Keira noted how one or two of them glanced her way before murmuring to each other. One in particular, an older man with dark-blond hair and beard, kept staring at her. She didn't like the hard, assessing look in his eyes.

Her breathing accelerated.

Connor had reacted better than she'd expected to her plainness, but she wagered that some of his men wouldn't be so kind.

Perhaps Connor was just being polite. The voice, cruel and cold, made her tense. It was her elder sister, Maire's, voice. One that had always plagued her whenever she'd dared to glance at herself in a looking glass. Maire was the most beautiful of all the sisters but also the haughtiest. She'd wed the MacLeod clan-chief's eldest son five years earlier, and Keira hadn't seen her since.

She hadn't missed Maire in the slightest, only it seemed she still wasn't rid of her sister's scorn. It dogged her steps, even now.

Especially now.

Watching the chieftain of the Mackays of Farr as he waded into the surf and shouted instructions to his men, Keira chastised herself for so readily believing the things he'd said to her. Her gaze lingered on the breadth of his shoulders and noted the powerful lines of his body.

The man could have any woman he wanted.

Why on earth would he find the likes of her *arresting?*

Stop it. Keira clenched her jaw. Rhianna had told her off a few times over the last year for running herself down. "Ye aren't with yer sisters anymore," her friend had reminded her sternly. "Ye don't have to spend yer days apologizing for yer existence."

Keira had appreciated Rhianna's frank advice. She was right of course, although old habits were hard to break.

"Yer betrothed isn't the beauty the Ross clan boasted of," Kennan grunted. They were heaving the birlinn onto the shore, a feat that required a lot of effort from the crew of ten men. Even so, Kennan managed to get his observation out.

Connor shrugged. "I find her pleasing enough to the eye."

Kennan caught his gaze, his own enquiring. "I wasn't being cruel ... merely stating a fact. The lady isn't what her people promised."

Next to him, Domhnall grunted in agreement. "Aye ... she has a face like a horse."

The comment made Connor's gaze narrow. He cut his uncle a warning look before replying to his cousin. "Many years have passed since we were betrothed to each other. Folk change ... they mature. I repeat, I find nothing offensive in her looks."

Kennan flashed him a smile then, and Connor realized that, unlike Domhnall, his cousin hadn't brought up the subject to be unkind. He'd been concerned that Connor would find his betrothed's appearance an issue. "I'm relieved to hear it," he replied.

Connor glanced then, farther up the shore to where a lone figure stood.

Rhianna pulled her blue cloak tightly around her as she watched them bring the boat in. Her pale face was solemn, her expression watchful. She had a strong, self-possessed aura about her. He'd sensed a real depth to this woman the moment their gazes locked shortly after departing Iona. His betrothed possessed a clever tongue and sharp gaze, and instinctively he felt he could trust her.

He'd known Rhianna Ross barely a day, but he was looking forward to talking to her again, to discovering who she was.

Unlike his uncle, he didn't think she had a face like a horse. He didn't appreciate the comment.

I should have fetched her sooner.

Suddenly, the freedom that Connor had once reveled in seemed empty. All these years, he'd been out hunting, hawking, and fighting, when he could have been spending time with Rhianna Ross.

Maybe a wife was exactly what he needed.

5

YE LOOK LOVELY

"WELCOME TO TALASGAIR!" Iain Fraser boomed, his voice echoing off the surrounding stone. A big man with a wild mane of vivid russet hair strode out into the bailey to meet them. His keen moss-green gaze swept over the party, traveling to Connor Mackay and the woman at his side.

"So, this is the famous Lady Ross. A woman of renowned beauty."

Keira's belly twisted. The man's tone wasn't snide, and yet she inwardly cringed. How many more times would she have to weather these comments?

How long before ye meet someone who has actually seen Rhianna Ross?

Keira swallowed, a cold sweat beading across her body. She thought hard then, trying to recall what Rhianna had told her about the clans she'd had contact with over the years. She hadn't mentioned the Frasers of Talasgair.

Keira's pulse slowed. She had to stop panicking every time a stranger looked her way; she'd be a nervous wreck by the time they reached Farr Castle if she didn't take her new role in her stride.

"Good eve, Laird," she replied with a polite dip of her head.

Iain Fraser continued to watch her for a few moments, an assessing expression on his face, before he smiled. "Pleased to meet ye ... it was time this warrior settled down." He cast a grin in Connor's direction. "I'm glad ye made a stop here ... Fiona will get the cooks to put on a fine supper for ye."

"We have given ye no warning," Connor replied with a wave of his hand. "Don't put the cooks to any trouble."

Fraser snorted. "It's no trouble at all." He gestured to the oaken doors behind him, which led into the squat broch. This close, Keira could see it was made of stacked stone that had been patched in many places. The newer tower had been added on the northern side of the broch. "Come ... let's pour ye a horn of mead and catch up on news." He glanced once more at Keira, smiling. "My wife will be keen to meet ye, lass."

"That sack does ye no favors at all." Fiona Fraser took a step back and ran a critical eye over the black habit Keira wore. "Ye can't go down to supper dressed as a nun."

Heat flushed through Keira's chest. "I'm afraid I don't have any other clothing with me," she said meekly. She would have brought her old clothes with her, if the prioress hadn't taken them away after her arrival at the nunnery.

"It's just as well ye and I are of a similar size then," the Lady of Talasgair replied with a toothy smile. It was true. Fiona Fraser was tall and buxom, with a mane of peat-brown hair that she wore loose this afternoon.

Keira tensed, not sure whether to be offended or pleased by the woman's comment. She remained silent, watching as Fiona turned and bustled over to the row of brightly-colored kirtles that hung up against the pitted stone wall.

The two women stood in the women's dressing room, high up in the tower. The small shuttered window was open. It afforded a view across the tawny hills to the south of the fortress, to where the bulk of the mountain rose against the sky.

"What a bonny view," Keira murmured. "There are no mountains on Iona ... I've missed them."

Fiona glanced over her shoulder, her full lips curving. "Aye, Preshal More is a lovely sight this time of day," she replied. She selected a dark-green kirtle and a pale cream lèine and carried them over to Keira. "A kirtle to match yer bonny husband's eyes," she said with a mischievous grin.

Connor was onto his third horn of mead when his betrothed appeared in the great hall. The wide, circular space had once been the feasting hall of the ancient people who'd resided here. The alcoves that lined the walls had been sleeping spaces years earlier, but now the laird of Talasgair used them for storage. A large hearth burned in the center of the wide space, and tables had been set out in a square around it.

The burnished light of sconces on the walls gilded Rhianna Ross as she followed Fiona Fraser through the archway into the hall. Both women then made their way across to the laird's table on the far side of the hearth.

Connor couldn't take his gaze from his bride-to-be.

It was like looking upon a different woman to the one he'd collected from Iona. Then, her form had been shrouded by a voluminous cloak, her brown hair coiled tightly around her crown.

This evening, the cloak and the black habit he'd caught glimpses of under it were both absent. Instead, she wore a form-hugging, pine-green kirtle that showed off a strong, curvaceous body. The low neckline of the kirtle, and the cream-colored lèine under it, revealed a deep cleavage and swelling bosom that made it difficult not to stare. The green contrasted against the milky texture of her skin and complemented the lustrous oaken-colored hair that flowed over her shoulders.

Rhianna Ross might not have been the classic beauty that her clan had boasted of, yet there was something about her that made Connor's pulse quicken.

He knew he was staring. However, he couldn't help himself.

"That's better." The approval in Iain Fraser's voice was evident. "I'm glad to see yer betrothed looking like the lady she is." He paused then, raising his horn of mead to Connor. "Like Fiona, she has the body of a goddess."

Connor grinned at the laird's frank appraisal of both his own wife and Rhianna. Iain Fraser had never been a man to hold back his thoughts, and Connor found his openness refreshing. Not all Highland chieftains were as candid as his host. Many watched every word when they met with men they considered to be potential rivals.

Connor's father, Rory, had once told him it was a lonely position—that of laird. "Ye always need to watch yer back lad," his father had advised, after one too many skins of ale on a hunting trip. "For there'll always be some cunning bastard sharpening his dirk at yer shoulder."

Iain Fraser wasn't a man to cross, but Connor always knew where he stood with him.

A few yards down the table, Domhnall was smirking at Fraser's comment, while next to him Kennan caught Connor's eye and winked.

Male stares tracked Keira across the hall, and by the time she reached the laird's table, she was sweating in her fine lèine and kirtle.

She wasn't used to being the center of attention.

All her life, she'd never been stared at like this.

Some of the stares that followed her path from the doors to her betrothed's side were hot, lustful. Keira felt as if she'd just paraded herself naked before them.

Hoping that her cheeks weren't aflame, she lowered herself onto the bench-seat next to Connor. And when she saw that he was watching her under hooded lids, her heart started to thud against her breastbone.

It was a look of pure male appreciation.

She'd seen men favor other women with gazes like that. She remembered Beltaines past, when her father's men would ogle at her sisters as they danced around the bonfire.

But until now, she'd never received a searing look like that; it robbed her of breath.

"Ye look lovely, Rhianna," he said when she sat next to him.

"Aye, doesn't she?" Fiona quipped, taking a seat beside her husband.

"Thank ye," Keira replied with a shy smile. She had to learn to take a compliment gracefully, as Rhianna would have done.

Even so, her heart was hammering and her palms were clammy. This was all mummery, and she was terrified of saying something that might bring everything crashing down.

Goose, she chided herself inwardly. *If ye keep yer nerve, no one shall ever know.*

Her pulse settled a little at the reminder. She had to remember that she was no longer Keira Gunn but Rhianna Ross. How long would it take her to settle into her new identity?

Servants appeared then, bringing in wheels of cheese, platters of salted pork, boiled eggs, cabbage cooked in butter, and large loaves of oaten bread. Grateful that their arrival distracted everyone's attention, Keira reached for a pewter goblet of sloe wine and took a sip.

A year of vegetable pottage, goat's cheese, and coarse bread made even this relatively simple fare seem like a banquet. She hadn't eaten salted pork since leaving her parents' broch.

Even so, the proximity of the big, blond man she would soon wed robbed her of appetite. They sat close together upon the bench-seat, so close that their thighs were just inches away from touching.

The heat of his body enveloped her, and Keira found that she was keenly aware of him. Maybe it was the tension that thrummed within her, but every sense was attuned. He was dressed in chamois braies and a white lèine this eve, his clan sash—cross-hatchings of forest-green, and various shades of blue—draped across his broad chest.

His golden hair was unbound and rippled over his shoulders. It almost appeared red-gold in the hallowed light of the nearby hearth and the burning cressets behind them.

The supper began, and the rumble of voices and laughter echoed off the stone walls. Taking another sip of wine, Keira slowly relaxed. Her fear of being unmasked as an imposter aside, she'd felt exposed when she'd walked into the great hall. This kirtle showed off far more cleavage than she was comfortable with, but Fiona had insisted the gown suited her.

"Many lasses would scratch each other's eyes out to have curves like yers." Fiona had said as she puffed out her own impressive bosom. "Let yer husband-to-be see what awaits him."

Keira had flushed red at that. If Lady Fraser hadn't been so obviously proud of her own curves, Keira might have taken offense. However, unlike the vicious comments of her slender sisters, there had been no malice in Fiona's voice.

The woman was simply paying her a compliment.

"Will there be reckoning for Harpsdale, Connor?" Iain Fraser's gruff voice intruded then. Keira glanced up from her meal to see that the chieftain wore a hard expression. This was the battle that Rhianna had mentioned to her: the one between the Mackays and the Gunns—her own people.

Guilt compressed her chest, tension coiling within her once more. Of course, she'd had nothing to do with that battle. But she was a *Gunn* nonetheless. The Mackays and the Gunns had been at each other's throats for a while now. Feuds among the Highland clans ran deep, although the warring had gotten more brutal over the last years.

A beat of silence followed, and Keira witnessed a shadow pass over her betrothed's handsome face. He then shook his head.

"Rory was a good friend ... I'd like to see his death avenged," Fraser continued.

"So would I." Connor's features tightened. "But it was a blood-bath. At one stage, Morgan and I fought back-to-back, knee-deep in the gore of our enemies. Their losses were as great as ours." He paused then, a nerve flickering in his cheek. "Don't worry, we made those bastards suffer."

Keira's breathing quickened, as did her pulse. The chill she saw in Connor Mackay's eyes warned her of the hatred he bore for her people.

Keira heaved in a deep breath in an effort to loosen the tightness in her chest. She may not have been close to her own family, but she was proud to be a Gunn. Had any of her relatives fallen at Harpsdale? No word had reached her at Iona, so she imagined her father was still alive. He was getting a little too old these days for battles, although she knew he loved a good skirmish. Maddoc Gunn had been a fearsome warrior in his youth. Her father had once proudly told her that although smaller than some of the other clans, theirs made up for it with their aggression. Indeed, their clan name came from the Norse word 'Gunnr', which meant 'war'.

The silence stretched out before Connor's expression changed. His gaze guttered. "I should have been able to save him," he said finally, his voice roughening.

Watching the younger man under hooded lids, Iain Fraser reached for a jug of wine and refilled Connor's pewter goblet. "It wasn't yer fault," he admonished him softly. "Rory was a leader, a born-warrior. He died as he lived."

Connor's throat bobbed. "Aye ... but till my dying day, I'll never forget the sight of him on his knees ... trying to push his guts back into his body. His screams still haunt my dreams."

Keira stilled at these words, while Iain Fraser's eyes widened. He was clearly surprised that the younger man had been so open with him.

"I'm so sorry about yer father, Connor," Keira murmured finally, when another uncomfortable silence drew out. "I would have liked to meet him."

Guilt clenched hard within her once more as she spoke. She wasn't lying—she would have liked to have met Rory Mackay. However, this pretense was proving even harder than she'd anticipated.

Oblivious to the turmoil churning within his bride-to-be, Connor's mouth lifted at the corners, although his gaze was still bleak. "Aye ... and he would have been pleased to meet ye too. He was the greatest chieftain the Mackays of Farr have ever known. The world is a darker place without him."

6

SHELTERING FROM THE STORM

SEATED AT THE stern of the birlinn, Keira clung on as a wave crashed over the side, drenching the occupants of the boat. Shivering, she glanced up at the leaden skies. The sky had been clear when they'd left Skye with the dawn, but the farther north they traveled, the worse the weather got. And now, the sea was so rough that her belly pitched with every roll.

Keira gripped the railing that ran along the stern and glanced over at where Connor was trimming the sail.

"It's too rough," he called to his cousin, Kennan. "Let's bring her in at Scourie."

"No complaints from me," the auburn-haired warrior shouted back above the roaring wind. "If this continues, we'll go over."

Nausea swept over Keira, and she clung on even tighter to the railing. The sky overhead was so dark now, it was difficult to tell what time of day it was; even so, she guessed that dusk was still a few hours off. They'd planned to travel farther before dropping anchor.

"Are ye well, Rhianna?" Connor's gaze sought hers.

She nodded, not trusting herself to speak. Her belly lurched with every roll of the boat, and the size of the waves they now crested terrified her. However, she was loath to admit such a thing; she didn't want her husband-to-be to think her a whining coward.

A woman mustn't take to complaining, Keira, her mother had once advised her. *A man won't suffer a whinger.*

It was an irony really, that her mother had given her such advice, for Keira had always thought her shrewish. And even more ironic still, her parents had announced barely a moon later that Keira was to take the veil at Iona. It didn't matter if she turned into a scold, for she wasn't destined to become a wife.

"We're docking at Scourie soon," he continued, raising his voice to be heard as another wave crashed across the bow. "There's an inn there."

Keira favored him with a weak smile, relief flooding through her. She couldn't wait till they got out of this storm, for she feared that if it worsened, she would soon throw up the bannock and cheese she'd eaten at noon.

Huddled against the stern, her belly lurching with each wave, Keira watched Connor Mackay masterfully take control of the birlinn. He shouted orders to his men, and they worked as one, bringing the craft into a wide bay.

A low, rocky headland greeted them as lightning illuminated the wild sky. A huddle of stone houses sheltered under the lee of the hill, near the shore. It was a dangerous approach, for dark rocks emerged from the churning waves, yet Connor's men maneuvered the birlinn with both sail and oars toward the pebbly shore. The tide was rising, and with the aid of the waves, they brought the boat hard into the beach.

The bow hit the pebbles with a loud 'crunch', and Connor and four of his men leaped from the birlinn, landing waist-deep in water. They then hauled the craft up onto the shore.

Hair whipping across his face, Connor clambered back onto the birlinn and took Keira by the hand, leading her onto the beach.

Keira's knees buckled as soon as she stepped down from the boat; solid ground felt strange after spending hours in a pitching boat. However, Connor's arm was there to steady her.

She leaned against the hard strength of his body for an instant, reveling in the contact, before he guided her farther up the beach.

Then, as he'd done the day before, Connor left her to rejoin his men. They needed to drag the boat up the beach, above the tideline, for it to be safe overnight.

Pulling her sodden cloak about her, Keira gritted her teeth to prevent the shivers that made her teeth chatter. She was still wearing the green kirtle of the night before, and although she much preferred it to her habit, it wasn't half as warm.

Fiona Fraser had gifted the kirtle to her that morning. "Ye need something pretty to arrive at Farr Castle in, lass," she'd said with a wink. "Consider it a wedding gift from the Frasers."

Keira had warmed to Lady Fraser, even if her bawdy sense of humor and direct manner had unbalanced her a little. The women of her own family were nothing like Fiona, and Mother Jean and the other nuns were largely humorless and closed in their manners.

But Rhianna had been different. Like Lady Fraser, she'd always been open and warm with Keira.

Keira thought of her friend then, for the first time all day. Truthfully, she'd been so caught up by nerves, and in Connor Mackay's company, that she'd forgotten all else. Guilt feathered through her now at the realization. Her own situation had taken her mind off the reason she'd agreed to swap places with her friend.

I wonder if she managed to get away.

She hoped Rhianna and her lover were both safe.

Never had a roaring fire been so welcome.

Keira inched closer to the hearth, stretching out her chilled fingers toward the flames. It was hard to believe it wasn't yet winter, although Scottish weather could be like this, could turn from one season to another in just one day.

"Careful ... get any closer to those flames, and you'll scorch yerself." Keira glanced up to see Kennan looming over her, a cup of something steaming in his hands. "Here, lass." He handed the cup to her. "This mutton broth should warm ye up."

Keira favored him with a shy smile. She liked Connor's cousin. Handsome, with wild auburn hair, he had an open face and laughing green eyes. She preferred him to Domhnall, the older warrior she'd discovered was Connor's uncle.

The man in question sat a few yards away, his leathery face inscrutable. During the day, she'd caught him watching her several times. The sharpness of his gaze made her nervous.

Does he suspect something?

Surely not. It was silly to worry about such things. Wrapping her chilled fingers around the cup, Keira took a tentative sip of broth. She then sighed. Never had a broth been so welcome.

Around them, the storm raged. The wind pummeled the stone walls of the inn, causing a draft that made the flames in the hearth gutter. It wasn't a night to be outdoors.

Keira sat in the inn's common room, a small space with a rush-covered floor and tightly-packed wooden tables. The Mackay party were the only patrons this eve. Connor was standing near the kitchen door, talking to the inn-keeper, while his men made themselves comfortable at the tables.

Connor appeared soaked-through, his blond hair hanging in dark tangles down his back. Finishing his conversation with the inn-keeper, the laird then turned and made his way to the hearth. "It's mutton and braised onions for supper tonight," he announced.

"Sounds good to me," Kennan replied with a grin. "And does he have the space to accommodate us all?"

"Aye ... although two of us are going to have to sleep in the stables." Connor flashed Kennan a grin then. "Ye'd better get ready to bed down with the horses, cousin."

Kennan snorted at this. "I think not. It'll be a soft bed for me." He then cast Domhnall a wicked smile. "Why don't ye draw straws with the others, uncle?"

"Aye," the older man replied. "Right after I kick yer arse."

Keira smiled at their banter. Although she could be timid around men, she'd missed male company during her year at Iona. Men always appeared less complicated than women—or maybe her view was clouded from being brought up with so many sisters.

The meal arrived then, platters of roast meat and onions served with coarse bread. The harsh journey had given the entire party ravenous appetites, and they fell upon their suppers, the common room quieting.

Keira ate with relish, enjoying the rich mutton while she listened to the howling wind rattling the shutters. A feeling of well-being suffused her then—a feeling of belonging. She wasn't Connor Mackay's wife yet, but she was no longer a novice nun either. Slowly, her old life was slipping away as she assumed her new identity.

Once supper ended, the men lingered over tankards of ale, before one by one, they drifted away to find their beds.

Eventually, only Connor and Keira remained by the fire.

Hands wrapped around warmed cups of bramble wine, they sat knee to knee before the roaring hearth, while the inn-keeper cleared and wiped down the surrounding tables.

"Apologies for the rough trip today," Connor said with a sheepish smile. "I should have made this journey earlier."

The shyness that had settled over Keira since taking her seat at the fire intensified for a moment. She was aware that she and Connor were alone for the first time since the journey had begun. "It sounds as if ye had a good reason for yer delay," she murmured. "After all the feuding."

His smile faded, his gaze shadowing. Unwittingly, she'd reminded him of his father, and she was sorry for it.

"Aye ... it's been a summer I'd rather forget," he admitted after a pause. "However, I can't blame the feuding for my late-coming." He offered her another smile, although this one was strained. "In truth, I'm a reluctant laird. I liked being young and unfettered. But fate decided it was time that changed."

Their gazes held for a long moment. "*Unfettered*," Keira said, shaking her head. "I can't imagine what that's like." It was true. Men, warriors especially, enjoyed a freedom that women could only dream of.

His gaze widened at her frankness, and panic suddenly quickened in her chest. For an instant there, she'd forgotten she was supposed to be Rhianna Ross.

"We know so little about each other, Rhianna," he replied after a pause, "despite being betrothed since we were bairns."

"Aye, it's a bit awkward," she admitted, glancing away. "Meeting someone who's been yer destiny for so long."

"It is. Our parents should have arranged a meeting when we were initially betrothed," he replied. "It would have made things easier."

Keira nodded, even if her heart started to hammer at his comment. Thank the Lord that hadn't happened.

"What was yer childhood like?" Connor asked gently.

Still not meeting his eye, Keira frantically searched her thoughts for details about Rhianna's past. Fortunately, her friend had told her a few things about life at Caisteal Nan Corr, the Ross holding where she'd grown up.

"It was a little lonely." She forced herself to look up then and meet his eye. "I lost my parents young, and my elder sister and I have never been close ... but there are worse starts in life, I'm sure."

Connor inclined his head, inviting her to continue.

Keira started to sweat. She was out of her depth here, and as such, she needed to tread carefully lest she trip herself up. "My uncle never wanted to bring up two troublesome nieces." Her mouth twisted as she thought of her own father. He'd never wanted six demanding daughters either. "He thought he'd rid himself of us both ... but my sister was widowed just over a year and a half ago, and now he's saddled with her."

"And why aren't ye and yer sister close?"

Sweat trickled down Keira's back, between her shoulder-blades. She knew very little about Rhianna's elder sister, Maggie, other than that she was, apparently, insufferably bossy. Once again, Keira delved into memories of her own childhood, bringing her sisters into her answer. "She was the one favored by my parents." Keira glanced away and focused on the dancing flames in the hearth. "And growing up, she never missed an opportunity to heap scorn upon me."

That was an understatement. Her elder sisters had wielded insults like boning knives over the years; she still bore the scars, deep inside where no one could see them.

"Sounds like ye are well rid of her then," Connor replied.

She glanced up, to see that he was watching her. "Aye," she murmured, forcing a smile. As much as she enjoyed this man's company, she wished they could steer the conversation into safer waters.

She might have been pretending to be someone else, but those answers had come straight from Keira Gunn. Straight from her own heart.

7

SLEEP WELL

CONNOR LED THE way up the creaking stairs to the rooms on the top floor of the inn. Outdoors, the storm still howled like a banshee, clawing at the thatched roof and rattling the shutters. "We've got the two chambers at the end of the hall," he said, glancing over his shoulder at his betrothed. "The inn-keeper assures me they're his best."

"I'm sure the room will do me well." His betrothed flashed him a warm smile. "Ye forget, I've spent the last while sleeping in a dormitory upon a hard wooden pallet."

Their gazes held for an instant, before Connor smiled back. He'd felt drawn to this woman all evening, had deliberately lengthened their time together before the fire. But finally, the inn-keeper had started clearing his throat and making a noise with pots and pans in the adjoining kitchen—making it evident that he wished to retire and hoped they'd do the same.

Rhianna Ross fascinated him. The way those dark-blue eyes rested on him, the soft sound of her voice when she replied to him, drew Connor in. She'd been initially reluctant to talk about herself, but he admired the honesty of her answers.

Eventually, they'd transitioned to lighter matters. He'd talked about his younger brother and sister, and of his own childhood, which had been a happy one. Rhianna had laughed when he told her about how his brother, Morgan, once got a thrashing for leaving a toad in their sister, Jaimee's, bed.

Rhianna was easy company, with a quick, dry wit that he enjoyed. He liked the way she responded to him, and as the evening had worn on, he'd found himself studying the planes of her face.

Arresting.

Aye, it was the right word for Rhianna Ross. Her eyes had been dark in the firelight, her high cheekbones flushed from the wine, and he'd found himself wondering how her lush, crooked mouth would taste.

She'd been a surprise—but what had he actually expected his betrothed to be like? Over the years, rumors had circulated that the lass was a beauty but haughty and spoiled. Such news hadn't made Connor any more eager to fetch her. And when he'd finally traveled to Iona, he'd braced himself to meet a woman who was pleasing to the eye but also difficult to warm to.

But there was nothing haughty or spoiled about the woman he'd just spent the evening with.

They stopped at the end of the hallway, before their respective doorways, and turned to each other. Rhianna was a tall woman, yet even so, she still had to lift her chin to hold his stare. Connor had inherited his father's breadth and height, and towered over most men.

Their gazes met and held, and as the moment drew out, Connor witnessed a becoming blush stain Rhianna's cheeks.

God's teeth, she drew him in. Her hair was tangled and damp from the storm, and he now fought the urge to reach out and run his fingers through it.

"I'm glad we finally met," he said, breaking the awkward silence between them. He then reached out and brushed a damp curl off her forehead. "I think ye and I are well matched, Rhianna Ross."

That crooked mouth curved, although her midnight-blue eyes held a veiled look now. Did she have any idea how alluring he found her?

He'd heard his uncle discussing her with one of his men at dawn, as they'd prepared to leave Talasgair. Domhnall had been muttering how this woman couldn't possibly be the vaunted Ross beauty the Highlands had been whispering about for years now. Connor's belly had clenched at his uncle's callousness, and when he'd sniggered that his nephew's betrothed had a face as long as his favorite nag's, Connor had stepped up behind him, making both men nearly jump out of their skin. A few sharp words had sent Connor's warrior slinking away wearing a shamefaced expression, although Domhnall had merely mumbled a half-hearted apology.

Fury had burned like an ember in Connor's belly for a while afterward.

In truth, he barely knew this woman, yet he was already protective over her.

And right now, her pale skin caressed by the light of a nearby cresset, she looked both sensual and vulnerable.

Without overthinking his actions, Connor leaned in, his mouth brushing hers. It was a feather-light, chaste kiss—and yet the contact sent a jolt of lust through his groin.

Her lips are so soft.

Rhianna remained still, her breathing hitching, her eyes drawing wide.

A heartbeat passed, and then Connor leaned in once more, his lips slanting across hers—again gently.

A sigh escaped her. Warmth spread through Connor's belly in response. She'd enjoyed that, and he wanted to give her more. He stepped closer, his hands lightly cupping her cheeks. He kissed her properly this time, parting her soft lips with his tongue and tasting the sweetness of her mouth.

Rhianna melted against him, giving herself up to the moment. Her pliancy, the sensuality of her lips open under his, unleashed something within him. He pulled her into his arms and devoured her mouth.

And when she whimpered, white-hot lust barreled into him, spiking through his groin with such force he groaned.

Drawing back from her, Connor stared down into Rhianna's face. His breathing now came in ragged pants, and she too was struggling to catch her breath. The kiss had gone from gentle to passionate in an instant, catching alight like wildfire in his veins.

He had to put some distance between them before he lost control.

We'll be wedded soon enough, he reminded himself. *Then I won't need to restrain myself.*

His aching rod protested at the thought that he'd have to wait, but he ignored it. As much as he wanted her, tonight was too soon.

"Goodnight, Rhianna," he said, a rasp to his voice. "Sleep well."

Keira let herself into her bed-chamber and then leaned back up against the closed door.

Heart pounding, she raised her fingers to her lips.

She'd never before been kissed. She'd always thought it appeared a bit awkward, that it would be an uncomfortable clash of lips, teeth, and tongue. She certainly hadn't expected her first kiss to be like that. He'd been achingly gentle, and then he'd taken her in his arms and plundered her mouth. The feel of his tongue sliding against hers—teasing, dancing—had made a strange yearning claw its way up from her lower belly.

Even now, she pulsed with it.

Mother Mary, is that a taste of what lies in store?

Her already galloping pulse quickened further. On shaky legs, Keira made her way across to the bed. The room was small and neat, with scrubbed wooden floors and white-washed walls, but Keira barely paid her surroundings any mind.

Instead, all she could think about was how his lips had felt on hers, about how he'd tasted.

A wave of dizziness swept over her then; she was out of her depth here, and she knew it.

It had been an unexpected evening. Not only was Connor breathtaking to look upon, but he was also fine company. She'd observed over the past two days how he treated others—his men and the Frasers at Talasgair— how he exuded a quiet strength, a warmth that drew people to him.

But their easy rapport surprised her. The only models of marriage she'd had over the years had been provided by her parents and elder sisters. Her parents barely tolerated each other at times; their union was one of practicality. On the rare occasions she'd seen her sisters with their husbands, it appeared that the couples lived separate lives. He did manly things, she did womanly things, and neither ventured into each other's sphere.

But every time she conversed with Connor Mackay, she saw the keen interest in his eyes and felt his need to *know* her. When he'd observed her by the fireside, a hot, prickly sensation had swept over her. This wasn't how men usually responded to her—and certainly not men like Connor. Back at her father's broch, the warriors had ignored her. No one had ever asked her to dance at Beltaine or Samhuinn. Instead, they'd all vied for her sisters' attention.

But Connor Mackay noticed her, 'saw' her. And his kiss had left her in no doubt of his desire for her.

For the woman he believes is Rhianna Ross.

Keira's breathing hitched. It was as if someone had just emptied a bucket of icy sea-water over her head.

She was living a lie, pretending to be someone she wasn't.

She was a Gunn—the clan that was responsible for his father's death. Would he have kissed her with such ardor if he'd known her real identity? Would he wish to have anything to do with her at all?

"There it is ... home."

The note of pride in her husband-to-be's voice made Keira look up, pushing away a lock of hair that had gotten free of its braid. The storm had spent itself overnight, although a chill wind now gusted in from the north, making the day's journey another rough one.

Relief flooded over her at this news. However, she stifled a gasp when she spied Farr Castle ahead.

Perched high upon a lush-green headland, its grey walls presiding over the sea like a great watchtower, it was a sight indeed.

"God's bones," Keira murmured, awed. "That's quite a drop." She spared Connor a quick look, to see that he was grinning.

"Aye, it's precipitous indeed," he agreed. He then pointed. "See how it's only joined to the mainland by a narrow neck?"

Keira's attention returned to the castle, and she spotted the high rampart that protected the castle's approach from the landward side. It wouldn't be an easy spot to lay siege to.

"How long have yer kin lived here?" she asked, her gaze never leaving the crenelated walls above.

"My clan has held this stronghold for the last century," he replied.

Keira nodded, her gaze still upon the fortress. Excitement feathered down her spine.

I am to be the lady of this place.

It hardly seemed real.

They approached the headland, sliding past a wall of sheer rock to a small white-sand cove tucked in on its northern side. There, Connor and his men moored the birlinn to a sturdy jetty, and the party disembarked.

It was a steep climb to the top of the cliffs, up winding stairs between nesting shags and gulls.

Breathing hard, Keira held up her skirts to avoid tripping and kept her gaze firmly placed on Connor's broad back as he led the way. With the wind buffeting her, and the steep drop to the cove below, she preferred not to look down.

It was a long way to fall.

By the time they reached the top of the cliff, a few yards from the rampart and the heavy gate leading onto the headland, Keira was out of breath. Life at the nunnery had been busy, and she'd thought she was relatively fit—however, that climb had nearly been too much.

Meanwhile, Connor appeared barely winded.

As she recovered her breath, Keira glanced around, taking in the velvet green landscape surrounding her. Her attention rested upon the knot of thatch-roofed cottages that formed Farr village about a furlong back from the cliff-top. On the southern edge of the village, the pitched roof of the kirk rose up, framed against the shadow of rugged mountains to the east. It was an exposed spot, especially with the wind howling across the hills, and there wasn't a tree to be seen. Winters would be chill here in the far north of the Highlands.

"What do ye think?" Connor asked, stepping close. His golden hair whipped around his face. She glimpsed the eagerness in his eyes; her approval mattered to him.

"I don't think I've ever seen a castle with such a breathtaking setting," she admitted. It was the truth. Her father's humble broch sat in a lonely moor.

He raised a dark-blond eyebrow, even if a smile bloomed across his face. "Not even Caisteal Nan Corr compares?"

Keira swallowed hard. *Goose.* Of course, Rhianna had grown up in a chieftain's hold. Panic fluttered up as she scrambled to remember what her friend had told her of the castle. It sat on the banks of a river, surrounded by meadowland.

"Aye," she said meekly. "Caisteal Nan Corr is pretty enough ... but it's much smaller than Farr, and it doesn't have a view such as this."

8

HERE IT BEGINS

KEIRA'S HEART BEAT a tattoo against her ribs as she followed Connor through the gate and into the bailey of Farr Castle.

I must be more careful.

She was so comfortable in this man's presence that she sometimes forgot herself. When she conversed with him, she wasn't trying to be anyone else, she wasn't playing a role. She wasn't Rhianna Ross but herself.

It was dangerous to let her guard down like this.

If she got too relaxed, she could easily let details of her own life slip. She needed to remember that she was Rhianna Ross of Caisteal Nan Corr, a woman with one elder, widowed sister and no living parents. A woman who was the niece of the chieftain Graeme Ross. And she needed to act like the lady she was supposed to be; she wasn't a wool merchant's daughter anymore.

Keira's throat constricted. She wasn't one for pretense. Her directness had been a constant source of discord in her family. Her father had cuffed her across the ear many a time for being too blunt, and her mother told her it was an unfeminine trait.

But Keira hadn't cared what they thought—and she still didn't. Connor Mackay didn't seem to mind her manner at least.

She followed her betrothed across the windswept landward bailey, taking in the low buildings that surrounded them: a byre, stables, storehouses, and an armory most likely. It was early afternoon, and as such there were a number of men about. They passed a forge, where the blacksmith straightened up from hammering a blade and waved a beefy arm at the returning laird.

Connor called out a greeting, favoring the smith with a wide smile.

The keep rose before them, a rectangular, solid structure with two stories looming above a set of stone stairs. A jagged row of crenellations flanked the staircase, protecting residents from the elements as they climbed to the first-floor entrance.

A large oaken door, weathered by age and the harsh climate this far north, greeted them. Connor led the way into the keep, through a small entrance hall with a stairwell off to the left, and into the great hall beyond.

Keira's gaze swept the wood-paneled interior, taking in the flickering hearth at one end, the long tables that covered the wooden floor, and the smoke-blackened rafters overhead. A mighty stag's head loomed over the fireplace, but that was the only ornamentation in here. The great hall of Farr Castle was an austere, masculine space.

A man and a woman stood upon the raised dais before the hearth, a grey wolfhound sitting between them.

Keira knew at a glance they were kin to the laird.

"Morgan, Jaimee ... come down to meet my betrothed," Connor called to them.

Keira's pulse quickened, her gaze riveted on the pair as they did as bid. A grin spread across Morgan Mackay's face when he stepped forward and clasped arms with his brother. Up close, Keira saw that he was of a leaner, lankier build than Connor. His hair, cut in a shorter, shaggier style, was a shade or two darker. However, he had those same penetrating pine-green eyes.

Morgan's attention then shifted to Keira.

She tensed, waiting for the grin to slip, for surprise to widen those green eyes. But if Connor's brother was surprised that Rhianna Ross wasn't the 'Jewel of the Highlands' everyone had expected, he didn't let it show. Instead, he favored Keira with a boyish, cocky smile, revealing a deep dimple on his left cheek. "Welcome to

Farr Castle, Lady Ross." He then reached down and ruffled the ears of the wolfhound that now pressed up against his leg. "And this is Gritta."

"Never mind yer damn dog, Morgan. Move out of the way, and let me greet my new sister." An irritated female voice intruded.

Morgan snorted and then winced when an elbow collided with his ribs. Muttering an oath, he drew back to let his sister through.

Jaimee Mackay stepped up, smiling. She was the same height as Keira and so their gazes were level. Tall and willowy, with red-gold hair, she too had vivid green eyes.

A weight settled in Keira's belly.

Of course, Connor's sister was always going to be bonny.

Yet Jaimee didn't possess Rhianna Ross's queenly beauty but something earthier. Her cheeks were slightly reddened as if she'd spent the day outdoors, and her red-gold hair looked as if it needed a good brush. Keira spied horse-hair and pieces of straw upon her kirtle. Most likely, the lass had been out riding earlier in the day.

Keira knew she shouldn't be so prejudiced against a beautiful woman. One didn't choose what the Lord blessed one with. It was just that she'd grown up in an environment where comeliness was held up as a prize— and Keira had always felt sadly lacking.

Her sisters had never wasted an opportunity to comment on her plainness.

And yet, as Jaimee reached out and took her hand, squeezing it firmly, she saw none of the slyness she'd often witnessed in her sisters' gazes. The woman before her was lovely indeed, but she gave the appearance of not knowing or caring about such matters.

"I'm so glad ye are finally here." Jaimee cast Connor a disapproving look. "My brother took far too long to fetch ye."

"Rhianna's with us now," Connor replied, a dry tone creeping into his voice. "Please don't keep berating me over this."

Jaimee drew herself up, "And the wedding? I hope ye don't intend to make us all wait for that too?"

Connor laughed, the warm sound echoing up into the smoke-blackened beams overhead. "No, sister. It will take place on the morrow ... as planned."

Connor turned to Keira then, meeting her gaze. He inclined his head, "Is that agreeable to ye, Rhianna?" he asked, his mouth lifting at the corners.

Keira's belly fluttered—a blend of nerves and excitement. "Aye," she murmured. She then looked down at the green kirtle that Fiona Fraser had gifted her. It was damp with sea-spray but would have to do.

As if reading her thoughts, Jaimee gave the hand she still held another squeeze. "Worry not, mother had many fine gowns ... we shall choose one for ye."

Seated by the window in the women's solar, Keira watched while Jaimee laid out a number of brightly-colored kirtles over the table. "These were Ma's favorites," she said, standing back and running a critical eye over them. "It shouldn't take much to alter a gown to fit ye."

Keira resisted the urge to frown. If Jaimee's mother had been as willowy as her daughter was, she seriously doubted altering a kirtle for her would be an easy task.

Jaimee glanced over her shoulder. "Come over, and see if any are to yer liking."

Rising to her feet, Keira approached the table. They were fine garments indeed, made of dyed wool, although some were edged in colored-ribbon. Reaching for one the hue of plum wine, she ran her fingers across the fine weave. "Shall we see if this kirtle fits?"

"That gown was my mother's favorite," Jaimee replied. Hearing the sadness tinging the lass's voice, Keira glanced her way. Jaimee's eyes shone with tears.

"It's been a year now," she continued, her voice lowering to a whisper, "but I miss her every day."

A lump rose in Keira's throat. She'd only just met Jaimee and didn't know what to say to her. It was difficult to know how to respond when faced with grief that was still so raw. Instinctively, Keira reached out and placed a comforting hand on Jaimee's forearm.

"I can choose another kirtle if this one brings back too many memories," she said softly. "They're *all* bonny."

Jaimee shook her head, knuckling away a tear that now trickled down her cheek. "Nonsense ... what good is a kirtle this pretty gathering dust? It needs to be worn." Jaimee favored Keira with a watery smile. "Ma would want that. It's just a pity she can't be there to see Connor wed."

Keira tried on the kirtle, and to her surprise, it fitted. The garment was a little tight around the bust, with a daring, low neckline—but it hugged Keira's curves like a glove. A surcoat of the same color went over the kirtle, a beautiful sleeveless garment that brushed the floor when Keira walked.

Staring at her reflection in the looking glass servants had brought in, Keira wondered at the woman who stared back at her.

Her face wasn't any prettier than she remembered. It was hard to look at her own reflection without remembering her sisters' taunts. And yet there was something different about her.

A faint blush stained her cheeks, accentuating her high cheekbones. The bright expression transformed her serious features and softened their irregularity. Her hair, unbound at present, tumbled in heavy brown curls over her shoulders.

"I suppose all of this must feel a bit overwhelming?" Jaimee spoke up from behind her. "Surrounded by strangers and about to wed a man ye barely know."

"Aye," Keira admitted. Jaimee had no idea just how out of her depth she felt.

"It's a shame none of yer kin are attending the wedding tomorrow," Jaimee continued.

Keira tensed, nerves suddenly twisting her belly. "I have few kin left," she murmured. "Just my uncle and sister ... and neither of them love me well enough to make the trip here."

Once again, she wasn't speaking about Rhianna but herself.

Silence fell in the chamber, and when Jaimee spoke again, her voice was subdued. "Will the gown do for yer wedding?"

Keira turned to her, smiling. "Aye, it will do very well, thank ye, Jaimee."

Their gazes met, and Jaimee smiled back. After a moment, she inclined her head. "Ye are different to the tales I've heard of ye, Rhianna," she admitted.

The warmth that had suffused Keira as she'd stared back at the tall, statuesque woman clad in plum in the looking glass faded.

Here it begins.

"Word in the Highlands is that for all yer beauty, ye are spoiled," Jaimee continued. "But I don't see it."

The comment came as a surprise, and the urge to laugh bubbled up within Keira. *Spoiled?* Did folk really think that of Rhianna? Keira had thought her friend was beloved by all—except that cruel uncle of hers. It was true that the nuns at Iona hadn't ever warmed to the oblate, but Rhianna had been a good friend to Keira. And in return, Keira had felt fiercely loyal.

"Well, I'm hardly a beauty, am I?" Keira replied with a sigh, glancing back at her reflection. "So maybe the stories about my character aren't true either."

An awkward silence fell then, and when Keira glanced back at Jaimee, she found the woman watching her. They were around the same age, Keira guessed. Both well past the age when most women wed. She wondered why Jaimee wasn't married. Surely, she had suitors lining up for her hand?

"Stories are just stories," Jaimee replied after a pause. "Folk like to gossip ... but I think ye are pretty." She favored Keira with a sly look then. "My brother certainly can't take his eyes off ye."

Keira's breathing caught, her cheeks flushing.

Seeing her shocked reaction, Jaimee laughed. "Don't pretend ye haven't noticed?"

"Well, no ... I ..."

Delight sparkled in Jaimee's eyes. "Ye haven't?"

Keira dropped her gaze. There had been that kiss the night before—but no, she'd thought Connor was just well-mannered and attentive by nature. She hadn't caught him *watching* her.

"Indeed, I think my brother is well pleased with the match others made for him," Jaimee continued, making her way over to the open jewelry box on the table. "It's unfortunate that he put this moment off for so long. Morgan and I have been teasing him for years about when he'd collect his wife-to-be from Iona." She peered into the small rosewood box. "Now ... I have just the brooch to match that kirtle and surcoat."

9

TOO PERFECT

"YE ARE FULL of surprises, brother."

Tensing, Connor took a gulp of ale. *Watch it, Morgan.* He'd already had to deal with his uncle's snide comments; if his brother started on at him too, he'd get the sharp edge of his tongue.

Oblivious to Connor's shift in mood, Morgan continued, "All these years, ye have avoided fetching yer betrothed ... and now that ye have, ye look decidedly smug."

A little of the tension eased in Connor's shoulders. Morgan wasn't going to run down Rhianna's looks after all.

"Well, that's what happens when ye are promised to someone at the age of eight," he grumbled. "I didn't like having my future planned out for me ... and if Da hadn't died, I still wouldn't have made the trip."

And what a pity that would have been.

Rhianna Ross captivated him. He'd found it difficult to concentrate all day, especially when she was near. The memory of their heated kiss before her bed-chamber door made him restless. He was relieved that their wedding would take place at noon the next day.

He was usually a patient man but not over this.

Three days in his betrothed's company, and he was yearning for her.

He wasn't sure what had come over him. Rhianna made all other women appear boring and insipid. He'd never known what longing was till he locked gazes with her on the morning he'd collected her from Iona.

"William Leslie and his sons paid us a visit while ye were away," Morgan spoke up once more, changing the subject. The pair of them sat at the laird's table upon the dais, sharing cups of ale before the women joined them for supper. Around them, the long tables farther down the hall were filling up and the aroma of mutton stew drifted in from the nearby kitchens.

Gritta, Morgan's loyal hound, sat under the table, awaiting any scraps that would come later.

Connor inclined his head. "He did?"

"Aye." Morgan pulled a face. "He seems to think our feuding with the Gunns has caught the king's eye ... and it seems King James is not best pleased with us at all."

Connor considered this news and took another pull of ale. He wasn't surprised that news of the bloody battles between the northern clans had been brought to King James's attention. The feuding of late had gotten out of hand. "I wouldn't be surprised if the king eventually intervenes," he replied after a pause.

As always when he thought of that last battle over the summer, a chill prickled Connor's skin. Likewise, Morgan looked unusually solemn. They'd both been there, wading through bodies piled high in gore.

They'd both seen their father fall.

Connor had only recently taken his father's place as chieftain of the Mackays of Farr, and already he was growing weary of the eternal squabbling between the clans. He understood the hate, for his belly burned too whenever he thought of the Gunns, but if the bloody feuding continued, King James was likely to take action against them.

And he couldn't exactly blame him.

Scotland would grow weak indeed if the clans continued to fight amongst themselves.

The appearance then of two women in the doorway to the hall, one red-blonde and the other with hair the color of burnished oak, drew Connor's attention from politics.

Pushing aside his concerns, he watched Rhianna approach the dais. She'd changed into a dark-blue kirtle, brushed out her hair, and then braided two plaits at the top, pulling it back off her face.

And as she stepped onto the dais, Connor rose to his feet.

Their gazes met, and he smiled. "All organized for tomorrow?"

She nodded.

"We have the perfect gown for the occasion," Jaimee chimed in with a grin as she took her seat next to Morgan.

Connor gestured to the empty place beside him. These days, he sat upon his father's oaken chair. The clan's crest—an arm with the hand gripping a dagger— had been carved into the back of it, along with the Mackay clan motto: *Manu forti*—with a strong hand.

Wordlessly, Rhianna took her seat, while Connor seated himself again. "That kirtle matches yer eyes," he murmured, leaning close to her. "The color of the sky just after sunset."

His betrothed's high cheekbones colored prettily, and she glanced up at him under long eyelashes. "Do ye like it then?"

"Aye."

He was keenly aware of Rhianna, of her nearness and the faint perfume of lavender that trailed after her like an invisible veil when she'd stepped up next to him upon the dais. He hadn't been lying; that kirtle suited her even better than the green one Lady Fraser had gifted her. Its tight-fitting sleeves and low-cut bodice revealed her long limbs and lush curves.

Connor was glad of the loose braies he wore this eve, for his shaft stiffened at her proximity.

God's teeth, he was reacting to her like a randy, wet-behind-the-ears lad. Nonetheless, he wished tomorrow were already here.

Servants appeared then, bringing in tureens of stew and baskets of bread. It was a simple meal, for folk ate their main meal at noon. Jaimee had assured him that the cooks were already hard at work on the wedding banquet for the following afternoon. However, they had made some of their preparations ahead of time, as they'd known a wedding was looming close.

"I spent the morning out picking brambles," Jaimee announced from farther down the table. She then held up her hands, the fingers still stained pink. "There will be fruit tarts and thickened cream for the banquet tomorrow."

Connor grinned at his sister, warmth flooding through him. "Sounds delicious." Jaimee was a handful, but her enthusiasm for life had been a balm to his soul these past months. She reminded him so much of their mother—Jaimee had the same practical nature, although she possessed her father's stubborn streak.

Like her brothers, Jaimee was leery of being wed. Their father had indulged her, but now that she'd just passed her twenty-first summer, the time was fast approaching when Connor, as the new laird, would need to bring the subject of marriage up with his headstrong sister once more.

He wasn't looking forward to that day.

Connor glanced at Rhianna then. She had just broken off a piece of bread and was dipping it in her stew. He watched her for a moment longer, drinking her in.

Marriage wasn't so bad. Not if one found the right partner. He needed to convince his sister of that.

Keira wanted to enjoy the supper, but her belly twisted itself in knots as the meal drew out.

It was all perfect—the food, the company. Too perfect.

These people were so kind, so welcoming.

And she was deceiving them all. It wasn't right.

Every time she glanced in Connor's direction, an ache that was both pleasure and pain constricted her chest.

Connor was laird of Farr Castle. Surrounded by his kin and warriors, he looked truly at home here. And the warmth in those pine-green eyes whenever he glanced her way made guilt tighten like a noose around her throat.

Keira had thought she could go through with this—
and she would have to. But she'd never been part of a
deceit like this before.

She glanced then, over at where Jaimee was laughing
at something Morgan had just said. She liked Connor's
siblings. Morgan possessed a devastating, boyish charm
that she wagered had broken a few hearts. Jaimee had a
carefree, independent spirit that Keira envied—that, she
supposed, was what came from growing up in an
environment where one was loved, wanted.

Keira's throat thickened. Swallowing a mouthful of
stew, she reached for her cup of ale.

This family stood in stark contrast to her own. How
she'd hated mealtimes. She'd sit at her father's table,
weathering his criticisms and defending herself from her
sisters' spite while her mother smirked at the other end
of the table. Once her sisters had all been wedded, it was
just Keira and her parents at the table; that had been
even worse than before, for she couldn't let her sisters
dominate the conversation, couldn't pretend she was
invisible.

She hadn't wanted to be packed off to Iona nunnery,
yet it had been a relief to be free of her family.

"Is everything to yer liking, Rhianna?" Connor's voice
drew her out of her dark thoughts. She glanced up, to see
he was frowning.

With a jolt, she realized she was gripping her cup so
tightly her knuckles had gone white. And for a few
moments, she'd let the anguish of the past and her
unhappy childhood show on her face.

Fool, ye must keep up pretenses.

"Of course," she said meekly, taking another sip from
her cup. "Why?"

"Ye looked ... sad ... just then," he observed, a groove
forming between his eyebrows. "Do ye miss Iona?"

Keira suppressed the urge to snort. "No," she replied
honestly, "not at all."

"What is it then?"

Of course, after their conversation the evening before, he knew she didn't miss her kin. She couldn't use that as an excuse.

Meeting his eye, she was tempted to say she was merely tired, that the journey and the rough seas had taken their toll. However, the directness of his gaze drew her in. The desire to forge a connection with him rose within her.

"I never thought this day would come," she murmured. Once again, she was speaking honestly. She hadn't. "I confess I'm nervous."

A slow smile stretched his mouth. "Aye, and so am I." He gave her a long, penetrating look then, and Keira felt as if she'd just been immersed in hot water. That gaze could melt stone. He then reached out and took her hand, entwining his fingers through hers. "This is all new to me as well."

Alone in her bed-chamber, Keira paced the floor.

Connor had given her a room next to his sister's, and Keira had retired early. Jaimee had been disappointed. She'd hoped for the pair of them to natter away together long into the night in the women's solar. However, Keira was too heart-sore for such light-hearted conversation.

Guilt dogged each step as she circuited the chamber. It made each indrawn breath an effort. The supper she'd eaten churned uneasily in her belly, and queasiness rose up within her.

I can't go through with this. I can't wed him pretending to be someone I'm not.

Connor Mackay was a good man; he deserved better than that.

Keira stopped pacing and raised her trembling hands to her face. Her eyes were gritty and sore. She suddenly felt exhausted, yet although it was now getting late, she couldn't bring herself to lie down on her bed.

She was still fully-dressed, her night-rail hanging over the chair by the bed.

Curse Rhianna for suggesting this folly ... and curse me for agreeing to it.

It began to dawn on her then that she'd held herself up like a sacrificial goat to have its throat cut. Rhianna had risked very little. Instead, she'd fled from the nunnery to run away with her lover. If the ruse was unmasked, it was Keira who'd suffer.

And if their places had been reversed, Keira wouldn't have been able to do such a thing to a friend.

Spoiled. Jaimee's words came back to her then. Had she really been so gullible? Perhaps she had. She'd felt so lonely at Iona, her friendship with Rhianna had saved her. She'd been so grateful to her friend—*too* grateful.

Now, here she was, on the eve of wedding a man who believed she was a chieftain's daughter, who believed she was a Ross, not one of the hated Gunns.

I can't do this.

Despite that it was a cool evening, and outdoors a wind whipped in off the sea and rattled the shutters, sweat now beaded on Keira's brow. Guilt mingled with a sense of impending doom. It was too much; she couldn't carry on with this deception.

I have to tell Connor it's all a lie.

Heart pounding, Keira made for the door. She needed to do this before her courage failed her.

10

THE RIGHT CHOICE

CONNOR WAS DOZING before the fire in his solar, his feet up on a settle, when there came a knock at the door.

It was soft—a woman's knock.

"Come in," he called, expecting his sister. It was a bit late in the evening for visitors, but he imagined Jaimee was so excited about the coming wedding that she was still up and about. He too should go to bed.

However, when the door opened, the woman who stepped through the threshold, closing the door behind her, wasn't his younger sister—but his betrothed.

Connor rose to his feet, blinking away the sleepy fog that had settled over him. "Rhianna ... what is it?" His gaze raked over her, taking in the fact she was still dressed in that dark-blue kirtle. "Why aren't ye abed?"

"I couldn't sleep." Her voice came out in a panicked rasp. Rhianna leaned up against the closed door, her gaze settling upon him. "Connor ... I can't do this."

A chill slid down his spine at these words. "What's happened?" When she didn't answer, he crossed the laird's solar and reached her in just a few long strides. He stopped before his bride-to-be, gazing down at her ashen face. "I don't understand, Rhianna," he murmured. "What's wrong?"

Her throat bobbed. "I ..." she began, before faltering. She wet her lips and tried again. "I'm not ..." Her voice choked off.

Connor frowned. He didn't like seeing her so upset. "Has someone said something cruel to ye?" he asked, his tone hardening. He'd thought his brother and sister had welcomed Rhianna, but perhaps one of the servants had been callous. Had his uncle insulted her?

Anger quickened in his belly at the thought. He was going to have to do something about Domhnall. Connor wouldn't have him intimidating Rhianna.

However, she shook her head, allaying his fears.

"What then?"

She stared up at him, her dark-blue eyes glistening. God's teeth, the lass was close to tears.

"I'm not what ye think," she finally whispered.

Tenderness rose up within Connor. From the first, he'd seen that this woman was tormented. She was reputed to be a great beauty, but he could tell she felt lacking. He couldn't understand why, for he'd made his desire for her clear. Yet although she'd spoken of her unpleasant sister, he didn't know just what folk had said to her over the years. Cruel words left scars that took far longer to heal than physical injuries.

"And what do I think?" he asked softly, moving closer to her. He raised a hand then, brushing her cheek with the back of it.

She drew in a slow, trembling breath. "I don't ... I'm not ..."

Once again her voice died away, a blush staining her cheeks. They stood close now, and heat rose up between them. It chased away the last of Connor's reserve as he stared down into her tear-filled eyes.

"I once berated my father for arranging this match," he admitted with a half-smile. "We quarreled more than once over it." His chest tightened as he recalled those angry words, which could never be taken back. "But the moment ye pushed back yer hood that morn at Iona and I stared into yer eyes, I realized what a fool I'd been." He stroked her cheek once more, before the pad of his thumb ran across her full lower lip. That mouth, with its sensual quirk, ached to be kissed. Yet he resisted the urge. She was upset, and he wanted to comfort her, not push her worries aside with a kiss. "We don't yet know each other, Rhianna," he continued, "but if ye give me a chance, I shall show ye that this is the right choice ... for both of us."

Keira closed the door to her bed-chamber and leaned up against it. Her eyes fluttered closed. *Idiot ... ye had yer chance ... why didn't ye tell him the truth?*

She'd wanted to.

She'd walked into the solar determined to reveal who she was to Connor Mackay. And yet, the moment he'd approached her, the moment she looked up at his face, his gaze clouded with concern, the words literally wouldn't come.

He'd thought she had cold feet, that some inner insecurity had driven her to seek him out in the wee hours of the night. And when he'd brushed her cheek with his knuckles, had traced her lower lip with his thumb, her determination had fled.

The tender things he'd said had made it difficult to think, to breathe. And so she'd left him, returned to her bed-chamber, and wondered what in Hades was wrong with her.

Coward.

Was that it, was she afraid of how he might respond when he discovered the truth? Or was it that she was terrified of losing this one chance at happiness?

Ever since setting foot in Farr Castle earlier in the day, she'd received a welcome like no other. It made her realize how ignored she'd felt till now. But ever since she'd arrived, she'd also felt like a fraud.

The Mackays of Farr were welcoming Rhianna Ross *not* Keira Gunn into their midst.

Connor didn't merit this lie—and yet she'd messed up her chance to put him right, her chance to end this farce.

Moving across to the bed, Keira sat down. She entwined her fingers upon her lap, clenching them so hard her joints started to ache dully. She paid the discomfort little mind though. She deserved no less for letting herself continue impersonating Rhianna Ross.

And tomorrow, a priest would unknowingly further the lie, binding her and Connor together before God.

A tear rolled down Keira's cheek, and an ache welled up deep within her chest. It was a mess—all of it—yet she had no idea how to stop what she had so foolishly begun.

11

TOO LATE FOR REGRETS

"WHAT A BEAUTIFUL spot this is." Keira halted, her gaze going over the squat stone kirk and the windswept graveyard surrounding it. It was a bright, breezy morning, although there was a sting in the air; they were well into autumn now, and soon Samhuinn would be upon them.

Keira and Jaimee had just taken a morning walk over the hills to the east after breaking their fast in the great hall. It felt good to get outdoors and stretch her legs. She needed to burn off the nervous energy that seethed within her, before the wedding ceremony.

"Aye ... I come here when I want to be alone with my thoughts," her companion replied, stopping next to her. Jaimee gestured then to two headstones on the southern edge of the kirkyard. "My parents are buried over there. I often visit them ... and sometimes find myself talking to them as if they were still alive." She broke off there, and when Keira glanced Jaimee's way, she saw the young woman wore an embarrassed expression. "It probably sounds daft."

"Not at all." Instead of continuing down the path that would take them back to the castle, Keira walked over to the headstones. Her gaze took in the two names etched onto the slabs of sandstone. "Rory Mackay, chieftain of the Mackays," she murmured. "And Rose Mackay, beloved wife and mother." She glanced then over at where Jaimee had joined her. "They were happily wed then, yer parents?"

Jaimee nodded, her eyes glittering. "They were inseparable."

Keira shifted her attention back to the headstones. *Inseparable.*

"Connor told me that ye lost yer parents young," Jaimee said after a pause. "But do ye remember them?"

"Aye." Keira's throat suddenly felt thick, her voice choked.

"And was it a good match?"

Keira swallowed. She had no idea whether Rhianna's parents had been happy or not, for her friend had barely mentioned them. Instead, she thought again of her own parents. "Not entirely," she murmured. "My father wanted sons ... he never forgave my mother for giving him daughters."

Jaimee gave an indelicate snort, making it clear what she thought of such a view. "What my parents had was rare," she replied. "That's why I don't wish to take a husband. My mother was fortunate to be promised to someone like my father. But she could have easily been married off to a brute."

Keira tore her gaze from the headstones and met Jaimee's eye once more. "Aye, a chieftain's daughter must often wed to please her kin ... and not herself."

Jaimee nodded, her jaw firming. She then flashed Keira a brittle smile. "But ye are one of the fortunate ones, Rhianna. My brother and ye are well-matched—all of us can see it." She linked her arm through Keira's and drew her away from the graves, back toward the path. "Come on ... let's get ye ready for the wedding."

Keira walked across the seaward bailey toward the chapel. A sturdy wall circled the cobbled space, and a watchtower rose up at the far end. This was a quieter courtyard than the landward bailey. There was a tiny walled garden to her left, and Farr Castle's chapel to the right, its peaked roof silhouetted against the windswept sky. A stone well dominated the heart of the bailey.

Drawing in a deep, steadying breath, and clutching a spray of heather as if her life depended upon it, Keira made her way across the cobbles to where her husband-to-be awaited her in the doorway to the chapel.

Connor's gaze tracked her path, although he wasn't the only one watching her. A small crowd had gathered before the steps of the chapel. Jaimee, Morgan, Domhnall, and Connor's cousin, Kennan, were among them. A small woman with thick black hair stood with Kennan, her pale, heart-shaped face alive with curiosity.

The chaplain stood in the chapel doorway with Connor, although when her attention shifted to his stocky, black-robed figure and solemn expression, Keira's belly twisted.

After a year in a nunnery, she knew how important it was not to lie before God.

And yet that was exactly what she was about to do.

The crowd parted, the faces of the well-wishers alive with warm smiles. Few folk could look miserable at a wedding, and it seemed that those at Farr Castle had been waiting a long while for this ceremony. Even Connor's uncle wasn't scowling at her for once.

Forcing herself to keep a smile plastered upon her face, Keira alighted the steps. Connor waited for her at the top. As was tradition, they would wed at the entrance to the chapel.

Reaching her husband-to-be, Keira stopped and turned to face him. He was breathtaking this morning, his golden mane catching the sunlight. Connor wore a snowy-white lèine, his clan sash, a pair of chamois braies, and gleaming hunting boots. A heavy broadsword—a claidheamh-mòr—hung at his left hip and a jeweled dirk at his right.

He'd pinned a brooch to his sash—a bright-green polished agate surrounded by smaller stones of amber and pearls nestled in silver—and that too caught the sun.

Keira wore a matching brooch upon the bodice of her plum-colored kirtle, just below where her cleavage was visible.

Jaimee had told her that these twin brooches belonged to the laird and lady of Farr Castle.

Connor's gaze flicked down to the brooch, and did she imagine it, or did his attention linger upon the swell of her breasts, exposed by the daring neckline of her kirtle?

An instant later, his attention returned to her face, and he favored her with a slow smile. "Ye look bonny indeed, Rhianna."

Rhianna.

Would she ever get used to him calling her that?

"Thank ye," she murmured, acknowledging the compliment gracefully, as Rhianna would have done.

The chaplain then cleared his throat, brandishing the length of Mackay plaid that he would use to bind their joined hands. "Are we ready, Mackay?"

Connor glanced his way. "Aye, Father Lachlan, let us begin."

Laughter and music filled the great hall of Farr Castle. An elderly woman sat at a harp near the hearth, her gnarled fingers flying across the strings with the nimbleness of someone half her age. The strains lifted high into the rafters, blending with the rumble of voices and punctuated by the odd merry laugh.

A great banquet had been served. To start, servants brought in wheels of aged cheese and cured meats, together with baskets of bread studded with seeds and nuts. And then lads carried in haunches of venison that had spent all morning spit-roasting outdoors. Wine, mead, and ale flowed—and as she ate and drank, Keira's knotted belly slowly relaxed.

It was done.

There was little point in bemoaning her lack of courage now.

She'd had her chance to put Connor and his kin right about her real identity, and yet she'd let the opportunity slip through her fingers like grains of fine sand.

The ceremony had been lovely and emotional. Her vision had blurred when they'd recited their vows together, her heart hammering against her ribs.

This was really happening. She'd taken the deception to the limit.

At the end of the ceremony, once Father Lachlan had unwound the ribbon of plaid from their joined hands, Connor had pulled her into his arms and kissed her passionately.

The gesture had delighted the onlookers. Their cheers, clapping, and whistling had reverberated off the surrounding stone.

And now, seated at her husband's side, Keira took a sip from the gem-encrusted silver goblet he held out to her.

Their gazes held as she drank and then passed the goblet back to him, so that he could do the same.

Suddenly, the laughter and voices surrounding them disappeared. All that existed was her and Connor. The knots in Keira's belly tightened once more. When he looked at her like that, a fierce longing rose within her, a sensation so strong that it robbed her of breath.

She wasn't sure exactly what it was she longed for, but Connor somehow held the key.

This was why she'd not been able to tell him the truth. Whenever this man held her gaze, nothing else in the world mattered.

Keira had fallen under Connor Mackay's spell, and it was an enchantment she never wanted to wake from.

"It's time for the bedding!" Connor's uncle, who was well into his cups as the evening drew out, swayed to his feet and raised his drinking horn. "Go on, Connor. Get the deed done!"

"Enough, Domhnall ... sit down," Connor growled, casting Keira a pained look. "Apologies ... my uncle forgets himself when he's had a surfeit of mead."

"Ye have delayed long enough, lad!" Domhnall boomed, his voice slurring. He then crashed back down into his seat. "The hour grows late."

Indeed it did.

The banquet had long ended, and hours of dancing had followed. Keira's feet now ached, although she'd enjoyed every moment of it. From the lively circle dances to the courtly *basse danse*, she'd loved each opportunity to step out onto the floor with her husband.

Husband.

But he wasn't really; he wouldn't be until they consummated their vows.

As his mouthy uncle had observed, Connor appeared to be deliberately delaying the moment. Keira wondered why. Was he as nervous as she was?

Farther down the table, Morgan grinned, before winking at his brother. "Go on ... if ye stay down here, Domhnall will only get more obnoxious." Next to him, Jaimee favored Keira with a sleepy smile.

Jaimee had danced with abandon and now looked as if she was about to fall asleep at the table.

It was getting late—and if they lingered here for much longer, things would get awkward.

Even so, Keira found that brownies danced in her belly, as a mixture of excitement and trepidation bubbled up inside her.

She'd spent four days in this man's company, but they were still in many ways strangers to each other. The idea of disrobing before him, of letting him take her maidenhead, made her break out in a cold sweat.

Wordlessly, Connor rose to his feet, took her hand, and led her from the dais.

Thunderous applause, as well as a few ribald comments, cat-calls, and whistles followed.

Keira's cheeks flushed hot. Was this all necessary?

However, she'd attended all of her sisters' weddings; she knew that it was tradition for the drunken revelers to heckle the newlyweds at the end of the night.

Grateful to leave the great hall, Keira silently followed Connor out into the entranceway and up the stairs to the top floor of the keep.

Hands clasped together, although they still hadn't exchanged a word since leaving the hall, the pair of them walked along the narrow corridor toward the laird's chambers. Guttering cressets studded the walls, their flames sending dancing shadows over the pitted stone.

They entered the laird's solar and crossed to the open doorway of Connor's bed-chamber.

The chaplain awaited them. The small man stood, hands clasped around a pot of holy water, as the couple entered the room.

Once again, the sight of Father Lachlan made Keira's pulse quicken.

It was yet another reminder that she'd lied before God.

And then, her gaze slid past the chaplain to the large bed behind him. Servants had scattered rose petals and sprays of heather over the soft woolen coverlet, and the light scent filled the room.

"Take a seat on the edge of the bed," Father Lachlan instructed gently.

Connor and Keira did as bid.

Keira swallowed, in an attempt to ease the tightness in her throat; the nerves were getting hold now. She was starting to feel sickly and light-headed.

Without further delay, the chaplain set about sprinkling holy water over the coverlet. "Let us bless this bed, Lord, so that this couple may remain firm in yer peace." Father Lachlan then moved before Connor and Keira and blessed them both with the holy water. "May ye have a strong union and be blessed with bairns, and finally arrive at the kingdom of heaven through Christ, Our Lord ... amen."

Keira's heart was now pounding so fiercely she was sure both the chaplain and her husband could hear it.

Don't think about what ye have done, she counseled herself. *Now is too late for regrets.*

She was bound to Connor Mackay, and she had to focus on building a life with him.

The chaplain left then, closing the door to the bed-chamber behind him. They sat listening to the soft pad of his footsteps as he walked away.

Only then did Connor turn to Keira.

Staring down at her clasped hands upon her lap, she could feel the weight and heat of his gaze upon her.

"Ye can look at me, ye know?" The wry humor in his voice made warmth settle over her. She felt safe in this man's presence; she just wished her nerves would settle a bit.

Gathering her courage, Keira lifted her chin, and for a long moment, the pair of them merely gazed at each other. And then, eventually, Connor's mouth quirked.

"I didn't think I'd be nervous about this ... but I find that I am," he admitted.

Keira cocked an eyebrow, relief slamming into her. "Ye *are*?"

"Aye." He gave a soft laugh. "Ye sound surprised?"

"I am," she admitted. Connor Mackay was confident and appeared at ease in his own skin. She hadn't expected him to be anxious about this in the least.

His smile widened. "Shall I pour us some wine? Maybe, it'll calm us both a little."

Keira nodded. They'd consumed a couple of goblets of bramble wine each during the banquet, but Keira suddenly felt terrifyingly clear-headed. Her gaze tracked him as he rose to his feet and crossed to the mantelpiece, where a jug of wine and two cups sat. A lump of peat glowed in the hearth, casting a warm, golden light over the bed-chamber.

Pouring the wine, Connor returned to her side.

"To being man and wife," he said, catching her eye once more as he held his cup up in a toast.

"Man and wife," she murmured, the brownies twirling in her belly once more. She took a gulp of wine, welcoming the heat that chased her nerves away. That was better.

12

LETTING GO

CONNOR TOOK A sip of wine and watched his wife under hooded lids.

She had no idea how much he wanted her.

Sitting there delicately sipping her wine, the firelight playing across her milky skin, Rhianna was a sensual sight. The plum kirtle and matching surcoat were lovely, but even lovelier was the skin they exposed. His mother's brooch had been pinned in a distracting spot, right below that creamy cleavage.

It had been an effort not to gawk at her like a mooncalf all afternoon and evening.

He hadn't been lying though—when they'd entered his bed-chamber, he found his belly tightening with nerves.

It was strange, for it had been a long while since he'd been uneasy with a woman.

However, the wine helped, and after a few sips, he took their cups and set them aside. A faint blush had crept onto her high cheekbones, and he reached out and stroked her face, his heart now thrumming.

Lord, he'd never experienced longing like this before. It made him want to draw these moments out, to savor them—while part of him wanted to yank her into his arms.

He settled for tangling his fingers in the soft waves of her oaken-colored hair.

"I've been looking forward to this," he admitted. "From the moment I set eyes on ye, Rhianna, I've wondered what yer hair would feel like to touch."

He'd wondered a lot more than that. Last night, when he'd finally gotten to bed, he'd lain in the darkness and imagined Rhianna naked. He'd then imagined exploring that lush body of hers. The visions had become so intense that he'd finally taken his shaft in hand and given himself the relief his body craved. However, it hadn't been enough.

Only touching her naked body, in reality, would appease him.

Rhianna's breasts started to rise and fall sharply as he tangled his fingers deeper into her hair. She felt this pull as much as he did, he realized. She wanted this too.

Rising to his feet, he drew her up to face him. And then, cupping her warm cheeks with his hands, he lowered his mouth to hers and kissed her.

It was a slow, exploratory kiss, gentle at first, and then deepening as his tongue parted her lips.

And when Rhianna let out a soft whimper against his mouth, Connor forgot his resolve to go slowly, to draw these precious moments out.

He pulled her hard against him and kissed her hungrily, his mouth now slanting against hers. And to his joy, she flattened her soft body along the length of his, her arms encircling his neck as she kissed him back with fervor equal to his own.

She was drowning in the heat and taste of him.

Connor Mackay was delicious, and when his tongue tangled with hers, and his hands traveled down her back, she melted against the hardness of his body. His hands explored her, even through the layers of clothing that separated them. She loved his touch, the tenderness yet possessiveness of it. And when he cupped her bottom, pulling her harder still against him, she felt the stiffness of his rod pressing against her belly.

Excitement reared up within her, wild and consuming.

She was a maid, hadn't kissed or touched any man but Connor, and yet suddenly the nervousness fled.

Suddenly, all she wanted was to tear off his clothes and explore the magnificence of his naked body.

As if reading her fevered thoughts, Connor broke off the kiss and stepped back from her. He was breathing hard, his green eyes dark with need. In one swift movement, he pulled off his lèine and sash and then began unlacing his braies.

And as he did so, he kept his gaze upon her.

Heat pulsed through Keira then, and, hands trembling, she reached up and started to unlace her bodice. She'd just managed to divest herself of her surcoat and kirtle, standing there only in her thin lèine, when Connor pushed down his braies and kicked them aside. He stood before her naked.

Keira wasn't sure how to react, or what to do.

Did proper ladies avert their gazes at moments like these? Or did they just blatantly stare, soaking up the first sight of their naked husband?

Keira chose the latter. She had never done what others expected anyway—what point was there in starting now?

He was *magnificent*. Tall and heavily muscled with broad shoulders, he had a warrior's body. A few scars marred his torso, one or two of them pink—recent scars most likely taken during the Battle of Harpsdale. Crisp blond curls covered his sculpted chest, although the hair at his groin was a little darker.

Keira's breathing caught when her gaze traveled down to his manhood.

It thrust impatiently against his flat belly: a thick rod with a glistening, swollen tip.

Wet heat flooded between Keira's thighs. Hades, how she wanted to touch him there. But was such an act too bold?

Moving close to her, he reached out, his fingers fisting the linen lèine that shrouded her nakedness. He then slowly drew the ankle-length tunic up. Lifting her arms, Keira let him pull it over her head.

Cool air feathered across her naked skin, although heat bloomed immediately afterward when Connor stepped back, his gaze scorching her.

Pulse racing, her attention went to his face. The sensual good humor of earlier was gone. A very different man stood before her. Connor's handsome features had gone taut, a faint blush tinging his cheekbones.

His expression was almost feral.

Excitement twisted once more, low in the cradle of Keira's hips. She wasn't sure what was supposed to happen next, or if she was even going to enjoy it, but right at that moment, she didn't care.

Right then, fire roared through her veins, dousing all nervousness, all trepidation.

And when Connor led her over to the stool by the fireplace, instead of the bed, she went willingly.

She'd thought he'd want her on the bed, but instead, Connor lowered himself onto the stool and drew her down to sit astride him.

The position was intimate, especially when he pulled her down for another hungry, consuming kiss, yet Keira gave herself up to it. His hands explored her nakedness as they kissed, sliding down the length of her back to her bottom; there he cupped her and drew her flush against him.

The hard, hot length of his shaft pressed against her belly as the kiss deepened. Raw, desperate need clawed its way up inside Keira. This was better than her wildest imaginings. His kiss pulled her into a whirling vortex of desire so heady that she utterly forgot herself.

She forgot that the world had dismissed her as plain and of little value.

She forgot she'd woven a deception and pretended to be someone she wasn't.

She forgot that she was Keira Gunn.

Names, identities, clans—none of it mattered at that moment. Not when this man kissed her as if his life depended on it.

He pulled her up then, bringing her naked breasts level with his face, and when he started to feast on them—drawing each aching nipple into the heated cavern of his mouth—Keira let out a soft, keening cry.

Liquid heat flooded once more between her thighs. The pulsing ache there was becoming unbearable.

Connor worshipped her breasts, burying his face in their softness before sucking each swollen tip till she whimpered and writhed against him. The rasp of his stubbled jaw and cheeks against her sensitive skin, the slick feel of his tongue, was almost too much.

And then, his own breathing now coming in rapid gasps, he released her from the sweet torture of his mouth.

Glancing down, Keira saw Connor take himself in hand, his fingers wrapping around the thickness of his jerking shaft. Then he positioned her above him and placed the swollen tip at her entrance.

Slowly, so slowly she could hardly bear it, he stroked her there with the tip of his shaft. A deep groan escaped Keira, her legs trembling as molten heat pooled low in her belly. And just when she felt she could no longer bear it, he guided her down onto him.

Keira's heart galloped, and her breathing became shallow. He slid into her, stretching her as he went. The sensation of him entering her felt so good that another groan escaped her, but as he lowered her farther onto his shaft, a sharp twinging pain caught her by surprise.

Keira's moan turned into a gasp.

"It's alright, mo leannan," he murmured. "The pain shall pass soon enough."

My lover.

The sensual husk to his voice made tremors of hot desire shiver through her. Did he have any idea what his voice did to her?

Moments passed, and then, gripping her hips, he pulled her fully onto him, seating himself completely within her.

Panting, Keira sat astride him, wondering at the aching pleasure that now started to throb within her. He was right, the pain had passed, and what lay on the other side was breathtaking. She threw back her head and groaned.

It was almost too much, and she curled her fingers over his shoulders, her nails biting into his flesh, clinging to him.

Connor let the moment draw out. Being buried deep in this woman's heat had almost undone him. Like a lad with his first woman, he'd nearly spilled when Rhianna had groaned.

The sound was so sensual, so lusty, that he'd almost forgotten himself.

For a few moments, they remained like that, locked together, while she got used to the new sensation, and while he regained control of himself.

He trailed his fingertips up over her hips and the soft curve of her belly to her breasts.

The devil take him, he could feast on those all day. Heavy, with silky skin, her breasts had large, ripe nipples.

She was all curves and sweet, soft skin. She was a goddess, and he was buried deep inside her.

There was no place else he wanted to be.

Gripping her hips, he slowly raised her up, sliding her up the length of his rod, and then impaling her on it once more.

Rhianna's eyes snapped wide, her sensual, crooked mouth opening. "Connor," she gasped his name. "I ..." She trailed off as he repeated the act, and soon she wasn't able to speak at all. Soon she writhed, sighed, and gasped, while he continued to guide her.

Deep shudders passed through her, and she threw back her head, a soft, ragged cry echoing through the room. "Connor," she choked out his name, bending forward then and resting her forehead in the hollow of his neck. "This feels so good ... it's almost too much."

Connor smiled. Sweat coated him, from the effort he was making to go slow. She had no idea of the leash he was holding himself on; his pulse now roared in his ears. "It's not, mo leannan," he murmured. "Just let go."

He longed to see this woman unravel. A few days in her company had fascinated him, and yet he realized that Rhianna Ross had many layers to her, and even a few secrets. He wanted to tear down her walls, one by one.

And he would start tonight.

Taking her with him, he leaned forward, sliding off the stool and sinking to his knees on the deerskin rug before the glowing hearth. Rhianna sprawled onto her back, her face flushed, her eyes glowing, and her lips swollen from his kisses.

Murmuring another endearment, he took hold of one of her knees, raising it high, while he spread the other wide. And then he took her in hard, deep strokes.

She was a maid, and he knew he should go gently tonight. But now that he was buried to the hilt within her, all reason fled from his mind. Instead, the need to possess this woman, the need to watch her lose control, took over.

Soon both their cries filled the bed-chamber. Rhianna's eyes fluttered shut as she arched back against him, meeting each thrust. Like him, her skin gleamed with sweat. She gasped out incoherent words, her voice cracking as she finally let herself go. And then her movements became jerky, desperate. Another ragged cry escaped her. Connor drove into her once more, and she bucked wildly against him, shattering.

13

NEW LIFE, NEW IDENTITY

LANGUID AND LOOSE-LIMBED, Keira stirred next to her husband on the big bed.

The sheets were tangled, for after they'd moved from the deerskin rug to the bed, he'd taken her again. Connor now lay on his back, utterly spent. He sprawled naked, one muscular arm flung over his face.

Keira watched the gentle rise and fall of his chest, before her gaze slid over the rest of him, taking in the full glory of the man she was now bound to.

Excitement feathered in the pit of her belly at the thought.

She was Lady Mackay, but more than that, she was Connor's wife.

She'd resisted this, and her conscience had very nearly bested her. But lying there in the early dawn, her gaze devouring her husband, Keira was relieved that he'd misunderstood her reason for coming to his solar in distress.

He thought she hadn't believed herself worthy, and although there was some truth in that—it was not for the reasons he thought.

He'd hate me if he knew.

A chill slid over Keira then, making the warm mantle of well-being that hugged her slip, just a little.

Then he must never know.

She'd acted foolishly the night before. Rhianna would have scolded her for doing something so daft. She'd agreed to this, she'd walked out of Iona nunnery pretending to be someone she wasn't. There wasn't any point in developing a conscience after the fact.

It was just that she hadn't expected to be met with such kindness. The Mackays welcomed her so warmly, and she felt like a beast for betraying their trust. However, she had very nearly ruined things—and she wouldn't make the same mistake again.

This was her life now, her identity. She would give herself entirely to her husband and build a future with him. It was time to look forward, and to cast away the memories of her old existence.

Reaching out, Keira traced a fingertip down the pink, puckered scar on Connor's ribs. It was a long scar and would eventually fade to silver. However, now it still looked fresh.

Connor groaned at her touch, stirring awake. Lowering his arm, he regarded her with a sleepy smile. "Are ye tickling me, woman?"

"No," she murmured, propping herself up on one elbow as her finger traced the line of the scar once more. "Just exploring."

He glanced down at the scar, and Keira saw a shadow pass over his eyes. "I got that at Harpsdale," he murmured.

"I thought as much ... it's new."

"A big brute got me with his claidheamh-mòr ... managed to slice right through my chain-mail."

Keira winced at this description. *A Gunn brute.*

"A huge bastard with wild dark hair and a short beard." Connor continued, his brow furrowing. "I remember he had eyes as grey as the winter sea and a long scar down one cheek."

Keira tensed, alarm coiling in her belly.

"Alexander Gunn," she breathed. She'd attended enough clan gatherings over the years to recognize this man's description.

Connor's gaze widened. "George Gunn's eldest?"

Keira nodded. "None other." She cleared her throat. "I met him once at a clan gathering." That wasn't a lie— she had.

Connor took this in, and Keira was relieved to note that she saw no suspicion in his eyes. The Ross clan had joined the Mackays in their feud against the Gunns of late, but up until a couple of years earlier, there had been an uneasy truce between the two clans. He didn't think there was anything strange about her knowing who the man was.

"Pity I didn't deal the bastard a similar blow," Connor growled, a hard look settling over his face. Watching the transformation, Keira realized that although he was gentle with those he cared for, Connor Mackay was probably not someone to cross swords with.

Keira swallowed. "Did he kill yer father?" she asked softly.

Connor shook his head, the hardness in his eyes fading as sadness rose in its place. "Another Gunn warrior did ... one I cut down. I was bleeding like a stuck pig at the time, but seeing my father fall turned me into a beast. I don't even remember how many men I killed that day." A tremor went through his big frame then. "Battle brings out the worst in men, Rhianna."

Keira's breathing slowed, horror chilling her blood. She knew he'd killed Gunn warriors, but to hear him state it so baldly made queasiness rise within her. She was masquerading as a Ross, yet she'd always be a Gunn in her heart.

Fighting her reaction, for it risked unmasking her, Keira slid her hand across his chest, resting her palm over his heart. To her surprise, she felt it thud fast.

"Ye did what ye had to," she said after a pause, focusing on how Rhianna Ross would have responded to such a tale. "And just as well, for ye'd be dead now otherwise ... and ye and I would never have met."

The edges of his mouth lifted slightly, although there was no humor in his eyes. "Aye, but by rights, I shouldn't even be chieftain now." Pain flickered over his face. "My father should have lived for a long while yet."

Keira heard the strain in his voice. "Ye looked up to him greatly, didn't ye?"

He turned his face to meet her eye squarely. "Aye," he admitted, his voice gruff. "Rory Mackay was admired by all." His gaze guttered then.

Keira watched him steadily. "Ye fear ye won't do his memory justice?"

His mouth thinned. "A couple of years ago, we attended a meeting at Castle Varrich. I'll never forget Angus Mackay roaring across the table: *Ye will have big boots to fill, Connor. But let's face it, ye will never live up to yer father.*"

Silence followed this admission. Keira exhaled slowly, her fingertips digging into his skin. "That's not true, Connor. Surely, ye realize that?"

Connor's gaze speared her, and in its depths, she saw a surprising vulnerability—one that he'd not likely ever shown to anyone before. "Isn't it?" he rasped. "I saw the look in Angus Mackay's eyes as he said those words. At every battle I've fought, my father always overshadowed me. Even in his last one. I've lost count of the times I've watched in awe as his blade sang." He paused then, his hand rising and covering hers. "All my life, I've felt as if I've lived under his shadow ... and as much as I loved him, it has become my curse."

"I saw Connor earlier ... with a big grin on his face."

Heat flushed through Keira at this observation. The woman who'd made it—Cait Mackay—was favoring her with a knowing smile that made her drop the spindle she was winding wool onto.

Cait, Kennan's spirited wife, had joined Keira and Jaimee in the women's solar this afternoon. The open window revealed overcast skies and a rough sea, yet it was warm in the solar, for a large brick of peat burned in the hearth.

"Really?" Keira replied lightly, feigning surprise.

"Aye." Cait's smiled widened to a grin. "And judging from the pretty blush upon yer cheeks, ye know exactly why."

Indeed, Keira's cheeks now felt as if they were aflame.

"Ye have the look of a woman who's been well-bedded," Cait continued, a wicked glint now in her eye.

Keira picked up her spindle. *Lord, please stop,* she inwardly pleaded. She wasn't used to such talk. However, Cait had no such qualms.

"And as for Connor, he looks as if—"

Across the solar, and seated at the window, Jaimee snorted, cutting Cait off. "Please ... no more! I don't want to think about my brother bedding his wife." She cast Keira an apologetic glance. "Sorry, but I don't."

"No offense taken," Keira assured her, resuming her task. "I'm not comfortable with such talk either."

It was Cait's turn to snort now. "Listen to the pair of ye ... where's yer sense of fun? It's just coupling ... both men and beasts do it."

Jaimee rolled her eyes. "Well, I don't."

Cait favored the younger woman with a slow smile. "That's only because ye haven't yet discovered the pleasure of bed sport ... once ye do, ye won't sit there so primly."

"I intend never to wed," Jaimee announced. She had a pile of sewing upon her lap but hadn't yet touched it. Instead, she glanced wistfully out the open window. "I want to remain free."

"Well, that's a grand notion, lass," Cait replied with a shake of her head. The small woman pursed her lips. "But yer brother will have other plans for ye."

Jaimee's attention snapped from the view outside the window, to Cait, a deep furrow appearing between her brows. "Connor won't make me wed anyone if I don't wish it."

Cait held her eye, her own brow furrowing. "Ye are a chieftain's daughter," she pointed out, her tone softening a little. Like Keira, she'd likely seen the alarm that flared in Jaimee's eyes, the panic. She really was against the idea of taking a husband. "With that role comes responsibility," Cait continued. "Connor didn't want to wed either." She flashed Keira a smile then. "But look how well that's worked out for him. All his worries were for nothing."

A mulish expression settled upon Jaimee's lovely face. "Aye, but he's a man ... things are different for him."

Cait huffed a frustrated sigh, throwing up her hands. She then met Keira's eye. "And are ye regretting marriage, Rhianna?" she asked, a sly look creeping into her blue eyes.

"No," Keira replied honestly. "Not at all."

"Well, neither do I," Cait replied, casting Jaimee a look of censure. "Kennan is the best thing that ever happened to me."

"But ye were best friends for years before ye fell in love," Jaimee countered. Red spots had appeared on her cheeks now. This conversation was clearly starting to vex her. "That's not the same as having suitors paraded before ye." Her gaze shadowed then. "Don't ye remember that awful gathering last year ... when Da invited those warriors to compete for my hand?"

"Aye, and ye wouldn't speak to any of them," Cait replied. The two women's gazes fused then, and Keira suddenly felt as if she was intruding. Of course, Cait and Jaimee knew each other well, while she was a newcomer to Farr Castle. It was best to keep quiet during discussions like these, until she felt comfortable enough to contribute.

A tense silence drew out, and then Cait gave a rueful shake of her head. "Ye must find a man who will be yer dearest friend, Jaimee," she advised softly. "Such men make the best husbands."

Warmth spread through Keira at these words, even if Jaimee screwed up her face at this wisdom. Indeed, she and Connor had forged a connection from the moment she'd drawn back her hood outside Iona nunnery and met his gaze.

It was a connection that grew gradually stronger with each passing day—a connection that filled her with wonder and excitement for their future together.

Aye, there was passion and tenderness between them, but there was also a growing trust. The things Connor had confided in her that morning were raw—secrets that he revealed to no one. And yet, he'd told her.

She would guard them with her life.

14

THE INVITATION

CONNOR LEANED BACK in his seat and let the rumble of voices in the great hall wash over him. Supper was approaching, a light meal—especially after all the feasting of the last two days. He'd taken his seat alongside his brother, uncle, and cousin, although they were still awaiting the arrival of the women.

After a largely sleepless night, Connor was exhausted today. However, he welcomed the tiredness. He'd happily forgo sleep again tonight, in favor of making love to his wife. Shifting in his chair, his gaze flicked to the doorway of the great hall.

He hadn't seen Rhianna all afternoon and found he was missing her.

"She'll join us soon enough, brother." Morgan's drawl drew Connor's attention from the doorway. Connor glanced over at him, to find Morgan grinning. "I don't think yer wife has run off ... not yet at least."

Connor snorted. "Wipe that smirk off yer face ... idiot."

Farther down the table, Kennan laughed. "Morgan does have a point though ... ye haven't been listening to a word either of us has been saying."

A servant appeared at the table, bearing a jug. "Wine?" The young woman asked. Comely, with curly blonde hair and a dimpled smile, the lass's gaze was riveted upon Morgan.

The other men at the table might as well have been invisible.

Morgan favored her with a cocky smile. "Aye, thank ye, bonny Chrissa."

Moving to the table, she filled his cup—before going to Connor, Domhnall, or Kennan. Then, after serving the others, she cast Morgan another lingering smile, placed the jug upon the table, turned, and walked away, her hips swaying.

Morgan watched her go, a grin remaining upon his lips.

"Careful," Kennan murmured, as soon as Chrissa was out of earshot. "Ye will get yerself in trouble one of these days."

Connor frowned, his attention flicking between his cousin and brother. He then stilled as realization filtered through him. "Ye haven't been swiving her, have ye, Morgan?"

"Who do ye think warmed his bed last night?" Kennan countered, raising his cup to his lips. Domhnall, who'd been nursing a sore head after the excesses of the night before, coughed a laugh.

Morgan scowled at his cousin. "Thanks for that, Kennan," he muttered. He then raised his hand, making a dismissive gesture before he picked up his own cup. "It's just a bit of fun ... it was yer wedding ... and I felt like celebrating."

"Ye won't be celebrating when her womb quickens with yer bastard," Domhnall cut in. "And neither will Chrissa when the laird throws her out of the castle."

Connor cast his uncle a look of censure. He didn't need Domhnall to speak on his behalf. He had a tongue and wits of his own to respond to his brother. "Our uncle is a bit free with his opinions," he murmured. "But he has a point. Have a care. A tumble in the sheets can have repercussions." He didn't bother to temper the note of warning in his voice. Morgan had always been wild. Unlike Connor, he'd often clashed with their father. Possibly, Morgan and Rory Mackay were too alike in many ways; Connor had heard that his father had been reckless in his youth—although marriage to a good woman had smoothed his rough edges.

The memory of their mother, Rose Mackay, cast a shadow over his mood. They'd lost her after a short yet dramatic illness. His father hadn't been the same after that—and in fact, Connor had sometimes wondered if some of his old recklessness hadn't returned following her death.

He'd lunged himself into the fray at Harpsdale as if he didn't care if he lived or died. A chill slid down Connor's spine at the thought. Maybe, he'd never intended to live through that battle?

The sight of three women entering the great hall drew his thoughts from dark memories.

Cait led the way, in her usual quick, determined strides, with Rhianna following close behind. Jaimee brought up the rear.

As always since she'd entered his life, Connor couldn't take his eyes off Rhianna.

Rhianna Mackay.

She wore the emerald kirtle that Fiona Fraser had gifted her. The gown's color complemented her pale complexion and rich brown hair. She carried herself tall and proud. There was something about her, a grace that shone from the inside, that made it difficult for him not to stare at her.

"Good eve," Rhianna greeted Connor, sinking into the chair next to him.

"Sorry we're late," Cait added, as she took her seat next to Kennan, "but Jaimee wanted us to take a walk along the cliffs before supper."

"I was tired of being cooped up indoors all day," Jaimee quipped. "There's nothing like a bit of sea air after a mind-numbing afternoon of sewing."

Connor smiled; his sister was a restless soul, ill-suited to women's work. She chafed at having to sew, weave, and spin and much preferred to be out walking, riding, or hunting. However, his sister didn't hold his attention for long. Instead, he glanced back at Rhianna. "Did ye enjoy yer walk?"

"Aye, we went down to the Bay of Swordly," Rhianna replied with an answering smile. "I hadn't realized there was another village so close-by."

"There are plenty of them throughout our lands," Connor replied. "If ye like, we can ride out tomorrow, and I shall give ye a tour?"

A smile blossomed across Rhianna's face. "I'd love that."

"Can I come too?" Jaimee piped up, her green eyes shining with excitement.

"Of course," Connor replied, although secretly he'd hoped to have his wife to himself for the day. "We can leave early and make a day of it."

He broke off then, as a group of servants entered the hall, bringing in baskets of bread and platters of cheese and apples.

Pouring Rhianna some wine, Connor met her eye once more. Around them, conversation resumed. He was vaguely aware of Jaimee and Morgan bickering, while Kennan and Cait laughed over something together. But Connor's attention was focused solely on his wife.

"I missed ye today," he admitted, before feeling slightly foolish. They'd hardly been parted for long. He was behaving like a love-sick youth; he needed to rein himself in. And yet, when Rhianna smiled back, her dark-blue eyes shining with warmth, his embarrassment faded. "And I missed ye … even if Cait and Jaimee are lively company." Her smile widened. "And I look forward to our ride tomorrow. This is a bonny corner of Scotland … I can hardly believe it is now my home."

He inclined his head, pride tightening his chest. "I've traveled the length and breadth of most of the Highlands," he admitted, "but I never feel quite myself until I'm standing upon Mackay soil once more. The winters can be harsh up here, but if ye stand on the cliffs on a fair evening, watching the sun set over the sea, there is nowhere more beautiful."

"I agree," she replied softly. "I love it here already."

"Mackay!" A man's voice jerked Connor's attention away from his wife's midnight-blue eyes, a gaze he could drown in. His attention swiveled back to the entrance to the great hall, to see one of his warriors striding toward him, a rolled parchment in hand.

"This has just come from Castle Varrich," the man announced.

Connor nodded, reaching for the missive. "Thank ye, Fergus."

Indeed, the wax seal bore the Mackay crest—a victorious hand, gripping a dagger, held aloft.

Around him, conversation at the table died as Connor broke the seal and swiftly read the message from the clan-chief. He hadn't heard from Angus Mackay since Harpsdale. That battle had left a bitter taste in all their mouths, for the bloody end hadn't yielded a victor. Both sides had limped away from the exchange. The Mackay had been vexed by that.

"It's an invitation," Connor announced after a moment, relief filtering through him. At least it wasn't another call to arms, not so soon after Harpsdale. Such a missive would arrive at Farr Castle soon enough. Connor just wanted to have some time with his wife before it did. "He invites us to spend Samhuinn at Castle Varrich."

"Samhuinn?" Morgan Mackay cocked a dark-blond eyebrow. "But that's only two days away ... he's left it late."

Keira swallowed a mouthful of bread and reached for her cup of wine. A chill seeped over her, dousing the warmth that had cocooned her all day.

Castle Varrich. She'd only just arrived at Farr Castle and had no wish to leave it so soon. Not only that, but she was safe here. No one here had ever seen Rhianna Ross or Keira Gunn. But the seat of the Mackay clan could be a different matter.

Keira had no idea whom the clan-chief would be inviting to the festivities.

Beside her, Connor heaved a sigh. He then flicked her an apologetic look. "We'll have to leave that tour for another time, Rhianna." He flashed her a smile then. "Fear not though ... the ride to Varrich is a fine one."

"We're all invited, I take it?" Jaimee asked.

Connor nodded. He then shifted his attention to his cousin. "Kennan will look after things in our absence."

Kennan smiled back. "Of course I shall."

Keira noted that Domhnall Mackay tensed. Connor's uncle hadn't uttered a word all supper; truthfully, his bloodshot eyes and sickly expression made him look as if he should be abed. Indeed, he'd over-indulged the night before.

Even so, his big hand tightened around the cup of ale he nursed. "As will I," he growled.

Connor cut his uncle a look then, his own gaze narrowing.

"It's been a while since I enjoyed Angus Mackay's hospitality." Seemingly oblivious to the sudden tension at the table, Morgan reached for the jug of wine and topped up his cup. "From memory, he puts on a fine feast." He grinned at Connor then. "Let's hope he has some comely female guests."

"Ye are to behave yerself," Connor growled, frowning. "Misbehave, and I'll leave ye at home the next time."

Watching the two brothers interact, Keira realized that Connor was referring to past incidents. Jaimee pursed her lips at the reminder, while Kennan took a sip from his cup to hide a smile. Next to him, Cait was watching Morgan with an exasperated expression.

The tableau was a reminder that, although these people had welcomed her into their midst, they were still very much strangers to her.

Keira tensed. She needed more time here at Farr Castle before she was ready to face the Mackay clan-chief. She just prayed he'd never seen Rhianna Ross in the flesh. Her friend had made it sound as if she hadn't met many beyond her clan, although news of her beauty seemed to have spread far and wide.

Keira's belly clenched. *I hope she wasn't lying to me.* She dismissed the thought then. Of course, Rhianna had told her the truth. She would have known what such a lie could do to Keira.

Shifting his attention from his brother, Connor caught Keira's eye once more. Perhaps mistaking her tension for disappointment, he offered her another smile. "As I said, it's a bonny ride to Castle Varrich, especially if the weather holds."

Keira nodded, forcing her lips to form a smile. "I look forward to it," she lied.

Satisfied, Connor glanced back at his siblings. "We'll ride out for Varrich tomorrow then."

Keira stared down at the collection of kirtles spread out upon the bed and tried to decide which to bring to Varrich. They were likely to be away around three to four days.

She'd never before been faced with such a choice. Her parents hadn't lavished her with fine gowns, for they weren't interested in showing her off to potential suitors, and then once she'd arrived at Iona nunnery, she'd worn nothing but a habit.

How things had changed.

This should have delighted her. However, after the arrival of the Mackay clan-chief's invitation—one that none of his chieftains would ignore—she felt on edge.

Keira was alone in their bed-chamber. Connor was off organizing his men for the following day's journey. It was the first spell she'd had on her own since their wedding ceremony, and the solitude caused all kinds of worries to bubble up inside her.

Folk will whisper and smirk when they see me.

What if one of them has met Rhianna Ross before?

What if someone asks me a question about the Ross clan I cannot answer?

Clenching her jaw, Keira plucked two kirtles off the bed, rolled them up, and pushed them into the leather saddle bag she would carry with her the following day.

Enough. She was tired of the mire of her own thoughts.

The folk of Farr Castle hadn't smirked and whispered upon her arrival. Although, when she remembered the initial reaction of some of Connor's men, his uncle included, a lump of ice settled in the pit of her belly.

She felt secure here, protected by Connor. She didn't want to venture elsewhere—especially not so soon. She already knew just how cruel the world could be, and now that she'd found a safe haven, she was loath to leave its sheltering walls.

Keira had just finished hanging up the kirtles she wouldn't be bringing on the trip, when the door to the bed-chamber whispered open, and her husband entered.

Husband.

Heat flushed over Keira at the sight of him. Dressed in a loose lèine and plaid braies, his hair spilling over his shoulders, Connor Mackay never failed to make her go weak at the knees.

His gaze went to the stuffed saddlebag at the foot of the bed. "All packed?"

Keira nodded, before motioning to another satchel upon a chair near the window. "I took the liberty of packing some clothing for ye ... I hope ye don't mind?"

He smiled. "Of course not ... although one of the servants would have done it."

"I know ... but I wanted to."

Connor approached her then, his gaze roaming over her face. "Do ye not want to go to Castle Varrich, Rhianna?"

Keira swallowed. "Of course I do ... why?"

"Ye went quiet after that missive arrived ... and even now, yer gaze is shadowed."

Curse the man, he was far too observant.

She considered continuing to deny his remark yet noted the glint in his eye. He wanted honesty from her.

Honesty. Mother Mary, it's far too late for that. However, she would share a little of her worries with him.

"I'm anxious how folk will respond to me," she admitted. Her voice had developed a husky edge, betraying her. "I want to make ye proud ... not a laughing-stock."

Connor's strong jaw tightened, his pine-green eyes darkening to jade. "A laughing-stock? Is that what ye believe yerself to be?"

Queasiness churned in Keira's stomach. The dear Lord preserve her, that hadn't come out at all as she'd wanted. The man before her thought she was lovely, and yet she constantly ran herself down before him.

Witless goose, are ye trying to ruin everything?

She was letting her sisters' cruel words and her parents' scorn jeopardize her happiness. She had to stop. Pulling herself together, Keira heaved in a deep breath. "Sorry ... that's not what I really meant. I've never been at ease with crowds ... I worry I'll say or do the wrong thing."

Connor's expression softened, and he took a step closer to her. "Ye have to stop torturing yerself like this, mo leannan," he murmured. Reaching out, he cupped her cheek. As always, his touch was a brand upon her skin. Without consciously meaning to, Keira swayed toward him. "I don't know exactly what the likes of yer sister have said to ye over the years, but none of it is true." He paused then, his mouth curving. "Just earlier, I was thinking how well ye carry yerself. I admire everything about ye."

Heat flushed through Keira's belly, chasing away her nerves. "Ye do?"

His smile widened, and then he reached up with his free hand and entwined his fingers in her hair. "Ye bring something into my life, Rhianna ... something I never realized was missing."

15

MEETING THE JEWEL

THEY RODE OUT from Farr Castle on a brisk, windy morning. Wispy clouds chased each other against the lightening sky, and Keira's hood kept blowing back as she urged her courser into a brisk trot. The bay gelding had a long, comfortable gait. His name was Outlaw, and he was a gift from her husband.

Connor rode at her side upon a powerful roan named Thunder. The stallion was high-spirited. He'd pawed the ground and tossed his head before leaving the landward bailey, but Connor handled him easily.

The rest of their party—Morgan, Jaimee, and an escort of ten Mackay warriors—rode close behind.

Leaving the cliff-tops at their backs, the party struck out over emerald hills. In the distance reared the outline of great mountains. Castle Varrich lay to the south-west. However, the party set off south for a spell, before they would take the narrow road that led over the rugged hills toward their destination.

Being a Gunn, Keira had never visited the seat of the Mackay clan. She'd heard it was an impressive sight. It was said to perch high over the lands it commanded, under the shadow of two great mountains: Ben Hope and Ben Loyal.

Keira glanced, once more, over at her husband. The wind whipped his unbound hair over his cheeks. Like her, he wore a fur-lined plaid cloak. With Samhuinn looming, the weather had definitely taken a turn. Even as the morning sun cast its friendly face upon them, the heat was waning.

Like most folk, Keira didn't look forward to the bitter season. But, this morning, riding alongside Connor Mackay, she found she didn't dread it as she usually did. This winter, she would sleep entwined with her husband and reside within the thick walls of Farr Castle.

A pleasant cloak of fatigue enveloped her this morning—the result of another sleepless night. She and Connor had fallen into an exhausted slumber in the early hours, but the rest of the night had been spent in a languorous exploration of each other's bodies.

Fire flickered in the base of Keira's belly as she allowed memories of what they'd done to flow over her. Connor was breathtakingly sensual. She hadn't thought he could bring her more pleasure than he had on their wedding night. Yet last night, he'd shown her that was only a glimpse of what they could experience together. He'd spread her out on the bed and taken a long time to show her exactly what her body was capable of experiencing.

Keira's face flushed then. They'd both made a lot of noise. Hopefully, the thick walls of the bed-chamber had dulled their groans and cries from the rest of the keep. She'd deliberately avoided looking at his kin when they'd joined them in the landward bailey earlier.

In the stark light of the morning, her sense of propriety had returned. Connor hardly seemed to care though. He met her eye then, a boyish smile creasing his face. The glint in his eye told her that he'd noted her blush and knew exactly what was behind it.

Had he been recalling the torrid night they'd just emerged from?

"When will we reach Castle Varrich?" Keira asked, forcing herself to concentrate on the here and now. When Connor looked at her like that, her wits scattered like a handful of straw in the wind. She needed to focus on her surroundings.

"Late afternoon most likely," Connor replied, his gaze sweeping toward the windswept hills to the west. "It's slow-going, and the road is rough."

"When was yer last visit?"

"In spring ... the clan-chief called a meeting to discuss our next move against the Gunns."

Keira swallowed. She couldn't help it; every time he mentioned her clan, it was a punch to the belly. Loyalty tugged at her. Would the sensation ever pass?

"The Battle of Harpsdale," she said after a pause. "Who instigated it?"

Connor cut her a sharp look. "The Gunns of course, with their aggressive, belligerent ways. They claimed the lands of Caithness, but we ... and the Sutherlands ... contested it." His mouth thinned. "Angus Mackay and Robert Sutherland assembled the forces of Strathnaver, and we marched upon them. The Gunns made their stand just south of Thurso ... and there we fought them."

His tone had turned flinty—as it always did when he spoke about her clan.

So, the Gunns hadn't been the aggressors after all, Keira noted. Despite the Gunn's 'belligerence', the Mackays had made the first move. She wasn't sure why she'd asked him about the battle. She supposed part of her wanted to understand the hate between the clans, to try and find a tangible reason for the feud that had caused so much blood-shed—and would likely cause much more.

But just like when she'd questioned her father about it, Connor's reply had left her dissatisfied.

Keira's first view of Castle Varrich didn't disappoint.

They approached the fortress from the north, riding through the village of Tongue—a scattering of cottages with smoke rising from their thatched roofs. To the west, the broad Kyle of Tongue glittered in the late afternoon sun.

The wind had settled to a whisper now, the sun deepening the colors of the surrounding hills and gilding the walls of the castle perched high upon the crag over the water. The peaks of Ben Loyal and Ben Hope, their majestic slopes etched against the pale blue sky, formed a dramatic backdrop.

Connor cut Keira a look as they approached the pathway that wound its way up to the summit. "Impressed?"

Keira nodded, casting him a smile in return. "Aye, it's almost as fine as Farr Castle ... almost."

Connor laughed. "I do believe ye are flattering me, wife."

She wasn't. There was something about Farr Castle's position, overlooking the wild sea, that called to her soul. Castle Varrich, despite that it appeared a larger fortress, didn't affect her in the same way.

"The castle was built upon a Norse fort ... like Farr," Connor explained, his gaze sweeping up to the towering stone walls. "There are caves at the base of the promontory, where the locals once lived."

Keira took this in with a nod, even if her belly now felt tight with nerves. She'd enjoyed the day's ride and the long conversations with her husband along the way. However, now that Castle Varrich loomed above them, her fears returned.

Connor had been kind last night, but if only her anxiety *was* related to something trifling, like her looks. Instead, there was so much more at stake.

Ye could always tell him, a voice whispered. *Ye could end this farce.*

Keira clenched her jaw. Curse her conscience. She thought she'd managed to smother it after the wedding. She'd told herself that the only way forward was to live the lie she'd woven.

But it had merely fallen silent for a day or two. Like it or not, she wasn't going to be able to forget what she'd done.

I must be careful here, she reminded herself as she followed Connor up the path. Leaning forward, she let Outlaw pick his way up the slope.

How she wished the Ross clan weren't friends of the Mackays. Whenever Connor or his kin had asked her of her family, she'd merely blended it with recollections of her own. However, that wouldn't wash if she met anyone who actually knew the Ross clan well.

Fortunately, Rhianna had assured her that her uncle rarely traveled from his broch these days.

The reminder settled Keira's nerves just a little. As long as she took care, there was no reason why things wouldn't go smoothly here. Like the rest of her party, she could enjoy the Samhuinn celebrations.

As they neared the high curtain wall of Castle Varrich, Keira spied a great pyre to the right of the pathway. A smile curved her lips. The fire festival was just a day away now, and the folk of Tongue were readying themselves. She too loved the fires of Samhuinn. She loved the drums after dark—and how folk would dress up as wulvers, selkies, and fae, and leave out cakes in their windows for the spirits of the dead.

Samhuinn was part of the old ways, and Keira felt close to her ancestors on this night.

Angus-Dow Mackay strode out into the bailey to meet them. Huge and bearlike, with greying brown hair, a long beard, and sharp blue eyes, the clan-chief dominated any space he stepped into. "Welcome back, lad!" His deep voice boomed off the surrounding walls.

Lad.

Connor gritted his teeth at the patronizing tone in the older man's voice, even as he forced a smile. "Greetings, Mackay." He swung down from Thunder and walked forward to meet the clan-chief, clasping arms with him.

"Ye had a pleasant ride from Farr, I take it?"

"Aye ... the weather is kind today. Hopefully, it will be a fine eve for Samhuinn on the morrow."

Angus slapped his back. "Aye, tomorrow we shall celebrate ... but I expect ye at my table tonight, lad. Now that yer father is gone ... ye and I need to talk."

Connor tensed. There was something in the clan-chief's voice that put him on edge—aside from his continuing to call him 'lad'. Rory Mackay had been close to his clan-chief, and Connor wondered what his father had agreed with Angus before his death.

Tonight, he'd find out.

"So, this is yer Ross bride?" the Mackay boomed. "Let's have a look at her."

The tension in Connor's gut coiled further. It wouldn't have mattered, if he didn't know that Rhianna hadn't been looking forward to this visit. He wanted to spare her being the center of attention, but as his wife, it would be impossible.

However, to his relief, Rhianna had swung down from her gelding and pushed back her hood. Head held high, a smile curving her lips, she stepped up to his side. "Good eve, Mackay," she greeted him with a respectful lowering of her gaze.

"Rhianna Ross." Angus eyed her with interest, those sharp blue eyes roving over her face. "Our lad Connor took his time fetching ye ... it is a pleasure to finally see ye in the flesh." He paused there, still taking her in. Connor could see from the look on the man's face that— like many of his men—the clan-chief was struggling to reconcile the woman before him with the 'Jewel of the Highlands'.

And not for the first time, anger quickened Connor's blood.

He was getting tired of this. He was glad he'd left Domhnall behind. His uncle's attitude had started to rankle of late. However, his uncle wasn't the only one with a cruel edge to him. If any of Angus Mackay's guests said a word against her, he wouldn't be responsible for his actions.

Rhianna Ross was the most alluring, sensual creature he'd ever met. The past two mornings, when he'd woken up cradling her in his arms, he'd thought himself the luckiest man alive.

The reactions of others infuriated him. No wonder Rhianna hadn't wanted to make this trip.

"And it is a pleasure to meet the Mackay," Rhianna replied, her tone suitably demure.

Turning from Rhianna, Angus caught Connor's eye and grinned. "Good to see ye finally wed, lad."

"Connor!" Another voice boomed through the bailey. Relieved that Angus had been stopped from going on about Connor's delayed wedding any longer, and that he hadn't made a rude comment, Connor looked over at where a tall man strode toward him. Niel Mackay, the clan-chief's only son, was the image of his father—or how he would have looked at twenty-six winters, before his hair greyed, he grew a beard, and thickened around the belly. Niel's brown hair was cropped short, an austere style that contrasted with the grin on his face.

Connor's own grin wasn't feigned when he stepped forward to clasp arms with him.

"It's been too long," Niel greeted him. "We need to organize a stag hunt before the weather turns against us."

Unlike Connor's relationship with the Mackay himself, which had always been strained, Connor considered Niel a good friend—even if their relationship had a certain edge to it. They were of almost identical age—born during the same month of the same year.

"Aye, a grand idea," Connor replied. He moved back then, gesturing for Rhianna to step forward. "I'd like ye to meet my wife."

Niel's attention shifted to Rhianna, and for an instant, Connor was sure he saw naked interest flicker in his friend's blue eyes. It flared for barely an instant and then disappeared. Nonetheless, Connor tensed. Perhaps he was mistaken?

Niel took one of Rhianna's hands and lifted it, before bestowing a kiss.

Connor snorted. "What's this ... ye have manners these days?"

Niel flashed him a grin. "In the presence of ladies, aye." He glanced then over to where Jaimee had dismounted and was watching the exchange with barely-concealed amusement. Morgan stood next to her, his wolfhound at his side, seemingly unconcerned with being ignored for the moment. "Good afternoon,

Jaimee," Niel called out. "Looking bonnier than ever, I see."

In response, Jaimee frowned.

"Enough of all this prattle," Angus Mackay interrupted. He then swept his thick arm toward the stone steps leading up to a vast oaken door behind him. "Leave yer horses with my lads, and come indoors for an ale."

16

TRULY BE MYSELF

KEIRA WASN'T COMFORTABLE at Castle Varrich.

From the moment she'd met the clan-chief, and weathered his sharp assessing look, and then been faced with his flirtatious son, she'd been on edge.

Both men were the sort to take note of everything, even if they didn't comment on some of their observations.

There was a sharpness to Angus-Dow Mackay she hadn't expected. And although Niel Mackay had greeted Connor with the heartiness of an old friend, she didn't trust him either.

Now seated in the great hall, she watched the clan-chief and his son engage Connor in conversation, while servants poured them horns of ale. It appeared that Connor was the first of the Mackay chieftains to arrive. The great hall of Varrich was a lofty, impressive space, at least twice the size of that at Farr. A hearth burned up each end, and an array of weapons—shields, axes, and blades—hung from the stone walls, iron and steel gleaming in the light of the cressets lining the hall.

Keira continued to observe the conversation. It was difficult to catch everything being said, for the roar of surrounding voices nearly drowned their words out, but she quickly realized that the clan-chief and his son were both ranting about the Gunns to Connor.

Keira's breathing quickened. This shouldn't have come as a surprise, but such news did alarm her.

"Interesting characters, aren't they?" Morgan's voice, barely audible above the rumble of conversation, drew

Keira's attention. She glanced at where her brother-by-marriage sat next to her. Like Connor, he had piercing green eyes, although during their short acquaintance, she'd noted he possessed an entirely different character. He was the feckless, wild, younger brother who needed reining in. However, his gaze this evening was watchful, shrewd.

"Aye," Keira agreed, observing Morgan closely now. "Do ye know them well?"

"Not really," he admitted, feeding Gritta a morsel of meat under the table. "As the younger brother, I'm barely worthy of notice." It was a blunt comment, yet there wasn't a trace of bitterness to his voice.

Taking this in, Keira glanced over at her husband once more. It was a heavy mantle he'd taken on. She'd noted the patronizing tone the clan-chief had used with him earlier. Every sentence was interspersed with 'lad'. And she recalled what Connor had told her, of how hard it was to follow in the footsteps of Rory Mackay. Although Connor was smiling and talking with the two of them, she noted the lines of strain that bracketed his mouth and nose now.

She could tell he wasn't enjoying himself.

Turning her attention back to Morgan, she was surprised to find him watching her. But unlike earlier, when Niel Mackay had greeted her, there was no heat in Morgan's eyes.

Relief flooded through her. That would have been awkward indeed. She wasn't sure how she'd respond if her brother-by-marriage started kissing her hand and flattering her.

"My brother looks decidedly smug these days," Morgan said after a pause, his mouth lifting at the corners. "Who would have thought that betrothal he'd resented for so long would work out in the end?"

Keira raised an eyebrow. "He resented it?"

"Didn't ye?" Morgan pulled a face then. "I wouldn't like to have my future decided at eight winters of age."

Keira considered his words. She wouldn't have resented it at all if her parents had promised her to the likes of Connor when she was a bairn, yet she knew what Morgan was trying to say. She and Connor had spoken of the betrothal a few times of late, and both agreed that it was a strange thing to have your fate bound with another person's at such a young age.

"I suppose it's different for women," she said after a pause. She needed to speak with Rhianna's voice, not her own. "I was just pleased that my parents were looking after my future." She paused then. "However, I was less happy when my uncle packed me off to the nunnery."

Morgan inclined his head. "Ye didn't like it at Iona?"

"Not one bit. The prioress was a shrew, and the hours of prayer bored me to death."

Morgan laughed, his eyes crinkling at the corners. "I can see why my brother likes ye."

Connor's neck was so tense that as the evening wore on his head started to ache in a dull throb. The pain was a distraction, and the ale and mead that the clan-chief kept plying him with just made it worse.

Not only that, but Angus Mackay chewed over the same things repeatedly. It felt as if they were going in circles. The man's gruff voice, filled with latent aggression, was slowly wearing Connor down.

Can't he just stop talking?

"The Gunns haven't learned their lesson, lad," the clan-chief growled, oblivious to Connor's unvoiced wish. "The bastards are still occupying lands that don't belong to them." A slight slur to his voice betrayed the copious amounts of mead the big man had sunk already.

Connor swallowed down irritation. God's teeth, this was at least the third time the clan-chief had returned to this topic. Angus's cheeks were now flushed red. Next to him, his wife, Estelle—a thin woman with a gaunt face and long-suffering gaze—looked on.

Connor drew in a deep breath. He needed to be careful with the clan-chief, especially when the man was in his cups. He'd seen Angus Mackay's temper flare in an instant when he was full of drink. Few men dared be blunt with the Mackay. Connor's father, Rory, had been one of the rare individuals who could, but then, the pair had grown up together. Angus had always seen Rory as an equal.

"They have always tried to provoke us," Connor replied after a pause. "Although I would have thought they'll take a break from raiding for a while ... especially after Harpsdale."

"That won't stop them from taunting us," Niel pointed out. His friend leaned across the table, his blue eyes sharp. "The longer we fail to stake a claim on our lands, the weaker they will think us."

Connor clenched his jaw. Niel wasn't helping things this evening. He was deliberately trying to stir his father's temper. The clan-chief was never going to let the matter drop with his son's meddling.

Predictably, the clan-chief's expression darkened. "Arrogant dogs," Angus muttered, reaching for the jug of mead to refill his horn.

"More of our cattle have gone missing in Forsinard," Niel continued, his gaze never leaving his father's face, "it will be their doing."

Connor tensed. The village of Forsinard lay upon their eastern border—the border they shared with the Gunns. Leaning back in his chair, Connor resisted the urge to reach up and massage his temples. This was just the news the clan-chief needed to restart his own raids against their enemies.

Angus growled an oath, before lifting the horn to his lips and taking a deep draft.

"We can't let them get away with such behavior," Niel said, eyeing his father over the brim of his cup.

"No, we can't." Angus agreed, wiping his mouth with the back of his forearm. He then pinned Connor with a sharp stare. "Yer father was full of strategies on how to deal with the Gunns ... are ye, *lad*?"

The devil's stinking backside, not again.

The aching in Connor's head increased; it now felt as if an iron band were slowly tightening around his crown. This wasn't the first time tonight that Angus had lobbed a direct challenge his way.

"My advice is to wait until spring before making our next move against them," he replied. "Increase patrols on our eastern border, if ye wish, but use the coming months to observe their behavior. George Gunn is just testing us."

Angus's heavy jaw tensed, the expression visible even under his thick beard. It wasn't the answer he was looking for. Rory Mackay had always been an aggressor; and although he'd paid for that with his life, the clan-chief liked having such men at his side.

The Mackay's gaze narrowed. "Sometimes I think ye lack the stomach for war, *lad*."

Connor's mouth compressed. The comment was ridiculous. The man knew that Connor Mackay could fight; his body bore the scars from many violent skirmishes. He'd killed his first man at fourteen and had fought at his father and brother's sides ever since. But as Connor didn't sit there gnashing his teeth and muttering threats, Angus thought him a weaker leader than his father.

Perhaps he's right.

The thought arose, unbidden, but Connor pushed it back. Even before Rory's death, the Mackay clan-chief had sought to undermine his friend's quiet, even-tempered son.

Even so, Connor's patience was rapidly thinning. He'd had enough of this pointless conversation. Leaning back once more in his seat, he met the clan-chief's eye and favored him with a thin smile. "No ... I just lack the patience for endless feuding." He paused then, letting his words sink in. "As, I hear, does the king."

"Are ye well, Connor?" Keira's gaze settled upon where Connor stood before the hearth. His gaze was shuttered as he stared at the glowing lump of peat there. It was growing late, and they'd retired to the bed-chamber the servants had prepared for them.

Observing her husband's face, Keira noted it was unusually pale and strained, the grooves either side of his mouth deep now.

Connor glanced up, a sigh escaping. "I've got the mother of headaches tonight, that's all."

Keira frowned. "Would ye like me to rub yer shoulders and neck?"

His face relaxed a little. "Aye, thank ye."

Taking a seat before the hearth, he stripped off his lèine. As always, the sight of his naked torso made Keira's breathing quicken and her belly flutter. He had such a strong chest and back, and powerful, broad shoulders that she loved to cling to when he took her.

Banishing heated thoughts, she approached him and began to massage his shoulders. "Mother Mary," she murmured. "Yer muscles are like planks of wood tonight ... no wonder ye have a headache."

He let out a pained grunt, dipping his head a little as she gently kneaded the rock-hard muscles of his neck. "Angus Mackay tends to have that effect on me," he admitted gruffly.

Keira's brow furrowed once more. "I noticed him and his son interrogating ye," she murmured. "Although I didn't hear much of what was said."

"Just as well ... the Mackay tended to repeat himself. It got wearisome after a while."

He didn't elaborate, and Keira didn't press further. After a few moments, Connor let out a moan of relief when she started to really work his shoulder muscles, kneading harder now.

"The Lord preserve me," he groaned, "ye know exactly what I need."

Keira's belly fluttered once more at these words. It pleased her that she was helping him; she didn't like to see Connor's usually relaxed face so tense. "Glad to be of assistance, husband," she murmured, her mouth curving.

"Sorry I'm not in the best of moods tonight," he replied. "I had no choice but to accept this invitation ... but the moment we arrived here, I was reminded why a little of Angus Mackay goes a long way. The man has borne a life-long hatred of the Gunns ... and that loathing taints every conversation I have with him."

"But ye hate the Gunns too, don't ye?" Her pulse sped up as she asked the question. Part of her wanted to know how he truly felt about her clan. After all, his father had died fighting them.

"Aye, but not like Angus does ... he nurses his hate like a bruise. It's an old friend to him these days." Connor paused then. "Niel doesn't help things either ... sometimes I think he deliberately goads his father."

"He seems a different man to the clan-chief," Keira murmured. "Quieter."

A beat of silence passed, before Connor replied, "Watch him, Rhianna."

She tensed. "Who? Niel?"

"Aye." Did she imagine it, or was there a hard edge to his voice now? With a jolt, she realized he was jealous.

Keira couldn't help herself. She smiled, even if Connor couldn't presently see it. "I thought he was yer friend?"

"He is ... but that doesn't mean I trust him."

Connor twisted then, caught her by the arm, and pulled her around to his side, before he drew her onto his lap.

Keira's humor faded when she saw her husband wasn't smiling. He was in an odd mood indeed tonight, different from his usual affable countenance. Before now, he'd appeared someone who smiled easily. However, a shadow lay across his eyes.

"Ye know that ye have nothing to worry about there?" she murmured. "I got the measure of Niel Mackay the moment I met him."

Connor's mouth lifted at the corners, although his green eyes were still shuttered. "Aye ... my sister's never responded to his charms either."

Keira laughed, remembering Jaimee's response to Niel's greeting. The man had tried to flirt with her later in the evening too, but she'd barely suffered him. However, he hadn't seemed to mind; if anything, her wintry reception only encouraged him.

Keira sensed that Niel Mackay liked a challenge.

"Well then, the lass has a sensible head on her shoulders," Keira replied, still holding Connor's gaze.

She then lowered her head toward her husband and kissed him.

Gasping, Keira collapsed upon the bed. She'd been on her hands and knees while Connor took her, but in the aftermath of the storm of passion that had consumed them both, her limbs had gone to porridge. She lay upon her belly, her pulse drumming in her ears. Sweat bathed her, and the ragged sound of her breathing filled the bed-chamber.

Connor lowered himself to the mattress as well. He then rolled onto his side, curved a large hand over Keira's belly, and pulled her toward him, so that they spooned together.

Unspeaking, they lay there for a short while, enjoying the languorous aftermath of their lovemaking.

Keira's pulse took a while to settle. The depth of passion Connor managed to arouse in her was overwhelming in its intensity. Truthfully, there were times when it almost frightened her. In those moments, she wasn't playing the role of Rhianna Ross—in those unguarded moments, she could have told him the truth, could have spilled the whole lie. He stripped away all her defenses, made her not care about the outcome.

But afterward, as she regained control of her senses, warning feathered over her skin, causing goosebumps to rise.

It was dangerous to lose control so completely. Who knew what she might blurt out one day?

Still not breaking the silence between them, Connor stroked the length of her flank with his fingertips, long sensual caresses that made her stretch like a cat against him.

"How is yer head?" she asked finally, smiling as his lips trailed a soft path down her nape.

"Much better, thank ye," he murmured. "Yer presence is a balm."

Her smile widened, and despite that her limbs were still weak, despite that she was weary after a long day of travel and a tense evening, she found herself pushing back against him. It didn't surprise her when she felt him harden against her bottom.

A groan escaped Keira, unbidden. How she loved the feel of him. He reached up, his hand cupping a breast, while the thumb caressed the nipple, bringing it to a tight, hard bud. His hand slid down to her waist then, holding her fast as he rolled his hips against hers, his shaft seeking entrance.

When he spoke, his voice was husky, with a raw edge that sent shivers across her skin. "I can truly be myself with ye, mo ghràdh."

17

LATECOMERS

THE POUNDING OF drums echoed through the darkness—a slow, ancient rhythm that mimicked a beating heart.

Wrapped up in a cloak, for a chill had settled across the promontory with the setting of the sun, Keira walked with her husband out to where men were lighting the Samhuinn fire. Behind them, the carven outlines of Ben Hope and Ben Loyal rose against the darkening sky.

Inhaling the aroma of roasting hazelnuts, from the braziers that burned next to the walls, Keira watched a man, dressed in wolf-pelts, chase a squealing woman around the fire. Behind her, a group of bairns were squabbling over handfuls of hot nuts.

A deep sense of contentment warmed Keira, and she turned, angling her face up to meet Connor's eye.

Mo ghràdh.

My love. He'd repeated the endearment a few times the night before as he'd taken her that last time. The coupling had been gentle, emotional. And Keira's face had been wet with tears when it ended. She'd wanted to respond in kind, to tell him that she'd never dreamed of winning the heart of such a man.

The firelight gleamed in Connor's eyes and gilded his unbound hair. They shared a smile then before Keira looked away. Holding his gaze for too long made her uncomfortable—almost as if, if he looked deeply enough, he'd see who she really was.

She'd wanted to tell him that she loved him—but the words had stuck in her throat.

In the day that had followed their arrival at Castle Varrich, a strange, reflective mood had settled upon her. Connor had been occupied for most of the time—for as other chieftains arrived, Angus Mackay wished to hold councils with them all. Most of the arrivals were Mackays and neighboring clans that the Mackays hadn't yet fallen out with, although there appeared to be few of them these days.

Keira had spent the morning walking with Jaimee and had been pleased to put some distance between her and Connor for a while. Her thoughts had been a churning melee all day, and there was a strange crushing sensation in her chest.

Fortunately, her sister-by-marriage was a restless soul, and only too happy to escape the keep. The two women had gone down the promontory a distance and watched as the last touches were added to the bonfire— men carried up branches of oak and fir from the village below, and wagons trundled up the winding path, bringing barrels of the first of the apple wine.

Hours later, the folk of Varrich and Tongue were outdoors again now, enjoying the evening's festivities.

Taking a sip from her cup of apple wine, Keira enjoyed the tartness on her tongue.

Her anxiety had settled. Even so, the subdued air that had dogged her steps all day persisted. She couldn't seem to shake it off, nor did she understand why she felt this way. Things between her and Connor just seemed to be getting better and better, and yet uneasiness now stole upon her like a thief.

"Is something on yer mind, Rhianna?" Connor asked, putting an arm about her shoulders and drawing her close. "Ye seem ... distracted."

"I'm just a little weary, that's all," she lied, glancing up at him once more. She then forced a smile. "Really, I appreciate the concern, but ye've no need to worry about me."

He smiled back. "I just want to make sure ye are happy."

Keira's pulse quickened. "I am," she replied huskily.

The truth was that his tenderness the night before, the way he'd huskily admitted his feelings, had opened his heart to her, had left her feeling ... guilty. *Connor loves Rhianna, not me.*

The realization caused an aching, hollowed-out feeling to rise under her ribcage. The sensation both saddened and vexed her.

Wasn't this what she'd wanted?

She'd dreamed of making a life with a husband who loved her. And here she was, wed to a chieftain who made no secret of his adoration.

She should have been delirious with joy, but the lie cast a shadow over her happiness.

Connor had opened himself up to her—had let her into his heart without reservation, and had given her his. And yet, she couldn't love him, not truly, while this deceit continued to play out.

It's too late for honesty now, she thought as she dipped her head and took another sip of apple wine. *If this is to be my punishment for lying to him, I must weather it.*

Having lived honestly until recently, she'd had no idea what toll weaving a lie like this would take. Indeed, it gave one an uneasy soul. The price was that she could never let herself go entirely, could never submit.

The lie would always keep something in reserve.

Laughter and booming male voices on the other side of the fire drew her attention then. Peering through the darkness, Keira saw figures on horseback appear on the pathway leading up the promontory. The riders at the front of the group carried torches aloft. They wore clan sashes across their chests, although since it was dark, Keira couldn't make out the color of the plaid.

"Looks like we've got some latecomers to the celebrations," Connor observed.

Angus strode toward the arrivals then, with Niel close behind him. "Graeme!" he boomed. "Ye came after all!"

A sturdy-looking man with short, thinning dark hair swung down from his horse and clasped arms with the Mackay clan-chief. "Apologies for the late hour of our arrival, Mackay," he rumbled. "My horse threw a shoe this afternoon, and we had to find ourselves a smithy."

"Ye made it in the end though," Niel spoke up with a grin, slapping the man on the back. "Here." He handed him a cup. "Slake yer thirst with some apple wine."

A yard or two behind the man, a small, dark-haired woman clad in black dismounted from her garron. She approached the knot of men, her pretty face weary.

Shifting his gaze to her, Niel's smile turned wolfish. "And who is this vision, Graeme?"

"My niece, Maggie," the older man replied with a frown, not bothering to look his companion's way. "Excuse her crow's garb ... she's been widowed a while, but I can't get her to come out of mourning. I'm keen to find her another husband, so if ye fancy her, just say the word."

"Uncle," the woman spoke up, her voice withering. "Please ... that's enough."

Her uncle snorted. "As ye can see, the woman has a mouth on her."

A rumble of male laughter reverberated over the hilltop, blending with the crackling of the Samhuinn fire. The flames now licked high into the night.

Maggie's mouth thinned at her uncle's comment, but she held her silence.

Watching the group a few yards distant, Keira's attention focused upon the woman. There was something familiar about her lovely, heart-shaped face. Had she seen her before?

Maggie. A sudden chill feathered down the nape of Keira's neck. *No ... it can't be.*

"I take it all is well at Caisteal Nan Corr?" Angus Mackay boomed.

"Aye, well enough ... although we had a poor harvest this year," Graeme grumbled. "Too much rain."

Caisteal Nan Corr. The chill deepened, seeping through Keira's limbs now. *Lord, save me.* Her worst fears were confirmed.

"Thank ye for the invitation," the newcomer continued, his attention shifting back to the Mackay clan-chief. "When I heard Connor Mackay was also coming here for Samhuinn, I wasn't going to miss this." He then peered over the clan-chief's shoulder, scanning the milling crowd upon the hilltop. "Where is he? It's a while since I've seen my niece."

Maggie was also now surveying her surroundings, her gaze bright with interest.

A boulder settled in Keira's belly.

Standing at Connor's side, she went rigid, caught like a hind in a hunter's sights. Time slowed down, and suddenly all she could hear was the pounding of her heart.

Angus swiveled and motioned to Keira. "Yer sight must be failing ye man, if ye can't recognize yer own niece. She's standing right behind me."

Keira's breathing stilled, and time slowed further still. She was painfully aware of Graeme and Maggie's gazes shifting to her. She watched then as the Ross chieftain's face darkened, his greying eyebrows crashing together in confusion.

And when he spoke, his rough voice ripped the fabric of Keira's world. "This woman isn't Rhianna Ross."

A terrible silence fell upon the hilltop at these words. The revelers ceased their merriment, and even the bairns, who were still bickering over roasted hazelnuts, stilled.

All gazes settled upon Keira.

Connor's arm remained slung across her shoulders, although she felt the tension emanating from him.

Keira's belly twisted. *He won't want to touch me for much longer.*

"Is that any way to greet yer niece?" Connor's voice, when he finally responded to Graeme Ross, held a low note of warning.

The Ross chieftain's jaw clenched, while next to him, Maggie Ross—Rhianna's elder sister—stepped up to his side. Her gaze was riveted upon Keira's face, a look of horrified fascination etched there.

"I'll say it again," Graeme growled. "This woman isn't Rhianna."

"What have ye done with my sister?" Maggie demanded then, her voice sharp now.

A wave of dizziness washed over Keira. And if Connor hadn't been holding her, she might have crumpled.

Moments passed, and then he lowered his arm. Swaying on her feet, Keira pulled her cloak close. She could feel Connor's gaze pressing down upon her, yet she refused to look at him.

She just couldn't.

It was about to get worse yet, and she needed to somehow prepare herself.

"Is there something ye need to tell me?" he asked finally. His voice was calm, emotionless—and the sound of it was like a fist to the belly.

This was her worst nightmare, to be outed so publicly—and she was living it.

Heaving in a deep breath, she did look at him then. His face was taut, his gaze veiled. But she could still sense his hope. He wanted her to tell him that these two people were mad. He wanted her to reassure him that all was well.

But all wasn't well. It was as far from well as it was possible to get.

And soon he'd hate her.

"Rhianna has eloped with her lover," she said after a lengthy pause. She was aware then that Morgan and Jaimee had drawn close. The shock on both their faces might have been comical, if this situation wasn't so dire. Doggedly, she continued, "I know not where she is now."

Maggie Ross's face blanched at this news, while Graeme Ross spat on the ground. "Callum ... that bastard ... I should have known."

"So, *who* are ye then?" Angus Mackay spoke up. He'd watched the scene unfold without interfering but had now roused himself. His bearded face had gone hard.

Swallowing, Keira squared her shoulders and clenched her hands at her sides. Danger prickled her skin. She was in deep trouble now; her senses screamed for her to flee, but it was too late for that.

The consequences were likely to be terrible, yet she had no choice but to face them.

"My name is Keira Gunn," she said softly. "Daughter of Maddoc Gunn of Camster broch."

18

NO MORE OF YER LIES

AS SHE'D EXPECTED, just uttering that hated clan name caused a collective gasp to ripple through the surrounding crowd, like a stone dropped into the midst of a still pond.

When no one said a word, Keira drew in a ragged breath, fighting another wave of dizziness as it crashed over her. "Rhianna and I met at Iona nunnery ... and swapped places." With a great effort, she forced herself to look at Connor once more. "I'm sorry, Connor ... I'm not who ye thought I was."

That was the understatement of her life.

Connor didn't reply. He merely stared at her, as if she were speaking in tongues. Nearby, Morgan and Jaimee also gaped at her, while Angus and Niel Mackay's faces had gone stony.

"Filthy Gunn spy!" Niel Mackay was the first to emerge from his shock. Gone was the easy smile and charm he'd wielded ever since Keira had been introduced to him. A feral, dangerous expression replaced it, and Keira's heart quailed. She took a hasty step backward, although there was nowhere to go. "What news were ye planning to take back to yer clan-chief?"

An instant later, the sound of steel scraping against leather rent the night, and gasps followed. Niel had just drawn his dirk and was stalking toward her. "Shall I cut out yer treacherous tongue?"

A scream rose in Keira's throat.

Mother Mary, have mercy. He was going to slay her, here and now.

"Lower yer blade, Niel." Connor's voice, harsh and cold, sliced through the smoky air. An instant later, he stepped in front of Keira, shielding her from Niel's wrath.

"Stand aside," Niel snarled. "That woman has wormed her way into our midst, lied to yer face, and made a fool of ye. She has to die!"

The rasp of another blade being drawn followed, and Keira saw that Connor now grasped his own dirk in his right hand.

"Touch her, and I'll cut yer throat." The threat was spoken low, although the hardness of Connor's voice sent a shiver through Keira. Folk underestimated this man at their peril, she realized. Niel Mackay was his clansman and friend, but Connor would kill him in a heartbeat if he went for her.

And everyone who looked on knew it.

A few feet away, shock rippled over Angus Mackay's bearded face. His gaze flicked between his son and Connor, his meaty hands fisting at his sides. They were moments away from an ugly scene.

"Put yer dirk away, Niel," the clan-chief growled. "Bloodshed isn't the answer to this."

Keira's heart leaped into her throat. It wasn't?

"But she's here to learn our secrets and take them back to her clan," Niel snarled. High spots of color had appeared on his cheekbones. He was barely controlling his wrath. "Ye can't let her get away with it."

"Oh, she won't," Connor replied, his voice ice-cold. "Of that, ye can be sure."

Another silence settled over the hilltop, the moments drawing out. Keira shifted her attention to Morgan and Jaimee once more. These two had become kin, but now they both stared at her as if she were a stranger. Morgan's handsome face was all taut angles, his gaze narrowed, while Jaimee had gone pale, her eyes huge in the firelight.

Keira had betrayed them all.

Angus Mackay eventually cleared his throat. "Get that woman out of our sight, Connor ... or I won't be responsible for what happens to her."

"I want answers first," Graeme Ross burst out then. His face had gone ruddy, the veins on his neck standing out. "This woman knows where Rhianna is, I'm sure of it."

Keira shook her head. "Callum picked her up from Iona," she whispered. Her voice, reed-thin, didn't even sound like her own now. "I know not where they went from there."

"I don't believe ye," the Ross chieftain roared, taking a threatening step toward her. "Ye are protecting her."

"Enough, Graeme," Angus Mackay interjected, his voice a low rumble of warning. "It grows late ... now isn't the time for this." His gaze swiveled to Connor. "Bring her to the great hall tomorrow morning, and we will decide what will be done."

Keira glanced at her husband then, forcing herself to look upon his face. The cold mask that had settled there chilled her. She barely recognized him.

Wordlessly, Connor nodded. He then took hold of Keira's arm and steered her away from the fire. Together, they walked back into the castle.

Connor didn't say a word while they mounted the stairs to the top level of the keep.

His silence was damning, far worse than if he'd ranted and raved at her. Likewise, Keira held her tongue. There was nothing she could say that would mend this. Misery twisted her up inside; each in-drawn breath hurt, and queasiness came over her in waves.

And all the while, he kept a firm grip upon her arm.

Reaching their bed-chamber, he led her inside and then pushed the door shut behind them.

Heartbeat pulsing in her ears, Keira turned to him, her gaze settling upon his stone-hewn face. Swallowing, she backed away and found herself standing flush against the door. There was nowhere to go.

To her consternation, Connor drew close then, before reaching out to put a hand onto the door, next to her head, bracketing her in. Leaning forward, his gaze swept over her face as if he were seeing her for the first time.

Keira wilted under the force of his stare.

There was no warmth, no gentleness in it.

"Keira. Gunn." He said her name slowly, testing out each word.

Meeting his eye, Keira started to sweat. He hadn't been rough or aggressive with her, and yet there was a coiled menace to him now, a leashed fury that pulsed between them.

For the first time, she was scared of Connor Mackay.

"Is that yer real name then?" he asked after a pause. "Or is it another lie?"

Keira swallowed. "It's the truth ... I'm so sorry, Connor ... I never—"

"Don't say 'sorry' to me again," he cut her off. His voice was still low, although it was flint-hard. "I do not need yer apologies."

It was hard not to shrink down under the wintry force of his anger, yet Keira held her ground. She'd known what she was getting into; she now had to deal with the consequences of what she'd done.

"What kind of woman does this?" he demanded then. His handsome face was strained, a muscle feathering in his jaw. "Ye wed me pretending to be someone else. Why would ye do that?"

"I didn't want to be a nun," she whispered. It was time for honesty now, and she wouldn't soften the truth. Strangely, despite the shock of being discovered, relief now weakened her limbs. Wearing a mask had taken its toll. She didn't have to pretend anymore, didn't have to watch her words. "My parents sent me to Iona because they couldn't find a husband for me ... and didn't want to pay a dowry. I'm the youngest of six daughters. My father's a wool merchant. My kin reside at Camster broch in the west of Gunn lands."

"And whose idea was this deception ... yers or Rhianna's?" His voice was ice-cold.

Keira cleared her throat. It felt tight, making it difficult to get the words out. "Rhianna's ... she told me she was in love with someone else and wanted to run away with him. Graeme Ross put her at Iona to separate the lovers ... but it only made them more determined to be together."

Staring up at his face, she saw no flicker of emotion, empathy, or understanding. He wanted the full story, but he wasn't looking to pardon her.

When Connor didn't speak, Keira pressed on. Telling him all this felt as if she were lancing a boil, one that had been festering for too long. "I resisted initially, but she was desperate ... I wanted to help her ... and myself."

Connor stared down at her, and she watched his lip curl, watched disdain darken those pine-green eyes. He'd truly hate her after this, and she couldn't expect any different. This tale wasn't painting her in a favorable light at all, but it was the truth at least.

"As I said ... I didn't want to take my vows," she continued after a brittle silence. "I longed to have a family of my own ... a husband and bairns. All my sisters were permitted to wed, but Keira—plain of face and speech—was destined to be locked away in a nunnery for the rest of her life. My parents never wanted me."

Tears threatened then, prickling the back of her eyes, yet she hastily blinked them back. Instinctively, she knew that weeping wouldn't help her now. Connor was too angry to be moved, and somewhere inside—in that stubborn place she'd always known she had within—she didn't want to crumple in front of him.

She'd known what she was doing. There wasn't any point in breaking down in sobs and pleading for forgiveness.

Pride was the only thing she had left.

"So, ye planned to live this lie forever?" he asked, not remotely moved by her tale.

The hardness in his voice cowed her, yet she nodded.

"How ye must have laughed at me," he said, fury pulsating off each word. "Taking ye in, making ye my wife, and believing ye to be Rhianna Ross, while all the time ye were a Gunn—a cuckoo in a blackbird's nest. God's teeth, I even opened up to ye about the loss of my father."

His words cut deep, worse than if he'd actually lashed out and struck her.

Without thinking, Keira raised a trembling hand and placed it over his heart. She felt the thunder of his heart under her palm. "No, I never laughed at ye, Connor ... these past days have been the happiest of my life. I *love* ye."

The admission made her catch her breath. Aye, it was true. Now that the deception had ended, she could freely admit it. There was no barrier between them. They hadn't known each other long, but already she was lost. And knowing that he hated her now made her feel as if someone had just torn her beating heart from her chest.

His fingers wrapped around her wrist, gripping hard. He then pulled her hand back, so that she was no longer touching him, before releasing her as if she were a leper. "Don't," he said through gritted teeth. "No more of yer lies, *Keira*."

He stepped back from her then, breathing hard. It was the only sign of the storm that raged within, for his voice was still cold.

"Sleep well, *wife*," he ground out, reaching for the door handle. "Tomorrow the clan-chief will decide yer fate."

Heart pounding, Keira stepped aside, watching her husband stalk from the room. The door crashed shut behind him, shaking the walls with its force. And for the longest while, Keira didn't move. She merely stood there, staring after him.

19

HER FATE IN YER HANDS

CONNOR FELT SICK to his stomach. Nausea rolled through him in waves, and his belly cramped.

Descending to the great hall, he was relieved to find it deserted. Everyone was outdoors enjoying the Samhuinn revelry. He could just hear the steady beat of the drums, audible even within the thick stone walls of the keep.

He wouldn't be rejoining the revelers this evening.

Right now, he felt as if he would never be able to raise a smile again.

Slumping down into a seat near one of the glowing hearths, Connor stared sightlessly at the flames.

Betrayed. Humiliated. Manipulated. A melee of emotions swirled within him, each vying for dominance, although a cocoon of shock kept it all under control.

And he'd not let it out, especially not here at Castle Varrich.

Such a display would be seen as weakness, and he wouldn't allow Angus and Niel to see just how devastated he was.

Keira Gunn had just torn his world apart.

He'd not known her long, the woman he'd thought was Rhianna Ross, but already she'd become his world. He'd fallen hard—harder than he'd thought was possible. For years, he'd believed he wouldn't be one of those men who lost their wits over a lass. Yet from the day he'd set eyes on his betrothed, he'd been fighting a losing battle.

She wasn't yer betrothed, he reminded himself. *She's an interloper, a liar. A Gunn.*

That should have been the worst part of it. Niel had drawn his dirk and intended to kill her—not because of what she'd done—but because of *who* she was.

Connor should have cared more about that, but he didn't. The fact that she'd lied about her identity, pretended to be someone she wasn't, felt as if someone had just rammed a dirk into his belly and twisted.

He let few people in, but with her, he'd lowered his defenses.

And in return, she'd humiliated him. Niel, curse him, was right. She'd made a fool of him.

Hearing footfalls, Connor dragged his gaze from the fire to see his brother approaching, Gritta padding along behind him.

Connor clenched his jaw. He wanted to be alone right now. Morgan would mean well, but he couldn't help.

However, Morgan didn't speak as he drew near. Instead, he pulled up a stool and warmed his hands before the fire. "It's chilling off out there," his brother said eventually. "Winter's going to come early this year, I can feel it."

Bitterness surged within Connor.

Winter was already here.

The brothers sat together for a while longer, neither speaking. Nonetheless, Connor felt Morgan's gaze flick to him, studying his face.

After a while, the force of his brother's stare got too much, and Connor looked his way. Morgan was eighteen months his junior and had always been the wilder of the pair. He never seemed to take anything seriously. The two of them had fought shoulder-to-shoulder at Harpsdale, had both seen their father cut down before them, and yet there had always been a reserve between them.

Connor was used to seeing mischief glint in his brother's eyes, to his mouth curving at something that only *he* thought was funny. However, there was no humor in his green eyes tonight.

Connor had never seen him look so grave.

"What will ye do?" he asked finally.

Connor's mouth twisted. "I don't know ... all will be decided tomorrow."

Morgan's gaze shadowed. "The clan-chief may be harsh with her."

"Aye ... and she'll deserve it."

Morgan's eyes widened. This wasn't a side to Connor he'd likely ever seen. The moment stretched out, before Morgan finally spoke once more. "Ye are in love with her."

A sour taste flooded Connor's mouth. "I *was*."

Morgan cocked a dark-blond eyebrow. He reached out then and stroked his dog as the wolfhound pressed up against him. "I'm not an expert in such matters," he admitted. "But as I understand it, ye can't dismiss such sentiment in an instant."

"Ye are right, ye *aren't* an expert in this," Connor growled. "As such, keep yer observations to yerself. I don't want to talk about Keira Gunn."

Not remotely offended by Connor's rudeness, Morgan flashed him a rueful smile. He lapsed into silence then, even if his gaze remained upon his brother. Connor shifted his attention back to the flames.

"I'm poor company, Morgan," he said finally. "Best ye return to the bonfire ... and keep an eye on Jaimee. I don't trust Niel around her."

Morgan snorted. "Ye don't need to worry about that ... he's too busy sniffing around Maggie Ross tonight." He paused then. "She's a comely lass ... even in that widow's black."

Connor scrubbed a hand over his face. His head suddenly felt as if it were filled with wool. "Curse Rhianna Ross," he muttered.

Morgan snorted. "Aye ... her uncle tells me that he'd feared something of the kind might happen. That was why he packed her off to Iona." Connor glanced back at his brother to see that Morgan was scowling. "Graeme Ross wants us to help him track her down."

Tension rippled through Connor at this news. He didn't want Rhianna Ross, any more than he wanted Keira Gunn. The pair of them could go to Hades for all he cared. "He can look for her on his own," Connor bit out the words. "And when he tracks her down, he can find another fool to wed her."

Seated at the clan-chief's table, Keira clasped her hands together upon her lap. Her gaze was riveted upon the man who would decide her fate.

Angus-Dow Mackay.

They weren't alone at the table. The clan-chief's wife sat at his side, her eyes gleaming with curiosity as she watched Keira.

This was likely the most exciting meeting to take place within these walls in a while.

Niel sat next to his mother, his face set in grim lines, while the Mackays of Farr—Connor, Morgan, and Jaimee—sat at the opposite end of the table next to Graeme and Maggie Ross.

The rest of the great hall was empty this morning; even the servants had vacated the space, leaving the clan-chief to conduct this meeting in peace.

"Ye don't want yer fate in my hands, lass," Angus Mackay rumbled, fixing Keira with a gimlet stare. "For the hate I bear yer clan is my ale ... my bread." He paused then, letting his words sink in. "Lucky for ye that ye are the daughter of a man of little importance ... for if ye had been George Gunn's get, I would take delight in severing yer head from yer shoulders and sending it back to yer father in a sack."

Ice slid down Keira's back, and she shivered. The threat in the clan-chief's voice was real. She didn't doubt him for an instant.

Her attention shifted then, to the opposite end of the table, where Connor Mackay looked on. He'd not uttered a word since coming to fetch her earlier, to bring her to the great hall. He was dressed for travel, in leather braies and a vest, a fur mantle about his shoulders. As soon as the Mackay made his pronouncement, Connor clearly meant to be off.

His gaze was detached, his expression shuttered.

At first glance, if one ignored the tension around his mouth, the hard set of his shoulders, one would believe he was completely unmoved by all of this.

"As it is, ye are a 'nobody'," Angus Mackay continued. "But all the same, my son has a valid point. Ye have been seated at my table, listening to our discussions. How do I know ye weren't sent here to take information back to the Gunns?"

Keira's throat constricted. "I wasn't," she croaked. "I swear. I'm no spy."

"She's lying," Niel murmured. The clan-chief's son's gaze was narrowed, hard, as he watched her.

"Maybe a spell in the dungeons will loosen her tongue," Angus Mackay growled. He paused then, before leaning across the table toward her. "Or perhaps, I'll let my men beat the truth out of ye."

Terror fluttered under Keira's ribcage, sweat bathing her body. *Mother Mary, have mercy.* She was in dire trouble and had no idea how to dig her way out.

Danger crackled through the air in the great hall now. Frozen in place, Keira continued to stare at the clan-chief. She didn't look Connor's way; she couldn't bear to.

"I'll take a horse-whip to her." Graeme Ross spoke up, his voice rough.
"Her treachery aside, the wench knows where my niece is ... I'm sure of it."

Swallowing, Keira shifted her attention to the heavyset man seated opposite. Her belly twisted when she met his eye. Beside the Ross chieftain, his niece Maggie sat stiff and pale, her blue eyes shadowed.

Rhianna lied to me ... she said he wouldn't visit the Mackays.

Betrayal and humiliation crushed her chest. She'd been played like a harp. What a foolish chit she was.

"I told ye already," she gasped. "I don't know where Rhianna is."

Graeme muttered a curse, his gaze shifting to the clan-chief. "Give me an hour alone with her ... I'll get the truth out of her. And when I—"

"Would ye listen to yerselves?" An angry female voice echoed through the hall, cutting the Ross chieftain off. "Ye speak as if the woman before ye is some dirk-wielding assassin. Has yer hatred for the Gunns turned yer wits to porridge?"

All gazes swiveled to the statuesque young woman with red-gold hair who sat flanked by her brothers at the far end of the table. Jaimee Mackay's winsome face was pale and taut, her jaw set. Her eyes had narrowed into glittering slits.

"Jaimee," Connor snapped, his gaze flashing a warning. "That's enough."

Connor's expression had altered since the beginning of the discussions. He no longer appeared unmoved. Like his sister, his face was pale and strained. A nerve flickered in his cheek.

"I don't condone what she's done," Jaimee continued, ignoring her brother's censure. She glanced Keira's way then, and sure enough, there was no warmth, no sympathy in her gaze. Jaimee's attention then snapped back to the clan-chief. "Aye, she's a liar, but she's no spy. I've spent some time with her ... and can assure ye she's never shown the slightest interest in our plans regarding the Gunns." The lass's brow furrowed then. "Besides, I've heard yer 'discussions' over the past few days ... ye lot are like a pack of hounds chasing yer own tails. Even if she were listening in, she'd have gleaned nothing of value."

A shocked silence settled over the great hall of Castle Varrich.

Angus Mackay stared at Jaimee as if she'd just slapped him around the face, while his wife gaped at her. Next to them, Niel looked like he'd just swallowed his tongue. Meanwhile, Graeme Ross's face had gone the color of raw liver.

Dizziness swept over Keira, and she released the breath she hadn't even realized she'd been holding. The last thing she needed was to faint in the midst of this.

She couldn't believe Jaimee had been so outspoken before her clan-chief.

It was both terrifying and thrilling.

The hush drew out. Slowly, the shock faded from the Mackay's face. He then reached for his cup of ale and took a long draft. Wiping his mouth with the back of his hand, his gaze speared Jaimee's.

The young woman stared back at him, as fearless as a she-wolf.

"Spy or not, the Gunn woman shouldn't be in my castle," he growled. "She has deceived us ... especially yer brother." Angus moved his focus to Connor then. The clan-chief's mouth twisted and a cunning look ignited in his blue eyes. "And for that reason ... I leave it to *ye* to decide her fate, Connor Mackay."

Keira's belly dropped through the floor. Her heart started to gallop.

She hadn't expected this.

Farther down the table, Connor's face had turned to stone. Another weighty pause followed. Suddenly, Keira could hear nothing save the hammering of her heart. Waiting for Connor's answer was torture.

The man hated her now. He'd want reckoning.

The moments drew out, and then Connor answered. "So be it, Mackay. In that case, I shall take Keira Gunn back to her father."

Shocked gasps echoed around the table.

Niel leaned forward, his face twisting. "What kind of punishment is that? Connor ... ye can't let her away with this."

"I can't believe ye're letting the bitch go free!" Graeme Ross roared.

Angus Mackay raised a meaty hand, silencing the outburst. His stare remained upon Connor. "Explain yerself."

Connor's mouth thinned. "This *is* punishment. By all accounts, her father is a heartless bastard. She's the unwanted youngest daughter he'd hoped never to set eyes on again. Believe me ... we aren't doing the lass a favor by returning her to him."

Keira stilled, a chill suffusing her breast. She couldn't believe it. Connor had used the things she'd confided in him the night before against her. She stared at him, willing him to look her way—but he wouldn't. Instead, he continued to hold the clan-chief's challenging gaze.

Niel shattered the tension with a snort. A smirk twisted his face. "Ye are a sly one, Connor," he murmured. "Are ye hoping that her father will slit her throat ... once he finds out a Mackay chieftain has been humping her?"

Connor's handsome face darkened at the accusation. He met Niel's eye, his lip curling. "How he deals with his daughter isn't my concern."

Keira dropped her gaze to her clasped hands upon her lap, struggling to contain the misery that thrummed through her. His voice was unrecognizable. Where was the gentle, gallant man she'd met at Iona? There was no warmth in him at all this morning. Her lie had stripped all tenderness from him.

Niel let it lie, and a strained hush settled over the table.

The Mackay would be deciding whether to agree to Connor's punishment. Would he think it harsh enough? Keira couldn't bear to look at the clan-chief. She couldn't look at any of them.

The sudden quiet drew her nerves to breaking point, but she had no choice other than to remain seated there—waiting for her fate to be decided.

"Very well." Angus Mackay eventually replied, his voice a deep, threatening rumble. "Take her back to her father ... but be it on yer head if the girl has fooled us all."

20

ENEMY TERRITORY

"ESCORT JAIMEE HOME, while I take my men and travel into Gunn lands," Connor instructed Morgan as they led their horses out of the stables and into the bailey. "I'll see ye back at Farr."

Morgan's step faltered, before he came to a halt and swiveled to face his brother. "I don't think so. We're not leaving ye to do this alone."

Irritation flared hot within Connor. "Yes, ye are."

"We're coming with ye, Connor." Jaimee stepped up next to Morgan. Her face was set in determined lines.

"Enough of this," Connor growled. His patience was on a short leash, as it had been all morning; he didn't need his siblings obstructing him. Jaimee had said enough already today. He couldn't believe how she'd lectured the clan-chief. More surprising still, Angus hadn't punished her for it. "Can't the pair of ye do as ye are told, just once?"

Morgan shook his head. "Not this time."

Jaimee folded her arms across her chest. "Ye need us with ye."

"It's not safe for ye, Jaimee," Connor countered, reaching out to steady Thunder as the huge dun stallion pawed at the cobbles and tossed his head. As always, Thunder was eager to stretch his legs. "Go back to Farr."

"I'll be safe enough with ye and Morgan," she replied, stubbornness hardening her voice. "We can stand here and argue it all day, but it'll change nothing. Morgan and I are coming with ye."

Connor muttered a curse. He'd always admired his sister's fire, her spirit—until today. Right now, he wished their father hadn't indulged her so much over the years. Around them, men and horses milled about the bailey. Keira sat atop Outlaw a few yards away, awaiting them. He didn't want a scene with his kin, not after the humiliation of the past few days. He was tired of fighting. Tired of talking.

He just wanted to kick Thunder into a flat gallop and outrun all of this.

But he had a task to fulfill first, one that his siblings had insisted on being part of.

Turning from Jaimee and Morgan, he swung up onto Thunder's back and urged him toward the gates. "Come on then," he grunted. "We ride for Camster broch."

A chill north wind whipped across the hills, chapping Keira's cheeks as she rode. Her father's broch was two days' ride from Castle Varrich—they would be the longest and shortest two days of her life: the longest because she would be an unwelcome companion for the whole journey, and the shortest because they'd get to Camster far too soon.

She wasn't ready to face her parents again.

Leaning forward, she urged Outlaw after the others, his heavy hooves churning up the turf.

Connor had set a cracking pace. He rode out front, with Morgan and Jaimee following side-by-side close behind. Gritta loped next to Morgan's courser. Keira followed behind them with the rest of Connor's party bringing up the rear.

Since leaving Castle Varrich, none of the Mackay siblings had spoken to Keira. None had even looked her way.

It was as if she were suddenly invisible.

Strangely, the sensation was familiar, and with a sinking heart, she realized why. Growing up in her father's broch, she'd either been ignored or insulted.

Her mouth thinned then, her gaze traveling to Connor's broad back. Of course, he knew all about that.

She'd told him about her unhappy childhood, and he'd used it against her—betrayed her confidence. She hadn't been angry in the great hall earlier in the day, for dread had consumed her. But now, as they rode over the hills north-east of Castle Varrich, resentment smoldered in her belly.

It had been a lowly act, and now she was going back to Camster—back to a place she'd never belonged.

Keira's belly twisted, dread closing its fingers around her throat.

Her parents would have likely heard about her disappearance from Iona by now. Connor and the others were right. They wouldn't welcome her home—especially when they heard that she'd married a Mackay.

Niel's comment on that subject had been cruel and crude, yet he wasn't wrong. She had no idea how her father would respond, but he wouldn't be gentle.

They rode hard that day, resting briefly mid-afternoon, before pressing on. By the time dusk settled across the land, the wind bringing droplets of rain with it now, Keira's legs and back ached with fatigue.

Exhausted, she sat upon a lichen-encrusted rock a few feet away from a burn, while Connor's men started a fire and put up tents.

The wind whipped her hair across her face, and she pushed it aside before drawing her cloak close. Samhuinn was only a day behind them, and already it felt as if winter were upon them.

A hollow sensation settled within her then, as she recalled how happy she'd been a few days earlier—how she'd looked forward to spending the winter at Farr Castle, curled up in bed with Connor, laughing at the fireside with Jaimee, and exchanging quips with Morgan.

But that life was lost to her now, like a dream she'd just been torn from. It had never been real—and deep down, she'd known her happiness wouldn't last.

Morgan brought her some bread and cheese.

His face, although not a hard mask like his brother's, wasn't friendly. He didn't enquire after her, but merely passed her the food, turned on his heel, and walked off. Sitting apart, Keira ate in silence, her gaze traveling over to where the three siblings sat by the fire.

During her brief time at Farr Castle, she'd watched them together. There was usually laughter, good-natured ribbing, and smiles. But not this eve. As the gloaming deepened, all three of them fell quiet, their faces shadowed. Sensing the mood, the rest of Connor's warriors kept their voices low. Even the horses were quiet.

A short while later, Keira was grateful to crawl into the solitude of her tent.

Connor's anger wouldn't subside. After the initial shock had faded, the rage continued to beat like a battle drum in his chest. And the closer they got to their destination, the quicker it beat. Ever since the eve of Samhuinn, he'd kept his temper leashed. But he could feel it writhing within him, a beast that wouldn't be tamed.

He needed to deliver Keira back to her kin before that beast got free.

Riding ahead in the misty dawn, Connor's gaze swept from side to side. They'd just entered Gunn lands and would need to be on their guard. He'd ordered his men to tuck away their Mackay-plaid sashes and cloaks—best not to draw attention to themselves while they rode through enemy territory.

Even so, his skin prickled, his senses on alert.

Connor glanced back, at where his brother and sister rode close behind. As always, Jaimee's face was determined, her gaze as watchful as his. She was a tough lass—stronger than he'd realized—yet he wished she and

Morgan had heeded him and returned to Farr Castle as he'd ordered.

Frustration bubbled up inside him, making the fury beat faster still.

Are ye hoping that her father will slit her throat ... once he finds out a Mackay chieftain has been humping her?

Niel Mackay's words taunted him, scalded him.

Humiliation made it hard to breathe. Connor knew Jaimee hadn't spoken up during the meeting to challenge his authority. And his siblings were only trying to help when they'd insisted on accompanying him on this journey. But this morning, as the last of the mist drifted across the heather-clad hills, he felt woefully inadequate—as a man, a husband, and a laird.

Keira recognized the landscape they rode through now. It was a wild moor—bare hills of brown and green— that stretched away in every direction.

Her belly tensed; they weren't far from Camster broch.

The reunion she dreaded as if she were going to her hanging was looming on the horizon.

Presently, they came upon two stacked-stone cairns. One was long and low to the ground, while the other was squat and round. Dark doorways led inside.

Connor and his siblings reined their horses to a halt and gazed upon the mounds before them.

One of the Mackay warriors muttered an oath under his breath.

Of course, many folk were superstitious of ancient barrows like these.

"The Grey Cairns," Keira announced, approaching them. These were the first words she'd spoken since leaving Castle Varrich. Her voice was husky, strained, which was hardly surprising, considering that her innards felt tied in knots and her heart ached.

Connor glanced at her then, his handsome face a cold mask.

"The locals say they're thousands of years old," she continued lamely. "Some say that the fairies come out at night here."

Connor's mouth twisted, his gaze narrowing.

"Let's move on, laird," one of the men called from behind. "This place gives me the chills."

Connor ignored him. Instead, his gaze remained upon Keira. "How much farther to Camster broch?"

Keira swallowed. "A short ride ... south over those hills."

Connor nodded, reined his stallion around, and continued on his way. An instant later, both Jaimee and Morgan did the same. However, just before she did so, Jaimee caught Keira's eye. The young woman's face was strained, her gaze shadowed. Then she looked away.

Jaimee might have spoken up in her defense before the clan-chief, but that didn't mean they were still friends.

Does she hate me now too?

Keira would never know, for this journey was fast coming to its conclusion.

Urging Outlaw on, Keira's attention returned to Connor. Soon he would ride away, and out of her life forever. But before that happened, she had to speak to him. She wasn't sure what she'd say, or why it was even necessary—only that something deep inside forced her to kick Outlaw into a fast canter, so that the horse overtook Jaimee and Morgan and drew up alongside Thunder and the laird himself.

"Connor," she gasped his name, her gaze swinging left at his profile. "I don't expect yer forgiveness, or yer understanding ... but please know that none of this lie came easily to me. I never wanted to deceive ye."

His attention swung to her, although his expression was cold, his gaze dangerous.

Keira's skin prickled. This was a side to Connor Mackay that she was having trouble reconciling. He was a good man, an honorable man—but once vexed he was deadly.

"Really?" The word came out in a snarl. "And there was me thinking that ye are an expert in mummery. Ye certainly had me fooled."

A pain rose under Keira's breastbone. "I tried to tell ye," she managed, her throat so tight now it was difficult to speak. "The eve before our wedding ... when I came to see ye."

His face tensed, his gaze shadowing. He too would remember how agitated she'd been, how she'd tried to speak to him. However, he'd taken control of the situation, had believed that she was merely struggling with low self-worth—and she'd let him believe that.

"Aye, that was yer chance," he growled finally. "And yet ye didn't take it."

"No," she agreed, misery churning through her. "Ye were so gentle with me ... I've known so little kindness in my life that I was loath to give it up." She heaved in a deep, shuddering breath, fighting down the sorrow that now clawed at her breast. "But I should have, and I will go to my grave regretting it."

Silence fell between them. The pain in Keira's throat made it difficult for her to continue, yet she forced herself on. She had one last thing left to say. "Ye must truly me hate me ... to take me back to my kin. I told ye how unhappy I was there. Ye know they don't want me."

His gaze snared hers, the moment drawing out. "Consider yerself lucky," he replied roughly. "If it were up to Angus and Niel, they'd have ye soundly beaten and locked in one of the caves below the castle ... till ye died of sickness or cold."

Keira's breathing caught. It occurred to her then that her husband's decision had actually been a merciful one. She tore her gaze from his, fighting the tears that blurred her vision.

This was her punishment, and she would have to weather it.

They reached the brow of the hill then, the wind pushing against their backs. Keira's gaze traveled south to where a burn wound its way through the valley below. Near its banks rose a solid grey broch. Flocks of sheep—

her father's livelihood—grazed the surrounding hillsides. And studding the bleak valley were a number of sod-roofed shielings, occupied by the shepherds who tended the flocks.

Keira's pulse quickened then, her fingers tightening around the reins.

This was a place she'd hoped never to see again.

21

SHE'S MY WIFE

THE RIDE DOWN the hill to her father's broch was over too fast. Few of her memories of this place were good. As a child, she'd run wild over the hills and played with the shepherds' bairns until her parents had forbidden her, but she'd spent most of her time within those thick stone walls weathering the scorn of her sisters and parents.

Unwanted—that's how she'd always felt here. And Connor knew it too.

Neither of her parents had looked bereft the day they'd seen her off on her journey to Iona just over a year earlier. They certainly wouldn't be pleased to see her back again. Especially not now.

The party rode through an arch in the high wall surrounding the broch, and into a dirt yard flanked with low stone buildings. The broch, shaped like a beehive with a thatched roof, rose above them, casting a deep shadow over the yard.

Keira drew up Outlaw, stroking his sweat-damp neck as she scanned her surroundings.

Her heart started to pound when she saw a bulky figure emerge from the doorway.

Maddoc Gunn lumbered down the steps toward the new arrivals, his greying brown hair catching in the wind. Behind him, a slight figure appeared in the doorway, her long, sharp-featured face peering down at the party gathered in the yard below.

Maddoc's gaze swept to Keira, his midnight-blue eyes growing wide. "Daughter?"

He'd rarely ever referred to her by her given name—sometimes Keira had wondered if he'd forgotten it, since he had so many daughters to deal with.

"Good morning, Da," Keira replied, her voice husky. She knew she should dismount, but suddenly she was frozen to the saddle. She felt safe upon Outlaw's back and didn't want to move from her current position.

Her father's expression hardened. "Where the devil have ye been?" he demanded. "We heard ye ran off from Iona ... ungrateful bitch!" His gaze swept to where Connor had drawn up his stallion next to Keira. She could see that he was searching for any sign of clan plaid, and disconcerted that he couldn't find any. "Who's this?"

"Connor Mackay of Farr," Connor introduced himself, his voice impassive. "We found yer daughter on our lands ... and escorted her home."

Shock rippled through Keira. Drawing in a sharp breath, she cast Connor a sidelong glance. She'd expected him to hurl the whole ugly truth in her father's face.

Instead, he'd come up with a lie of his own.

Maddoc Gunn's face turned to granite, his shoulders stiffening. "Mackay whoreson," he growled. "How dare ye venture on my land?"

Connor cocked an eyebrow. "Is that the thanks I get for returning yer daughter safely to ye?"

"Ye'd have done better to escort the useless wench back to the nunnery," her father snarled back. "I have no use for her."

"Camster was closer," Connor replied.

Keira swallowed a lump in her throat, her attention remaining upon her father. It was just as well he didn't know the truth; even so, he wasn't making any effort to hide his displeasure at her arrival. She glanced up then, at where her mother still stood in the doorway.

Moira Gunn was scowling, her thin body vibrating in outrage. "Willful, selfish chit!" Moira called down to her. "How dare ye run away from the nunnery?"

Keira wasn't surprised by her mother's reaction; nonetheless, seeing that shrewish face again made her belly twist. Still she didn't swing down from Outlaw's back.

This was the last place she wanted to be right now.

Keira lifted her chin, heat igniting in her belly. "I hated it there, Ma," she called back. "And I wouldn't have returned here either if given the chance."

The words were inflammatory, and both her parents stiffened as if she'd just struck them.

She'd pay for that later—neither Maddoc nor Moira were shy about raising a hand to her. Keira's fingers tightened further upon the reins.

If either of them touched her this time, she'd strike back. She'd had enough of being bullied by these people. She was no longer the lass who slunk around the broch, hugging the shadows and hoping no one saw her. Her time at Iona had altered her, but more than that, her marriage to Connor had opened up her world.

He showed me more kindness than my family ever did.

For a short time, she'd believed in happiness. Despite that the dream was gone now, part of her still clung to its ghost, to those days when she'd belonged somewhere.

These two angry people before Keira were her kin, but they no longer had any power over her.

"Get down off that horse now, girl, and get inside," Maddoc growled. "Ye will take a beating for that. I'll see to it that ye can't walk for a week." He then shifted his gimlet stare to Connor. "And ye ..." He spat on the ground then. "Get off my lands before I set my dogs on ye."

Long moments passed. Silence fell in the yard, broken only by the soft bleat of sheep on the surrounding hills.

Keira didn't look at Connor, or at Morgan and Jaimee, who'd drawn their horses up just behind them. She couldn't bear to look Connor's siblings' way. The kindness she'd experienced at Farr Castle seemed to belong to another lifetime now.

But this was what her life really was.

Behind her, Gritta issued a low, threatening growl. Clearly, the wolfhound had picked up on the aggression in her father's voice.

Heaving in a deep breath, Keira leaned forward and loosed her feet from the stirrups, preparing to dismount. *Best to get this over with.*

"Wait, Keira." Connor's voice, flint-hard, forestalled her. "Stay where ye are."

Stiffening, Keira glanced over at him. He sat there, green eyes dark with fury as he glared across at her father.

Keira frowned, confused. "Connor?"

"*Connor?*" Her father mimicked, scorn dripping from his voice. "What's this? Have ye been spreading yer legs for the Mackays?"

Heat pulsed through Keira. Lord, if only he knew.

Connor shifted his attention to her, a nerve ticking in his jaw. "We're leaving," he said tightly. "And ye are coming with us."

Her gaze widened. "What?"

"Connor," Morgan interrupted from behind them. His brother's voice held a warning edge. "This isn't—"

"We're leaving," Connor repeated, cutting off Morgan. "I'll not leave Keira with these people."

"She's my daughter!" Maddoc roared, his voice booming across the yard. "Ye have no say in what happens to her!"

Connor shifted his attention back to Maddoc Gunn. Looking on, a strange numbness seeped through Keira. It felt as if this were happening to someone else. She didn't understand what was transpiring here.

"I'd say I do," Connor ground out. "For she's my *wife*."

With that, he leaned forward, caught one of Outlaw's reins with one hand, and turned Thunder around with the other. A heartbeat later, he headed for the gateway.

Now that she'd turned from her father, Keira could see the faces of her escort. The shock on both Morgan and Jaimee's faces was a sight to behold. Keira imagined their reaction mirrored her own.

What in Hades was Connor doing?

Her father's roared threats followed them out of the broch, reverberating off the stone walls. Danger crackled through the air now; she hoped Connor knew what he was doing. She should have warned him that Maddoc Gunn had a volatile temperament and had been a formidable fighter in his youth. He also had a party of loyal warriors who followed him.

Connor had just roused his ire, in the midst of Gunn lands.

They rode out of the yard, back under the stone arch and along the banks of the burn.

Keira didn't glance back, didn't take one more look at the dark stone bulk of Camster broch, although the skin between her shoulder-blades burned the whole way back up the hill. She rode directly behind Connor, the rest of the party thundering at their heels.

Keira's belly knotted, her palms now slick with sweat.

What would her father do? Would he send out a party to retrieve her, to take his reckoning on Connor Mackay? Or was he just glad to be rid of her?

Whatever his reaction, the sooner they rode from these lands, the better.

Heart galloping in time with Outlaw's heavy hooves, Keira leaned forward and let the wind sting her cheeks.

She still didn't understand why Connor had stood up for her. Why, after making the journey here, was he taking her away again?

None of it made any sense.

Dull-wit.

Connor had taken some wrong turns in his life, and honoring that betrothal was one.

Clod-head!

He'd wanted to rid himself of Keira Gunn, and here he was riding away with her.

Yet Connor hadn't been able to stop himself. He'd sat there, astride Thunder, staring up at Maddoc Gunn's pugnacious face, and had wanted to sink his dirk into the man's belly. Although he'd known Keira wasn't welcome at Camster, seeing her parents' reaction to their daughter's return had jolted him from the fog of vengeance-filled rage that had driven him here.

Suddenly, he couldn't let Keira remain in such a place. He'd told himself this would be his reckoning, that she deserved her father's wrath. But the reality of it had hit him like a mallet in the chest.

Whatever Keira had done, he couldn't leave her with those people.

Now, as he rode north once more, the wind tangling his hair, he emerged from the red haze of fury that had descended upon him in that yard.

Stubbornness rose in its place. A different kind of heat kindled in his belly now, as he reflected on events back in Castle Varrich.

The devil take them all.

He was done with letting others decide his fate. Many members of his clan would likely not be happy with Connor's latest decision, but he didn't care. Angus Mackay might be clan-chief, but Connor was his own man.

Spying movement out of the corner of his eye, Connor saw Morgan draw level with him. His brother's face was unusually grim.

"Maddoc Gunn won't let ye get away with that," Morgan pointed out, raising his voice to be heard over the rushing wind and thunder of hoofbeats. "Ye better hope we reach our lands before he and his men catch up with us."

"I don't give a damn what that bastard does," Connor growled. "If he comes after us, he does so at his own peril."

Morgan fell silent, clearly surprised by his brother's response.

"This changes nothing between me and Keira," Connor continued, answering Morgan's unvoiced question. He didn't look his brother's way as he spoke, his gaze still fixed upon the shadow of the mountains that reared up in the distance. "The woman betrayed me, and I won't forget it."

"So what will ye do with her?"

Connor didn't answer. Right now, he had no idea.

They rode hard that day, stopping only briefly on hilltops so that Connor could check if they were being followed.

Peering south now, Connor turned, fixing Keira with a shuttered look. It was the first time he'd looked at her directly since leaving her father's broch.

"Yer father is on his way," he informed her curtly. "A small party ... but traveling fast." He then glanced north, at where a line of dark mountains crested the windswept sky. "We'll be crossing into Mackay lands shortly."

Keira watched him, unclenching her jaw as relief flooded through her.

Connor's attention shifted toward the heart of Gunn territory once more. His expression grew hard.

Keira's relief dissolved, fear knotting in her belly.

He looked like he wanted a fight.

"My father has a terrible temper," she murmured. "And he loathes yer clan."

A harsh smile split Connor's face, and he swung back to her. "If he's foolish enough to follow us onto Mackay lands, I look forward to drawing my dirk against him."

They set off once more, the tattoo of their horses' hooves upon the peaty ground rejoining the whine of the wind once more.

Keira's cheeks were chapped from the harsh wind, and as dusk settled and the air grew chill, her fingers numbed. Her belly ached from hunger—for she hadn't eaten since breaking her fast at dawn—and anxiety gnawed at her.

The scene at Camster didn't make any sense. She didn't understand Connor's behavior at all. Angus Mackay would be furious to discover what he'd done, but Connor didn't appear to care. Instead, he seemed to be spoiling for a fight with her father.

Connor rode a few yards ahead now, his hair flowing behind him. However, she noted the rigid, stubborn set of his shoulders.

Aye, she had no idea why he hadn't left her at Camster, yet sooner or later, she was going to find out.

22

MERCY

THE PARTY MADE camp for the night in the midst of a pine stand, at the foot of a forest-clad mountain. They were well inside Mackay territory now, yet Keira was even tenser than earlier. A confrontation with Connor wasn't far off—she could sense it.

He would turn that penetrating gaze on her soon, and when he did, she had to be ready.

Standing behind Jaimee, she watched as Connor sent five of his men, including Morgan, out to set a watch around their campsite. He then instructed the others, including his sister, to put up tents and start a fire.

Keira stood amid all the activity, her heart in the throat, waiting for him to turn his attention on her.

And eventually, Connor approached.

"Ye and I need to talk," he greeted her, his voice clipped. "Follow me."

A few yards away, Jaimee glanced up from where she was attempting to light a fire. Her smooth brow furrowed, her attention flicking from Connor to Keira. Like Keira, she'd heard the edge to her brother's voice.

However, she said nothing, and neither did Keira.

Instead, she followed Connor into the trees, dread dogging her steps.

Connor led her some distance away, to a small glade where a burn trickled. A carpet of soft pine needles lay underfoot, their scent drifting through the clearing. Walking to the center of the space, Connor turned, legs apart, and faced her, folding his muscular arms over his broad chest.

Keira approached him, her pulse fluttering in the hollow of her neck.

Breathe, she reminded herself. *He's just a man.*

Indeed, he was. Only, she suddenly felt a bit of a coward.

The past couple of days had shown her another side to Connor Mackay. He could be kind, warm, and fair-minded. But he could also be stubborn and ruthless. Today she had learned that although the connection between them had grown swiftly, there were still many depths to this man she had yet to discover.

"Connor," she greeted him softly. "Please explain what happened at Camster."

The handsome planes of his face tensed. "Sometimes I think ye are a witch," he growled, "that ye have cast an enchantment over me."

Keira's belly clenched. This wasn't a good start.

"I'm no witch," she assured him, "and I certainly didn't expect ye to come to my rescue back there. Why did ye?"

Connor stared at her for an instant, and then he stepped back, dragging a hand through his hair. Growling a curse, he started to pace before her.

Watching him, Keira realized he was a hair's breadth away from losing his temper. Her breathing grew shallow. She didn't want to push him, and yet she had to know.

"Curse ye, Keira Gunn," he snarled, as he continued to pace. "I wish ye had never entered my life."

Keira clasped her hands together before her, entwining her fingers nervously. An apology bubbled up within her, yet she choked it back. Connor didn't respond well whenever she said she was sorry. And she didn't blame him.

No amount of apology could change what she'd done.

Wretchedness twisted under her ribcage. She had no idea what to say.

Spitting out another curse, Connor circled the clearing. The air was thick with tension. "Ye weren't exaggerating ... ye have a truly foul family. I intended to throw ye back into their midst, but when it came to it, I couldn't leave ye with them. I just couldn't." He broke off there, his voice choked.

Keira's breathing hitched, her throat thickening. What had she ever done to deserve such mercy? Certainly, she didn't warrant it from the man she'd willfully tricked.

"So, what will ye do with me now?" she asked after a pause. Did she want to know?

He strode to Keira then, looming over her, his eyes gleaming in the gloaming. "Ye are coming back to Farr Castle ... with me."

Keira stared up at him. "As yer wife?"

He watched her, with a look that made her wish the ground would open up and swallow her. She'd never seen such pain in someone's eyes. "Aye," he rasped. "I wed ye, didn't I?"

Keira's throat constricted painfully now. Suddenly, it was hard to breathe. What a terrible mess she'd made of things. Tears escaped then, despite her best efforts to hold them back, flowing silently down her cheeks. She wished now that he'd left her behind at Camster. Her father's wrath, and even a good beating, would be preferable to witnessing the suffering she had caused him.

"When I said I loved ye, I wasn't lying," she said softly, cursing how her voice wobbled. She was on the verge of breaking down completely. "I still feel the same way. My heart is yers, Connor."

He shook his head, denying her words, his expression hardening. "Enough."

"But this isn't a lie, it's—"

"Enough, I said," he cut her off, his voice slicing through the glade. "I won't hear any more of yer poison. Aye, ye are still my wife, but that doesn't mean things will go back to the way they were. They can't."

Keira didn't sleep that night. Instead, she remained by the fireside, her cloak pulled tight around her shoulders as she stared into the glowing embers.

Connor's men had erected a tent for her, but she didn't use it.

Over the course of the evening, those also seated around the fire drifted away to their beds, or to take their turn at the watch.

Keira ignored them all.

Belly twisted in knots and fighting nausea, she continued to stare sightlessly into the fire.

Connor had disappeared shortly after they'd returned from the glade and hadn't returned to the camp. He was likely keeping watch with his men—and after the bitter words they'd shared, she didn't think he'd return all night.

Keira imagined that sleep would eventually drag her down into its clutches—that she would slump onto her side, letting oblivion take her—but it didn't.

Instead, she remained awake, eyes gritty, chest aching with the need to weep.

Only, things were too much of a mess for tears.

Connor Mackay was taking her home to Farr Castle, but things wouldn't be as they were when they'd left before Samhuinn. The servants and residents of the castle had once greeted her with warm smiles. They wouldn't this time, not when they knew who she really was.

Gunns weren't welcome at Farr Castle.

They would all wonder why their laird didn't just rid himself of her. Surely, he could get the union annulled by the church, especially since he'd wed a woman believing she was someone else?

Truly, Keira didn't understand it either.

But the past day had taught her that Connor Mackay wasn't a cruel man.

Maybe, with time, he would seek to annul their marriage, but for now, he was in too much pain to do so.

Keira swallowed, as despair settled over her like a heavy, smothering blanket. She had wounded him that deeply.

Connor ran a tired hand over his face and peered into the trees. His eyes burned with fatigue, and his body cried out for rest. However, he'd deliberately patrolled all night. Anything to be away from Keira.

Why are ye doing this to yerself?

He couldn't answer that. Taking Keira back to Farr would only hurt them both ultimately, and yet he'd backed himself into a corner.

I could take her back to the nunnery.

He could, and yet Connor balked at the idea. No, despite that he could hardly bear the sight of her at present, Keira was staying with him.

"Dawn's not far off." Morgan's whispered comment drew his attention then. His brother's face was cast in shadow, while around them, the silhouettes of his men were ghosts in the predawn light. Somewhere in the shadows, Gritta also stalked, on patrol.

Connor nodded, his attention returning to the southern tree-line. Just a few moments ago, he thought he'd seen movement there. He blinked, trying to ease the grittiness in his eyes. Perhaps it was just exhaustion playing tricks upon him.

"Ye should return to camp and get some rest," Morgan whispered.

Connor shook his head. They'd all taken turns at the watch during the night. "I'm fine," he grunted, keeping his gaze upon the trees. "As soon as the sun rises, we'll break camp and move on anyway."

"Maddoc Gunn didn't cross the border after all then?" Keeping his voice hushed, Morgan moved closer to Connor.

"It seems not," Connor murmured. Yet as he spoke, the fine hairs on the back of his arms prickled. Something was amiss. "But—"

His voice cut off there. Reaching out, he gripped his brother by the wrist in silent warning. Together, the pair of them looked south, at where shadowy figures crept out from the trees, moving cautiously toward them. "Look ... we've got company," Connor whispered.

Morgan's answering grin flashed white in the shadows. "Aye ... and they don't realize we've seen them."

Slowly, silently, Connor drew his dirk. Excitement quickened within him. How he needed to draw blood right now. "Come on, brother," he murmured. "Let's have some sport."

The night stretched out. As the first glimmers of dawn lightened the eastern sky, Keira blearily glanced up from the now dead fire to see that the camp was starting to stir.

Jaimee emerged from her tent and stretched. Then, braiding her thick hair into a long plait, she approached the fire, where Keira sat.

The two women watched each other for a long moment, before Keira cleared her throat. "What ye did back at Castle Varrich, Jaimee ... I appreciate it."

Jaimee frowned. "No woman deserves to be treated with such disrespect," she said coldly, "not even ye." She glanced around then, her expression shuttered. "Where is Connor?"

Keira swallowed. Her sister-by-marriage's cutting response stung, yet it was hardly unexpected. "He went out on patrol shortly after dark," she replied, her voice husky, "but hasn't yet returned."

Jaimee turned back to Keira. Her lips parted, as she prepared to say something else. But movement in the trees to the southern edge of their camp forestalled her.

Men emerged.

Keira's breathing hitched, and she scrambled to her feet, her cramped leg muscles protesting from the sudden movement. For a terrible moment, she believed her father had found her, but then she recognized her husband and his men.

Her breath gusted out of her, before a chill seeped through her limbs.

Connor was splattered in blood.

Next to him, two of his men were helping Morgan. Connor's brother hung between them, his face ashen. As always, his wolfhound trailed behind him.

Jaimee spat out an extremely unladylike curse and stepped forward. "What happened?"

"Are ye alright?" Keira asked.

Connor's expression was stone-hewn as his gaze shifted to Keira, pinning her to the spot. "Yer father and his men crossed the border after all," he replied, deliberately ignoring her question.

Keira's heart started to pound. "Where is he now?" Contrasting sensations warred within her then: outrage that her father had dared track them this far, fear that Connor might have killed him, and dread that the Mackays had another reason to hate her.

"We bested them in the end," Connor assured her. He was quite a sight standing there, his face and clothing stained with Gunn blood, his skin pulled tight across his cheekbones. He might have been keeping his wrath to himself, yet Keira could feel it pulsing between them. "Yer father escaped with his life ... as did three of his men." His mouth twisted then. "They won't be bothering us again."

An unexpected surge of relief flooded through Keira, weakening her limbs. As much as she resented her father, she didn't wish him ill. She was grateful that Connor had spared his life.

"Sent them running, we did," Morgan piped up from behind Connor. His tone was hearty, although the brittle edge to it betrayed that he was in pain. "Gunn bastards." His breathing caught then, and his legs gave way. He would have collapsed to the ground if the two warriors hadn't been supporting him.

Gritta pushed her nose against his leg and gave a low whine.

"Morgan!" Jaimee rushed to her brother. "What did they do to ye?"

"Just a scratch," Morgan replied, although his voice was much weaker now, and his eyelids flickered. He was struggling to remain conscious.

"One of them got him on the left flank," Connor replied, his voice grim. He turned to his men. "Lay Morgan down by the fire ... let's have a look."

"Stop fussing," Morgan protested weakly.

"Stop talking, ye big oaf," Jaimee retorted. However, her pretty face was now strained.

Standing on the edge of the group, Keira watched them lower Morgan to the ground. Jaimee then knelt at his side and peeled away the blood-soaked leather vest.

As Connor had warned, he bore a wound upon his flank. Even from this distance, Keira could see that a dirk-blade had found its mark. Blood trickled from the gash.

Jaimee muttered another curse under her breath, before she glanced up, her gaze fusing with Keira's. "I need some wine to wash the wound and cloths to bind it."

The two women's gazes held for a heartbeat. Of course, like Jaimee, this wasn't the first time Keira had seen battle wounds. She'd grown up watching her mother stitch her father up after a skirmish, and helping tend the other warriors who came back to Camster worse for wear.

With a nod, she turned and hurried over to where their saddlebags sat piled up near the horses. Grabbing a bladder of wine, she then dug into her own saddlebag and pulled out a lèine. She carried both items back to Jaimee, and while her sister-by-marriage began to tend her brother's injury, Keira began ripping the fine linen tunic into long strips.

23

TEARS CHANGE NOTHING

THE AFTERNOON WAS on the wane when Farr Castle hove into sight in the distance.

Keira rode behind Connor and Morgan—the latter sat awkwardly in the saddle, shoulders rounded. No doubt, his wound was now paining him greatly. However, he said nothing.

Riding next to Jaimee, Keira stared ahead at where the high walls of the castle rose against the cloudy sky. Gulls wheeled overhead, their screams echoing across the cliffs as the party drew close to the eastern ramparts.

They rode through the cluster of sod cottages east of the castle, where women were getting in washing and bairns played in the dirt.

The folk of Farr called out to their laird and his kin as they passed by, and Connor acknowledged them with a wave. He had his back to her, so Keira couldn't see his expression. However, she imagined it was grim.

As it had been while they patched up his brother.

Keira had done her best to assist Jaimee, although the linen bandages weren't good enough. Morgan needed to be stitched up by a healer.

"Is Cullodina here?" Connor called to a group of women who were tanning hides on the edge of the village.

"Aye," one of them called back.

"Go find her," Connor replied, his voice gruff now. "Tell her we need her in the keep urgently."

"Stop fussing, brother," Morgan wheezed. "I don't need a healer ... Jaimee can look after me."

Connor ignored him, watching as the woman who'd answered him picked up her skirts and hurried off to find Cullodina.

They continued on their way, passing through the castle gates into the landward bailey. Then, ignoring all else, Connor swung down from Thunder's back and helped Morgan off his horse. Despite Morgan's best efforts, he staggered as soon as he tried to walk on his own. As such, Connor and another warrior supported him as they helped him up the steps and into the keep.

Jaimee rushed off after them, leaving Keira and the others to stable the horses.

Grateful to be ignored for a spell, although dreading the moment when she would have to enter the castle too, Keira dismounted Outlaw and led him into the stables.

The bay gelding was a fine beast. She'd noted that he was one of the best in Connor's stables—a wonderful wedding gift. However, the horse was now a sharp reminder of everything she'd lost.

Some men never recovered from betrayal. Would Connor?

Breathing in the dusty scent of straw and hay, mixed with the stronger smell of horse, Keira led Outlaw into his stall and started to unsaddle him. Men now filled the stables, their rough voices rising and falling around her.

Her throat suddenly tightened, her vision blurring.

Don't weep, she berated herself inwardly. *Tears change nothing.*

It was wise advice, yet the misery within her couldn't be contained. It beat its wings against her like an angry netted bird, demanding to be released.

Grabbing a hog-bristle brush, Keira started to groom the gelding in long strokes. Yet a few moments later, tears blinded her.

It was no good.

Her actions had brought strong repercussions.

Morgan bore a deep wound, a dangerous one. If it festered, he could die—and if he did perish, the hatred of those residing here would know no bounds.

Morgan Mackay was loved by all at Farr Castle; she'd seen that upon her arrival here. His boyish charm and easy smiles drew others to him.

They'd never forgive her if he died. Never. And she wouldn't forgive herself either.

Tears scalded Keira's cheeks. Giving up trying to groom Outlaw for the moment, she leaned forward, resting her face against his sweat-damp neck, and wept.

***

"What do ye think, Cullodina?" Connor asked. He stood a few feet back from the bed, watching as the healer finished sewing up the wound in his brother's side.

The woman glanced up, her round face creasing into a cautious smile. "The blade missed his vitals, I believe … the bleeding has stopped now. I will cover the cut with woundwort tonight. That should help stop it from festering."

Connor exhaled slowly, the tightness in his shoulders easing just a little.

Cullodina was an able healer; she'd sewn both brothers up a few times over the years. Her knowledge of healing herbs was legendary throughout Mackay lands; once or twice, the clan-chief himself had even sent for her. As such, Connor trusted her judgment.

Connor glanced at his brother's serene face. Cullodina had given him a special draft that had made him sleep and would dull the pain when he awoke. His attention shifted to where Jaimee sat, her face drawn with fatigue and worry, her gaze riveted upon Morgan.

Morgan and Jaimee mattered more to him than anyone, although he was also close to his cousin Kennan. And strangely, after this humiliation, he felt closer still to them. But Keira had distracted him. It scared him how quickly the woman had become his world.

I will never let my guard down like that again.

Neither his brother nor sister had said much to him since; instead, their support had been implicit and steadfast.

He appreciated that, especially since wrath, and the need to lash out at someone, still pulsed in his gut like a burning lump of peat in a draft.

"Go and get some rest, Jaimee," he said gently, moving forward and placing a hand on his sister's shoulder. "Morgan isn't going to wake up for a while."

"Aye, lass ... I'll stay with yer brother tonight." Cullodina motioned to the chaise longue by the window. "I'll let ye know if anything changes."

They put Keira in a bed-chamber down the hallway from the laird's quarters.

The servant led her inside, left her with a tray of food, and departed without a word. She was a pretty lass with curly blonde hair, one that Keira had spied serving them in the great hall. She recalled the lass favoring Morgan with sultry gazes at mealtimes.

However, there was no friendliness in the woman's face this eve when she'd led the laird's wife to her new bed-chamber. The lass's reaction didn't surprise her though.

News of her real identity would have circuited the castle by now.

Keira didn't touch the tray of bannocks and goat's cheese; she had no appetite tonight. After seeing to her horse, she'd re-entered the keep, weathering wintry stares as she made her way up to the women's solar. Seated by the fire, while she wound wool onto a spindle to keep herself occupied, Keira had waited for Jaimee or Cait to join her. She'd hoped for word on how Morgan was faring, but as the day drew out, no news arrived. And then, finally, the servant had come to take her to her bed-chamber.

Loosing a deep sigh, Keira started to undress. She felt so weary—in body and spirit—that she could barely summon the energy. Yet she forced herself to strip off her lèine and kirtle—both in need of a wash after the journey. Standing naked at the washbowl, she lathered up a cake of lye soap and went through her ablutions. Then, shivering, she pulled on a night-rail and crawled into bed.

At least she'd avoided seeing Connor again tonight.

Lying abed, she stared up at the rafters, where long shadows cast from the dying glow of the small hearth played. Exhaustion stole over Keira, pulling her into its clutches.

What now? The question played repeatedly in her head. Was Connor going to simply ignore her going forward?

As she lay there, thoughts of Rhianna intruded. Bitterness twisted in her gut.

Rhianna had sent her into this. She felt like a goose that had been fattened over the summer and then offered up for the Yuletide feast. Rhianna had waved her off knowing that the ruse would be exposed sooner rather than later.

Where was Rhianna now? She hoped the lovers had managed to flee to a corner of Scotland where no one would ever find them. At least the sacrifice she'd made wouldn't be for nothing if Rhianna got the life she wanted.

Keira shouldn't have wished her well. And yet in all this mess, she found solace in knowing that one person, at least, was happy.

24

CAN BE FORGIVEN

"I DON'T WANT to look at that bitch's face every time I sit down to eat," Domhnall Mackay's belligerent voice rumbled across the table. "I'll not break bread with a Gunn."

Glancing up from his boar stew, Connor frowned. "Try to temper yer language, uncle ... there are ladies present."

Nonetheless, his uncle's anger didn't surprise him. He'd expected a harsh response from Domhnall; the man bore a hatred toward the Gunns that rivaled the clan-chief's. Two days had passed since their return to Farr, and in that time, news of what happened at Varrich, and then at Camster, circulated the castle with the speed of a deadly pestilence.

The folk of Farr were still getting used to the fact that Keira Gunn and not Rhianna Ross had wed their laird. Many of them, his uncle included, had urged him to send her away, but Connor refused.

Steeling himself, Connor shifted his gaze to where Keira sat, back ramrod straight, at his side. He observed the woman's stoic expression and felt a grudging pang of respect. She was tough. It was as if Domhnall hadn't spoken, hadn't just insulted her.

Connor insisted that Keira join them at mealtimes. She was still his wife after all. However, he'd spoken little to her, and likewise, she didn't attempt to draw him into conversation. Since their return, he'd avoided even looking squarely at her, although he forced himself to do so now.

Her features were schooled into a neutral expression, her midnight-blue gaze shuttered. She was dressed in a plain blue woolen kirtle today, her thick oak-brown hair pulled back from her face. His gaze lingered for an instant on the thick tresses that tumbled down her back. A memory returned then, of how he'd tangled his fingers through her hair, how, when he'd buried his face in it, he'd inhaled the fresh scent of rosemary.

Heart thudding against his ribs, Connor clenched his jaw.

Such memories were a betrayal. He wouldn't allow them.

"Apologies if my wife puts ye off yer stew, Domhnall," he spoke once more, picking up his pewter goblet of wine and taking a sip. "But she'll continue to join us."

Farther down the table, Kennan frowned. He was watching Connor, his expression guarded. "She's a distraction, Connor," his cousin pointed out. Next to him, his wife, Cait, wore an unusually brittle expression. "Please do us all a favor and have her take her meals elsewhere."

Connor shook his head, setting his goblet down with a thud. "No, Kennan. If ye don't like the company I keep, ye can choose to eat elsewhere. Keira is my good lady wife, and as such, she will take her seat at this table." His gaze swept over the tense faces of those surrounding him in a silent challenge. Only Morgan was absent. His brother was on the mend but still not strong enough to come downstairs for his meals.

"This is an outrage," Domhnall growled, his large hands gripping his eating knife.

"Just ignore her, uncle," Jaimee spoke up then, her tone clipped.

Domhnall's heavy-featured face reddened. Connor watched him across the table, awaiting his uncle's reaction. Looking at the man's florid face, he could see the resentment that burned in his eyes.

"Why would ye keep her here?" Domhnall accused. "Yer father would turn in his cairn if he knew."

Connor scowled, his own temper quickening. "My reasons are my own. I don't need to justify myself to ye, or anyone else, Domhnall."

"And what will ye tell the Mackay? Angus won't suffer one of his chieftains remaining wed to a Gunn."

"I've already sent him a missive, informing him of my decision." Connor's mouth twisted. In the note, he'd told the clan-chief that he couldn't bear to be parted with his wife. Gunn or not, he loved her, and so he'd taken her back to Farr Castle with him.

Writing the missive had made his belly hurt. He'd thrown away three drafts and wasted costly parchment before he managed to finish the letter. How would the clan-chief respond to the news? Niel would likely be incensed and whip his father into a frenzy about the matter.

Nonetheless, if Connor stood firm, they might eventually let things be.

His jaw clenched. Truthfully, he wasn't comfortable with her presence here either, but God's teeth, he was weary of others deciding things for him.

Connor's last comment did finally rouse a response from his wife. Her gaze widened as it swung in his direction—and for an instant, she met his gaze. He saw her confusion, the same expression that was echoed in the faces surrounding him.

They all thought he was losing his wits over this.

And maybe he was.

But he wouldn't have anyone question him over it.

Keira crossed the seaward bailey, basket under one arm, heading toward the chapel. She carried the last of the autumn flowers, sprays of heather and daisies, which she would use to decorate the altar.

At the squat stone well in the center of the bailey, two servants were drawing water. They both ignored her, and she did likewise. A month after her return to Farr Castle, she was used to being a shadow here. Truthfully, it was a relief in many ways, for she'd braced herself for their scorn.

Leaving the chill afternoon behind, she stepped into the silent interior of the chapel and breathed in the scent of incense mingled with the fatty odor of tallow. Looking around, she was relieved to see that the chapel was empty.

Her slippered feet scuffed on the stone as she made her way up to the altar and started laying out the flowers.

"Good afternoon, Lady Keira."

Breath catching, she swung around to see the chaplain standing a few feet behind her. Father Lachlan had entered the chapel so silently that she hadn't heard him approach.

"Father," she gasped, putting a hand to her erratically beating heart. "I didn't realize ye were here."

"Don't mind me, My Lady," he said. And then, to her surprise, a smile creased his round face. "Thank ye for the flowers ... they do brighten up the altar."

"It's the last of them before winter," Keira replied. The gentleness of his tone made her throat thicken. She was touched by the warmth in his words.

He nodded, his gaze searching her face. "I hear ye were to take yer vows at Iona?" he said after a pause.

Keira swallowed a lump in her throat. "Aye," she murmured. "But ye will have also heard the rest of the sorry tale."

"Aye ... I had trouble believing it though, I must admit." He paused there, his gaze searching. "Ye don't seem the lying kind."

Keira swallowed down a bitter laugh. "Appearances can be deceiving, Father, I'm afraid." She looked down at the empty basket she held before her. "I behaved stupidly."

He didn't disagree with her, although when she glanced up once more, she saw sympathy in his eyes.

"Aye, well ... none of us were born faultless," he replied. "Most folk spend their lives making mistakes and then paying for them."

"Not mistakes like mine though," Keira said quietly. Her fingers clenched around the handle of her basket. Nonetheless, it was a relief to talk to the chaplain. It was lonely being an outcast. "I sinned terribly, Father ... and I repent for it."

He held her gaze. "The Lord hears ye, My Lady ... but ye aren't a black-hearted lass. Ye lost yer way, that's all. And ye'll find yer way back onto the right path again soon enough." He paused then, his expression softening further. "Ye set out to deceive, but yer motives were pure ... ye were trying to help a friend. And because of that, I believe ye can be forgiven."

Keira was pondering the chaplain's words, and clinging to his kindness, when she entered the women's solar a short while later.

However, she stopped abruptly when she realized that Jaimee and Cait were seated there. Cait perched before a loom, while Jaimee was winding wool for her. Their presence was a surprise, for she'd gotten used to spending afternoons in here alone.

Both women glanced up at her entry, and for a few instants silence fell in the solar.

Then Keira cleared her throat. "Apologies," she muttered. "I didn't realize anyone was in here."

Swiveling on her heel, she turned to leave.

"Wait, Keira," Cait called out. "Don't go ... neither of us will bite."

Keira halted and turned back. Although Cait was looking at her, a tight smile upon her lips, Jaimee looked less than pleased. High spots of color stained Jaimee's cheeks, and her fingers now clenched the spindle she held.

"I don't want to intrude," Keira murmured.

"Ye aren't." Cait motioned over to the empty chairs near the hearth. "Ye are still Lady of Farr ... there's little point in ye hiding away."

Jaimee's thinned mouth told Keira that her sister-by-marriage wasn't in agreement about that.

Nevertheless, Cait's words encouraged her. She moved across to the hearth, picked up the embroidery she'd been working on, and settled into one of the chairs.

Across the solar, Jaimee had resumed winding wool onto the spindle, although her movements were now jerky, betraying her ire.

Moments passed, the silence tense rather than companionable, before Cait finally shattered it. Stepping back from her loom, she turned to Keira. The intensity of her bright blue eyes was unsettling. "Why did ye do it?" she asked, her gaze never wavering. "What sort of person would weave such a lie?"

Next to Cait, the red spots on Jaimee's cheeks deepened, and Keira wagered the woman had a few choice words to say on the subject of Keira's character. However, she managed to hold her tongue, allowing Keira to answer. No doubt, all of them wanted to know why—and clearly, Connor hadn't spoken of it.

"A desperate one," Keira replied softly. She dropped her gaze to the roses she'd been embroidering upon the pillowcase. "Rhianna Ross offered me a way out of a life I didn't want ... and I took it." She glanced up then and saw that both Cait and Jaimee wore wintry expressions now. Her answer wasn't improving their opinion of her. Heaving in a deep breath, Keira continued. "Ye met my parents, Jaimee. To them, I was nothing but an encumbrance. My elder sisters are all beauties, but Da spent all his money marrying them off. There was nothing left for me, and Ma and Da made it clear that my face was never going to win me a husband. So, they packed me off to Iona."

Silence followed this admission. Keira was aware then that her pulse had quickened, and that her palms were now damp. It was humiliating to admit that she was unwanted, especially to these two beautiful women who had likely never known what it was like to be mistreated.

"At the nunnery, I didn't fit in either," she continued. She'd begun the tale now—she might as well complete it.

"And then I became friends with Rhianna Ross. She'd been at the nunnery a while, waiting for her betrothed to fetch her. But when she discovered Connor was making the trip, she panicked and revealed to me that her lover, Callum, was already in hiding on Iona. He wanted her to flee with him, but she was afraid to." Keira swallowed then, to ease the tightness in her throat. "Swapping places with me bought them time to get away."

"What a self-centered bitch!" Jaimee burst out, unable to hold her tongue any longer. "Rhianna used ye." Anger smoldered in her sister-by-marriage's eyes. "And I can't believe ye let her!"

Keira stared back at her. She felt wretched now, for Jaimee had voiced what she'd known for a while—that she'd played straight into Rhianna's hands. The lass was determined to have her freedom, even if it meant sacrificing her best friend. Keira had been terribly gullible. "She told me that no one would ever discover the ruse," Keira admitted huskily. "But from the moment I sailed away with Connor, I struggled with it. I tried to tell him ... the eve before our wedding ... but when it came time, I lacked the courage."

Heaving in a deep breath, she looked back at Jaimee. "I never belonged anywhere until I arrived at Farr. Ye all were so kind to me, I was loath to give up my new life."

"But to live a lie?" Cait asked, incredulous. "That is a prison of another kind."

"Aye," Keira agreed softly. "But since I fell in love with Connor, I decided I would just have to carry my secret forever."

"Ye *love* my brother?" Jaimee's voice held a rasp now. Her eyes glittered as if she was on the verge of tears. "Despite everything? Despite all the lies?"

"Not everything was a lie," Keira whispered, dropping her gaze to her lap. "Although it matters not now ... for I've ruined everything. Whatever my reasons, what I did was inexcusable."

25

DO YE DISAPPROVE?

"FANCY A CUP of wine?" Connor held aloft the jug he'd just picked up on the mantelpiece and turned to his brother. "We should celebrate the fact ye are no longer an invalid."

Morgan snorted. "When ye put it that way, how can I refuse?" He lowered himself into a chair, wincing just a little as his injury made itself known.

Nearly six weeks had passed since they'd returned to Farr, and in that time, Morgan had recovered from the deep dirk-wound to his flank. However, he still had to be careful with it. The brothers had been out for a gentle ride that afternoon, although the outing had been cut short by the arrival of bad weather.

Icy rain and sleet now pelted the closed shutters, and the wind howled against the castle's thick stone walls, driving in through the gaps. The large fire in the solar guttered and flared in the drafts. In front of the hearth, Gritta lay asleep, snoring gently.

They were approaching the 'Long Night' now. The days were short, and outdoors this eve, a grey, wintry gloaming had settled over the coast.

Connor poured each of them a drink, handing Morgan his cup. It was definitely an evening for wine. The jug had been sitting above the fire, so the bramble wine was warm.

Sighing as the wine pooled in his belly, Connor sank down into a chair opposite his brother and put his booted legs up on a settle, crossing them at the ankle.

Morgan raised his cup in a silent toast before he lifted it to his lips. The brothers settled into a companionable silence then, as they listened to the foul weather clawing at the walls and the crackle of the fire.

A knock at the door interrupted them.

"Come in," Connor called out. "Jaimee, pour yerself some—"

He'd expected it was Jaimee, as she often did join them after supper. However, it wasn't his sister who stepped into the solar but his wife.

Immediately, the warmth in Connor's belly chilled, and the sense of well-being that had begun to steal over him dissipated.

"Keira," he greeted her coolly. "What do ye want?"

Halting, his wife's gaze swiveled to him. Connor noted that she carried a garment slung over one arm. "I've made ye a new lèine, Connor," she said, before holding it up for him to see. Made of finely woven linen, the neckline, sleeves, and hems were embroidered in blue and green thread.

"That's beautiful work," Morgan spoke up, only to earn a quelling look from Connor.

"Thank ye," Connor added curtly, before motioning to the table that dominated the solar. "Just leave it there."

Keira hesitated a moment, her gaze settling upon his face.

Connor held her stare, his belly clenching. How he wished this woman's presence didn't have a visceral effect on him. Whenever she was near, he had trouble concentrating.

They continued to sit together at the laird's table at mealtimes with barely a word spoken between them. Other than that, they had very little contact with each other. Connor's responsibilities as laird kept him busy. He'd spent that afternoon poring over detailed accounts of this year's harvest. There had been a lot of rain in late summer, and so it had been a poor one. The following day, he would spend the morning in the great hall, arbitrating disputes between his tenants.

Indeed, he had very little time to brood, but with each passing day, he was growing increasingly unhappy.

Every time Keira entered the great hall, he had to fight not to stare at her.

There was a challenge in her gaze now. She wanted a reaction from him, but he wouldn't give her one.

"Leave it there," he repeated, turning his gaze from her to the guttering flames in the hearth. "Goodnight."

Silence followed these words.

Her anger and disappointment washed over him in a cold wave. His belly clenched once more. He knew he was behaving badly, yet he just wanted her gone from his presence.

Moments later, the door thudded shut, leaving the brothers alone once more.

Connor took a gulp of wine, welcoming its heat. Curse the woman. He'd been on the cusp of enjoying his evening—something he hadn't done in a while—before Keira had entered the solar. But when she'd gone, she'd taken his mellow mood with her.

And once again, the familiar sensation of emptiness gnawed at his chest.

"What's happened to ye?" Morgan spoke up finally. His voice was quiet, reflective, and when Connor glanced up, he saw his brother's gaze was shadowed.

Connor tensed. "Excuse me?"

"Since when did ye turn into such a shit?"

Connor scowled. "Since my wife turned out to be someone else." Morgan continued to hold his eye, although his mouth flattened into a rare expression of censure. In other circumstances, Connor would have found such a reaction amusing, to be chastised by his laddish younger brother. But this eve, it just soured his mood further. "What? Do ye disapprove?"

Morgan snorted. "I wouldn't waste the energy." He paused then, frowning. "I understand yer anger. We were all horrified to discover ye had been tricked—and had unwittingly married a Gunn. But time passes ... and it was yer decision to bring her back here after all. I've watched ye over the past weeks ... witnessed the change within ye. How long are ye going to go on punishing Keira ... and yerself?"

Connor's mouth twisted. "I'm not punishing anyone."

"Aye, ye are. Ye haven't smiled once since we got back." Connor shrugged, making it clear he didn't care about such trifling matters. Yet Morgan wasn't finished. "Ye have grown so bitter."

"And so would ye," Connor shot back, his temper flaring. It often did these days; he'd once been so easy-going. But of late, it took very little to put him in an ill mood. Morgan had just succeeded. "I wed a liar."

"A liar ye are plainly still smitten with."

Connor had just taken a sip of wine, and he choked it down, before coughing. "Stop talking rot."

Morgan leaned forward, wincing as his flank pained him once more. "Ye have most folk fooled ... but not me. Ye are sick with love for her, Connor."

"Idiot," Connor snarled. "What do ye know of such things? Ye wouldn't recognize love if it bit ye on the arse."

Morgan shrugged, the insult washing off him. "Maybe I know nothing of love, but at least I don't torture women," he countered. "Lie to us all, if ye wish ... but not to yerself. It's eating ye up ... and it'll consume ye if ye don't face it."

Keira strode down the hallway, fury pulsing through her.

She'd spent the past days working on that lèine. She'd even sewn Connor's initials into the collar. But he hadn't even taken a look at the tunic. His 'thanks' had been insincere and deliberately aloof.

Initially, when she'd returned here, she'd dreaded seeing him. She'd been so sorry about what she'd done that it was an effort not to keep apologizing. But, strangely, with the passing of the days, and then weeks, a strange mood had settled over her.

She wasn't as alone here as she'd feared. She visited the chapel daily to pray, and afterward, she chatted to Father Lachlan. Then, in the safety of the women's solar, she now spent her afternoons with Jaimee and Cait. Her relationship with them had thawed considerably since she had spoken with them two weeks earlier.

Jaimee had revealed just how deeply shocked and hurt they'd been by her deception. But as the days passed, both Jaimee and Cait had agreed that Keira deserved an opportunity to explain herself. Before her ruse had been revealed, she'd been developing a strong friendship with them—and now, that friendship could flourish once more.

Jaimee and Cait's company had calmed something within Keira. And, unlike before, when she'd been pretending to be Rhianna Ross, Keira didn't have to keep her shields raised. She could make observations, and voice opinions, without filtering them—without lying to the people who made her feel so welcome.

Even the atmosphere within the keep toward her was thawing. Some folk still looked at her askance, and Connor's uncle never missed an opportunity to mutter an insult under his breath when she passed by. Yet most residents of the keep just let her be.

Nonetheless, it appeared that Connor had hardened his heart toward her—something that both saddened and infuriated her. Back there in the solar, she'd wanted to throw that lèine in his face.

Who would have thought that her kind, gallant husband, could behave like a cur?

She headed toward her bed-chamber, rather than returning to the women's solar, where Jaimee and Cait would be chatting by the fireside. The mood she was in, she wasn't good company. She'd almost reached her door, when a familiar, if unwelcome, figure emerged from the stairwell.

Domhnall Mackay.

The man's heavy features twisted into a belligerent expression as he approached Keira.

"Gunn witch," he growled, looming over her. "Yer days are numbered here. Connor's too soft-hearted by far ... but when he comes to his senses, I'll make sure ye are stoned."

Soft-hearted?

Keira held her ground, folding her arms over her chest. Fortunately, she was a tall woman, so she didn't have to lift her gaze far to meet his. The anger in her belly burned hotter still. She'd had enough of Connor's uncle.

"Why are ye wasting yer time here then? Ye had better get down to the shore and start collecting yerself a cache of stones, Domhnall," she replied coldly. She knew the response was goading, but after weathering this man's scorn at each mealtime, her patience had grown thin indeed. "Ye want to be ready for that day."

Heart hammering, Keira let herself into her chamber and shut the door quickly.

She hadn't shown her nerves before Connor's uncle, yet she believed his threats. When he looked at her, he saw a liar, a traitor.

Connor might have been lenient, might tolerate her, but Domhnall would enjoy making her pay for her crimes.

She crossed to the bed on shaky legs and lowered herself onto the edge, letting her galloping heart settle.

I must make sure never to be alone with him.

Keira's belly clenched then, and she placed a hand over it. The sensation reminded her of how queasy she'd been feeling over the past few mornings.

Her monthly flow was nearly three weeks late now, and she felt oddly tired, detached from her surroundings. Having five elder sisters, she knew what these signs meant.

Keira's eyes fluttered shut. She was likely with bairn.

I should say something to Connor.

Despite that she'd felt like slapping the man a short while earlier, she didn't want there to be any more secrets between them. However, she needed to make sure that she was indeed with child before telling him.

The healer, Cullodina, lived in the village. She would go to her the next morning and get her opinion.

A heaviness settled over Keira then. She opened her eyes and surveyed the small bed-chamber. Flames danced in the hearth, creating a welcoming atmosphere. Yet the room suddenly felt as cold as a tomb.

Some women would be delighted by such news, would see it as a way to build a bridge with their estranged husband. But the last thing Keira wanted to do was manipulate the man she'd already wounded deeply. Despite that he'd vexed her this evening, Connor deserved much more than that.

Keira ran a tired hand over her face and fervently hoped that her womb hadn't indeed quickened. Such a development would likely only widen the gulf between her and Connor.

26

BREATHE

"AYE, MY LADY ... ye are over six weeks gone with
bairn." Cullodina straightened up, removing her hands
from where she'd been examining Keira's abdomen.
"Congratulations."

Keira clenched her jaw, before nodding. She then
pushed herself up into a sitting position on the narrow
bed in the healer's cottage. A cluttered space surrounded
her. Bunches of drying herbs hung from the low rafters.
Clay bottles and small wooden boxes of healing herbs
and powders sat upon dusty shelves. A modest-sized
lump of peat glowed in the fire pit that dominated the
space. The smoke created a blue haze in the cottage, the
odor catching in Keira's throat.

"Ye don't look overjoyed, lass," Cullodina murmured
when Keira didn't respond.

Keira shook her head. "Aye, well ... since my husband
can barely look at me these days, things are ...
complicated." Her hand strayed to her belly, and without
thinking, she cupped it protectively. Memories flooded
her then, of the times she and Connor had lain together.
Her heart had ached with joy in the aftermath. Had
things remained as they were, she'd have been delighted
to know she carried her husband's child.

But as things stood, the confirmation just filled her
with dread.

"Maybe, he will soften when he hears the news," the
healer suggested, her round face tensing with sympathy.

"He likely won't," Keira replied, her voice catching.
"Things have gone too far for that." She reached for her

fur mantle and slung it across her shoulders, before favoring the healer with a tight smile. "Please keep this to yerself for now, Cullodina. Connor needs to hear the news from me."

Stepping outdoors, Keira sucked in a lungful of cold, clean, salt-laced air—a relief after the fug of peat smoke within. A sharp wind whipped in off the water this morning, and the sea was a wide expanse of churning white-caps. The rain had spent itself overnight, although judging from the leaden skies to the north, more bad weather was on its way.

Keira was tempted to take a walk along the cliffs, to be alone with her thoughts for a while, but as a particularly strong gust of wind hit her, bringing with it spots of rain, she decided against it.

The wind could be perilous on the cliff-top track.

And after Domhnall's threats the night before, she didn't want to venture out too far afield alone. She wouldn't be surprised if Connor's uncle was taking note of her movements and looking for a chance to strike. He hated her enough to toss her off the cliffs to her death if given the chance.

A shiver passed through Keira then, and she resisted the urge to cover her belly with her hand once more.

She had to stop doing that, or folk would get suspicious.

I must tell Connor.

Keira rounded her shoulders against the wind and walked through the village, toward the road that led back to the castle. Aye, and she would tell him. Tonight. She would intrude upon his solar once more and demand that they finally cleared the air.

She'd just stepped out on the road, when the thunder of hooves to the north drew her attention. Halting, she saw men on horseback approaching.

Connor was leading the way, while Morgan, Kennan, Domhnall, and three leggy wolfhounds—one of them Gritta—followed close behind.

Keira's breathing caught at the sight of her husband. He rode his stallion as easily as if he'd been born in the saddle, his golden hair streaming like a banner behind him. It didn't matter that he despised her now, just the sight of him still robbed her of breath.

Gathering her wits, Keira took a quick step back, drawing her cloak close, as Connor drew Thunder up before her.

"What are ye doing?" he demanded, frowning down at her. Gritta loped up to Keira and pushed her wet nose against her. Keira reached out and ruffled the hound's ears, although her gaze remained locked with her husband's.

"I took a walk," she replied.

His frown deepened to a scowl. "Ye shouldn't wander out here alone," he warned. Did she imagine it, or was there a different edge to his voice this morning—a note of concern that cut through the coldness?

Keira nodded. She wasn't going to argue the point with him. Just feeling Domhnall's baleful glance upon her from a few yards away was warning enough. The man wore an expression that could curdle milk. Next to him, Morgan and Kennan also looked on, although there was no hostility in either of their gazes. The two men hadn't yet taken to talking to her, unlike Jaimee and Cait, but they no longer viewed her with a jaundiced eye.

No, it wasn't wise for her to be out here alone, but this morning she'd had a valid reason.

"I'm on my way back now," she murmured.

Their gazes remained locked for a moment longer, before Connor urged Thunder on and headed back to the gates. Morgan and Kennan followed, both favoring Keira with nods, while Domhnall brought up the rear.

Connor's uncle lobbed a gob of spittle Keira's way, although she took a smart step back and the spit missed its mark. With a muttered curse, Domhnall returned to the keep with the others.

Connor took his seat in the great hall and inhaled the savory aroma of mutton stew. This morning's ride had given him a hearty appetite, the first decent one in weeks. Of late, he'd had little interest in food. His stomach had closed.

His attention shifted then, to where a tall woman with unbound brown hair, dressed in flowing green, crossed the great hall.

Connor couldn't keep his eyes off her.

Morgan's comments the night before still stung.

At least I don't torture women.

Was his brother actually right? It had never been his intention to hurt Keira, but he would indeed wound them both if he continued in this way. His gaze remained upon Keira as she drew closer, and his brother's closing comment now taunted him.

It's eating ye up ... and it'll consume ye if ye don't face it.

Aye, it was gnawing at him. Every damn day. Sometimes his gut felt tied up in knots and his head pounded. It was ripping him up on the inside. The disappointment, the humiliation—all entwined with longing. He couldn't bear it.

He wasn't sure he could ever feel the same way about the woman he'd wed, but he couldn't continue to act as if she didn't exist.

After Morgan had left him the night before, Connor crossed to the table, picking up the lèine she'd lain there. She'd embroidered his initials into the collar, and he'd run the pad of his thumb over the fine needlework. No one had ever made him something so fine.

Keira slid into her seat next to him now, while conversation at the table ebbed and flowed like a bubbling burn around them.

Jaimee was in high spirits this morning, for one of the hounds had just given birth to a litter of pups. Morgan was teasing her about it. Kennan and Cait were discussing something intently, their heads bowed together, their hands entwined upon the table.

Something deep inside Connor's chest twisted at the sight. Kennan and Cait had been childhood friends before their relationship changed forever at a summer clan gathering. These days, they made no secret of their love, their passion for each other. Connor had never envied them—but he did now.

He too had thought he'd found his life companion, a woman he could build a future with. But instead, it had been a lie. How could he trust her again?

Only Domhnall looked in an ill mood today. His uncle wore a fierce scowl as he barked at a passing servant to bring him some cheese.

Connor observed the man for a few long moments. Domhnall was an example of what bitterness could do.

Do I want to end up like him?

The question was a sobering one.

Shifting his attention to his wife, Connor inhaled sharply and reached for a basket of bread, holding it out to her.

Keira's gaze widened. That was the first time he'd made such a gesture since their return to Farr. However, her expression was shuttered, wary. He didn't blame her. He'd been a cold bastard of late.

Cautiously, she took a bread roll.

Connor cleared his throat, suddenly ill at ease. "Can ye join me for supper in the solar this eve, Keira?" he asked. "I wish to speak to ye."

Slowly, her gaze still shadowed, she nodded.

Keira had no appetite for supper that evening. The mutton stew she'd eaten at noon still churned uneasily in her belly. She wasn't sure if it was the bairn or nerves. Either way, she felt queasy as she walked the last steps to the chieftain's solar and knocked upon the door.

"Come in." The rumble of Connor's voice greeted her.

Heaving in a deep breath, she pushed the door open and went inside, her breathing catching when her gaze settled upon the tall figure standing before the hearth.

As always, Connor's presence sucked all the air from the room.

Breathe. Keira forced herself to exhale and then draw in another breath. Her attention shifted to his face, noting the signs of strain there.

Ever since Samhuinn, grooves had appeared either side of his mouth, and his face looked thinner, his eyes hollowed.

Keira's belly clenched. It was the last thing she wanted, yet she'd made him suffer.

"Supper will be served shortly," he said gruffly, gesturing to one of the high-backed chairs before the fire. "Take a seat, and I'll pour us some wine."

Keira did as bid, even if tension now rippled through her. She'd planned to visit Connor this eve, to tell him about the bairn, but now that they were finally alone, her courage was failing. Keira set her jaw as she settled into her chair.

No, this wouldn't do. Enough of being afraid of telling the truth. She wouldn't leave this solar without speaking plainly.

Watching the tense line of Connor's jaw, she sensed his discomfort. He'd said he wanted to speak to her, but she would say her piece first.

He handed her a pewter goblet of wine, their fingers brushing accidentally. A frisson of warmth shivered up her arm in the aftermath, and her breathing caught once more. Pushing aside the distracting sensation, Keira wrapped her fingers around the goblet, before raising her gaze to his, holding it firmly.

"Connor," she began. "Is there no hope of reconciliation between us?"

His pine-green gaze narrowed, a strained silence falling in the solar.

Keira's pulse quickened, misery twisting in her belly. His reaction made his feelings toward her clear.

"Some things are difficult to forgive," he said, his voice roughening. "But I don't want to go on like this, Keira. I can't."

Her spine stiffened, even as grief clutched at her chest. "Ye won't have to," she said quietly, her voice brittle now. "I shall return to the nunnery and rid ye of my presence." His eyes snapped wide, his lips parting, but Keira continued, forestalling him. "I wasn't taking a walk this morning ... I went to see Cullodina ... and discovered I'm with bairn."

She paused there, watching the shock ripple over his face. His reaction made hysteria bubble up within her. They'd lain together many times—surely, he couldn't be surprised that this was the result. Such things happened. Two of her sisters had gotten with bairn on their wedding nights.

"But worry not, the babe will be born in Iona," she pressed on, choking the words out. "Far from yer sight."

27

BEST FOR US BOTH

CONNOR STARED AT her, his eyes wide, his expression frozen. When he eventually spoke, his voice was hoarse. "Is that what ye think of me, Keira ... that I'd send my pregnant wife away from my side?"

Keira swallowed in an attempt to ease the tightness in her throat. She didn't want to weep, not now. She had to remain strong. "I know that ye take on far too much responsibility," she replied, cursing the tremble in her voice. "Ye shouldn't have brought me back here. It's killing us both." She heaved in a deep breath. "Aye, it's true, ye didn't wed beautiful Rhianna Ross but me, Keira Gunn, a wool merchant's daughter. I know what I did was wrong, but the fact remains that I do love ye. I thought that in time ye could find it in yer heart to forgive me, to love me back, but now I see it is useless. It is best for us both if I leave."

Her words echoed in the solar, dying away to silence.

Moments passed, and then Connor set down his goblet of wine on the mantelpiece and walked away from the hearth. Keira remained where she was, her pulse fluttering in the base of her throat.

He lowered himself onto the wide window ledge, leaning up against the wooden shutters. Her husband wore a stunned expression, as if she'd just belted him across the face.

Keira's heart drummed against her ribcage as she waited for him to speak.

"Ye are right ... this is killing us," he finally replied. "I didn't think it was possible to suffer so. But I'd willingly take bloody battle wounds over this."

Keira swallowed. She understood what he meant. Like him, each day she awoke with a boulder on her chest. Her head and stomach hurt, and her heart ached.

She knew now what folk meant when they spoke of those who had died of 'a broken heart'. It was an awful, crushing sensation that dogged every waking moment and sapped the joy from life.

"I've been an idiot," he admitted. His eyes opened then, and he shifted his attention to her. The pain in his eyes was palpable. "I wanted to hate ye, to cast ye from my heart ... but the harder I try, the worse I feel. As much as I fight it, my soul knows it needs ye."

Keira's breathing grew shallow at these words. She didn't know how to respond, and so held her tongue, allowing him to continue.

"Ye have become part of me." His face twisted then, as if he were in real physical pain. "And I can't give ye up. I'm not sending ye away, Keira. Not now, not ever."

"So what do ye plan to do about *us*, Connor?" she asked softly. She hadn't yet taken a sip of the wine she cradled. Truthfully, she felt too queasy to drink any of it. Instead, her gaze remained riveted upon her husband, awaiting his response.

Connor rose to his feet and approached the hearth. Her pulse quickened as she watched him draw near. Suddenly, it felt overly hot seated by the fire.

Gently, he took her goblet from her and set it down next to his upon the mantelpiece. And then he leaned down, took her hands, and drew Keira to her feet. His gaze speared hers. "I want us to start again."

Keira urged Outlaw into a brisk canter, following Connor and Thunder across the hills east of Farr. It was a bright, brisk winter's morning.

The perfect day to take a ride out with her husband—the perfect day to start mending things between them.

The conversation of the night before had left her reeling. She'd retired to her bed-chamber and lain awake for hours, going over the things they'd said to each other.

Emotions were still raw, and they were still circling each other, wary and afraid of getting hurt—but hopefully, with time Connor would trust her again. Hopefully, with time she'd believe that his heart actually wanted her to remain at Farr.

The tattoo of their horses' hooves drifted across the bare hills, and above, Keira caught a glimpse of a hawk gliding on the air currents.

She could see why Connor loved this wild corner of the Highlands so much. She too had fallen for its rugged charms. Her gaze shifted to her husband's broad shoulders up ahead. But she'd fallen for this man first.

Nervousness tightened her belly. They'd reached a crossroads. Soon the future of their relationship would be decided. Could they start again?

They rode high into the hills, finally stopping to rest the horses and take their noon meal in a sheltered valley carpeted in heather and clumps of broom.

Connor swung down from his dun stallion and retrieved the rolled blanket strapped behind the saddle. He then spread it out on the ground while Keira carried over the bag stuffed with food and drink that they'd brought from Farr.

Seated upon the blanket, they enjoyed a meal of bannocks, cheese, and tart apples washed down with ale. Meanwhile, the horses cropped at grass a few yards away. Despite that winter was now upon them, it was pleasant here, sitting under the noon sun.

Keira ate slowly, savoring the simple yet delicious fare. They sat in a secluded spot, far from any village or broch. The only sounds were the whisper of the wind and the screech of a kite that hunted in the distance.

For a while, neither of them spoke. Eventually, Keira dusted crumbs off her skirts, her gaze meeting Connor's. He had finished eating and now reclined on his side, watching her.

"This was a bonny idea," she murmured. "It's so peaceful in this valley."

"Aye." He favored her with a gentle smile. "I didn't want us to be interrupted today. Not when we're trying to mend things."

"I hope ye will learn to trust me again." Keira dropped her gaze to the blanket on which she sat, suddenly overcome with shyness. "I don't want our bairn growing up watching its parents at war."

"I'm not at war with ye," he said quietly. "I never was. This has been a battle I've been waging with myself."

He sat up and faced her. Keira raised her gaze, and they stared at each other for a long moment. He then reached out and took her hands. "I hate what ye did," he admitted after a pause, "but I don't hate *ye*." He paused there, his grip on her hands tightening. The strength and warmth of his fingers wrapped through hers was an anchor. "Yer strength and kindness ... yer natural way with folk ... and the passion ye kindle within me are impossible to condemn." He lapsed into silence then, before clearing his throat. "I've missed ye."

"And I've missed ye, Connor," she whispered. "But all this has taught me that we don't know each other at all." She held his gaze, her pulse racing now.

His gaze shadowed. "So, how ye behaved with me ... before Samhuinn ... was it all a lie?"

She shook her head. "My name, my identity, was false ... but nothing in how I behaved with ye was feigned. No one has ever listened to me like ye do. Before I became yer wife, I felt like a shadow. Only ye have ever truly seen me."

His mouth twisted. "Even when ye were pretending to be someone else?"

Keira tightened her grip on his hands. "Aye, even then."

They stared at each other, gazes locked. Connor's throat bobbed, and the air between them grew heavy, drawn taut by what they were now revealing to each other.

"It's ye I want, Keira Gunn." His eyes glittered now. "I have learned enough about ye to know that I'd be a fool to let ye go."

"And I'd be a fool not to fight for ye," she whispered back.

He released her hands then, his own rising so they cupped her cheeks. The feel of his palms—and the rough callouses caused by riding, hunting, and sword practice—made her draw in a sharp, needy breath.

Did he have any idea what his touch did to her?

His mouth slanted across hers—hungry, possessive. With a gasp, Keira's lips parted beneath his and she kissed him back greedily. Their tongues danced, tangled, and then with a pained groan, Connor pulled her into his arms.

A moment later, she was on his lap, her arms linking around his neck. Her hands tangled in his long hair as the kiss deepened to something bordering on desperation. Keira kissed him wildly, her pulse roaring in her ears. She clung to his shoulders, dizziness sweeping over her.

She hadn't realized just how much she'd missed this, how the taste and feel of him brought her alive. She couldn't get enough of Connor Mackay. She never would.

His hands slid down her back, before he cupped her bottom and hauled her hard against him.

Suddenly, there was too much separating them—their clothing a smothering, restrictive barrier between their skin.

Connor hauled up her skirts, his hands sliding along the bare skin underneath.

Meanwhile, Keira's fingers fumbled, such was her desperation, with the laces of his braies.

Breathing hard, Keira reached down, her fingers wrapping around his throbbing shaft. The wanting was driving her mad. She couldn't bear *not* to have him right now.

They rolled together on the blanket, knocking aside the remnants of their meal. Keira spread her thighs wide for him. A heartbeat later, Connor thrust into her.

Keira's cry echoed down the vale. Having him inside her felt even more glorious than she remembered. He stretched her, filled her, and turned her lower belly molten. She unraveled at his touch.

She clung to Connor's shoulders, arching her hips up to meet him.

He drove into her in hard strokes, and she took each one with a gasp of pleasure. Her fingernails dug hard into the fur cloak covering his shoulders, and their kisses turned bruising now.

They were erasing the last few weeks and all the heartache and turmoil that had turned their lives inside out. The lies, the anger, and the guilt—all of it faded under the heat of the passion that ignited between them.

And when Keira finally shattered, her cries joined those of the birds of prey high above. The past faded into shadow, and the future lay before them, unwritten. This was their new beginning.

Connor's climax ripped a hoarse shout from him. He arched back, his face twisting in such rapture that it almost looked as if he was in pain.

Panting, he lowered himself to the blanket and pulled her hard against him, wrapping his arms tightly around her as he buried his face in her neck.

28

THE ANNOUNCEMENT

FOR THE LONGEST while they didn't speak. They just clung together, sweat-slicked, the ragged sound of their breathing mingling with the whisper of the wind.

Connor *couldn't* speak. His heart was too full. Tears burned beneath his closed lids. He buried his face in the soft hollow of his wife's neck and breathed her in till his wild pulse calmed, and till the world stopped spinning.

Eventually though, he raised his face, pulling back slightly so that he could meet Keira's eye.

She watched him, her expression soft, her midnight-blue eyes luminous.

"Was I too rough?" he asked, concern suddenly constricting his chest. In the madness of passion, he'd forgotten she carried his child. "I don't want to hurt the bairn."

"Ye haven't," she murmured, a smile lifting the corners of that sensual, crooked mouth. "Worry not ... I have five elder sisters remember ... and they talk about such things."

Connor cocked an eyebrow. He didn't doubt her. He'd once overheard Cait gossiping with two of the female servants, and had been taken aback by how frank women were with each other about intimate matters.

Their gazes held for long moments, and tenderness swept over Connor.

This was what he'd been resisting for so long. He couldn't be in this woman's company and not love her, not look out for her. The past weeks, during which he'd tried to wall off his heart, had been the hardest of his life.

Reaching up, he brushed away a lock of hair that had fallen over her face. He captured a tress of her silky hair then, winding it around his fingers. How he'd ached to do this. He'd been tortured by the memories of what it had been like between them. And the thought that he might have to spend the rest of his life without the woman he loved had made him feel sick to his stomach.

"I love ye, Keira," he said softly. "And I'm sorry that I've been cruel to ye."

Her gaze shadowed. "Ye were hurt ... folk lash out in such situations."

"Aye, but I didn't need to take it so far." He swallowed then, dislodging the lump that had risen in his throat. "Ye didn't deserve that."

Her mouth pursed. "I couldn't believe it ... when ye didn't leave me at Camster."

"I couldn't leave ye there to be mistreated," Connor growled. And he meant it.

Maddoc Gunn was a bully. It had been an effort to let the bastard escape with his life that morning after the ambush. He'd let him live for Keira's sake. He hadn't wanted to see the horror on her face when he returned to the camp and told her that he'd cut her father's throat.

Bully or not, Maddoc Gunn was still her father. And there were some acts there was no coming back from.

"Thanks to ye, I'm free of them," Keira replied. She reached up, her fingertips tracing the line of his jaw. "Thanks to ye, I have discovered who I really was meant to be."

They lingered awhile in that valley, making love once more upon the blanket, until clouds moved across the friendly face of the sun and the air grew cold.

"It's time we got back, mo ghràdh," Connor announced eventually, rolling to his feet. He then favored Keira with a slow, sensual smile that made excitement flutter low in her belly.

How she'd missed his smiles. She didn't want to return right now. Instead, she wanted Connor to herself for just a short while longer.

However, he was right. The days had grown much shorter as Yule approached. They didn't want to be traveling after dark.

They packed up and headed west toward the coast, riding home side by side.

Home.

Indeed, Farr Castle was where she belonged.

However, a little nervousness fluttered in her belly then, as she anticipated how the folk of Farr would react to seeing the chieftain and his wife reconciled. The thought cast a shadow over her happiness, and she turned to Connor. "What if the others don't accept me as yer lady?"

He snorted. "Of course they will."

"The rift between our clans is a deep one. Yer uncle doesn't miss an opportunity to snarl threats at me."

Connor's dark-blond eyebrows crashed together. "I thought I'd made things clear to Domhnall." His voice hardened then. "I will have words with him again."

Relief fluttered through Keira at this news. Truthfully, Connor's uncle scared her.

"I apologize for my uncle," Connor continued, still frowning. "He lost his wife and bairn years ago ... and has been a bitter husk ever since. Nonetheless, I won't tolerate him mistreating ye."

Keira smiled back, warmth filtering through her. He had no idea how relieved his assurance made her.

"The past lies behind us now," Connor added, holding her gaze. "I won't have anyone threaten our happiness."

They arrived back at Farr Castle as the last of the daylight faded from the western sky. Torches had been lit upon the walls, welcoming them home.

They'd just ridden into the landward bailey and dismounted from their horses when Kennan Mackay strode across the yard to greet them.

The auburn-haired man halted a few feet back, his gaze shifting from Connor to Keira before he raised his eyebrows.

Connor met his cousin's eye. "Aye, Kennan." His voice held a warning edge. "Just in case ye are wondering, we have mended things."

Keira tensed, unsure what Kennan's response would be. Unexpectedly, his mouth lifted at the corners. "Far be it for me to pass judgment," he replied. "I was wondering when ye would get back though." He then motioned to the dark bulk of the castle behind him. "We have a visitor ... from Castle Varrich. Niel Mackay is here."

They met Niel downstairs in the great hall.

Their guest was waiting for them, lounging on his chair upon the raised dais at the far end of the hall.

Connor strode forward to meet him, forcing a welcoming smile. Niel rose from his seat and stepped down from the dais. Connor clasped arms with him, with the man who until recently he'd considered a good friend. However, the events at Samhuinn had altered things, had cast a shadow over their relationship. He understood Niel's suspicion of Keira, his fears that she might have been a spy. But he had taken things too far.

Niel was the last person, besides Keira's father perhaps, that he felt like seeing today. He'd intended to announce his change of heart toward his wife to his kin and warriors at supper, but the arrival of the clan-chief's son had forced his hand.

He'd asked Kennan to call everyone to the great hall this evening before supper was served. He heard his kin and warriors filing in behind him now, murmuring and whispering amongst themselves as they settled onto the bench-seats at the long tables below the dais.

Of course, the servants who'd seen him and Keira ride out that morning would have already sent word through the castle that something was afoot with the laird and his wife.

However, Connor wanted to make their reconciliation official.

He also wanted to make it clear that he would not tolerate any sign of disrespect toward Keira.

Guilt twisted under his ribcage as he remembered how cruelly he'd treated her over the past weeks.

"This is unexpected," he greeted Niel, keeping his smile firmly in place. "I didn't realize ye were that keen to go out stag hunting." He was aware then of his wife standing behind him, and stepped aside so that the clan-chief's son could see her.

Niel's expression froze when he did.

"I'm always keen for a good hunt," Niel replied, his tone cooling. "Although I have more of an appetite for a border raid these days." His gaze remained briefly on Keira before he flashed Jaimee a charming smile. "And of course, I had to pay the prettiest lass in Scotland a visit ... looking ravishing as usual, Jaimee."

Connor's smile slipped. He tired of Niel's heavy-handed attempts to flatter his sister.

"Enough of that," he muttered. "Come ... join us for an ale before supper. Ye are in time for an announcement."

Niel raised a dark eyebrow. "Announcement?"

"Aye ... one that's been long overdue."

They all took their places at the laird's table, and Connor waited for the rumble of conversation in the hall to die down. Usually, the others at the table talked amongst themselves, but this evening Morgan, Kennan, Cait, and Jaimee watched him closely, their expressions tense with anticipation.

Domhnall also joined them, and despite that his uncle was currently silent, Connor could see the outrage vibrating off his big frame. His expression was thunderous, his color high. Domhnall likely realized why the chieftain of Farr had called them all early into the great hall.

Connor rose to his feet. Then, turning to Keira, he reached down and drew her up so that she stood at his side.

Silence fell. Connor spied servants clustered in the doorway, but he let them remain. Everyone could hear what he had to say. At least this way, few folk within the castle would find out the news secondhand.

"Ye all know about what happened at Samhuinn," he began. He held Keira's hand and gave it a gentle, reassuring squeeze as he continued, "I discovered that the woman I'd wed wasn't Rhianna Ross, as I'd thought, but Keira Gunn. The two women swapped places."

Many of the surrounding faces darkened at his blunt tale. It was a galling reminder, and Connor had deliberately not tried to soften the truth with pretty words. He glanced back at Keira and saw that her face had paled. She was worried, but she didn't need to be.

"Well that is all in the past," he continued, turning to face her squarely. "I've been an arse, mo ghràdh ... I have mistreated ye terribly, but that ends now. Forgive me for my behavior of late. I'm sorry ye have suffered at my hands. I love ye, Keira ... and I can't wait to be a father to our bairn." The sucked in breaths of shock, the murmured oaths that followed, didn't surprise him. Connor pushed on, his gaze never leaving his wife's. Keira's cheeks had flushed, and her dark-blue eyes glistened. "Ye are the only woman for me."

More muttering followed this admission. Connor turned from Keira, his attention sweeping over those amassed in the great hall this evening. "My wife has treated all of ye with gentleness and respect. I will say this only once. Anyone who speaks against Keira, who abuses her in any way, will no longer be welcome at Farr." He paused then, letting his declaration sink in. "This is Keira's home now ... and *we* are her family."

He shifted his attention back to his wife, to see her staring at him. Her lips had parted, for she'd clearly not expected such a speech. A wave of protectiveness washed over Connor.

He meant every word he'd just said. This woman was his life. She understood him like no one ever had. He would never give her up.

The other expressions at the laird's table were quite a collection. Jaimee's face was flushed. Next to her, Cait was brushing away tears. Kennan wore a pole-axed expression, while Morgan was grinning. However, Niel

Mackay's face was an inscrutable mask. He leaned back in his chair, surveying Connor with a veiled look.

A few feet away, Domhnall had gone the color of raw venison. The veins on his forehead stood out, and his green eyes glittered.

"Lovesick fool." Domhnall's rough voice split the silence. "That Gunn witch has cast a spell over ye … she will be all of our ruin. Ye forget all the wrongs done to us over the years by that clan. They have stolen our lands and raped our women. Ye don't remember the bitter winters of the past, where we almost starved because the Gunns had razed our crops and stolen our cattle. Yer father lies rotting in the ground because of them … and he would be ashamed to see this day come to pass." Heaving himself to his feet, Domhnall drew the dirk from his hip. "Any man who defends a Gunn isn't fit to rule the Mackays of Farr."

29

A DEADLY DANCE

A STUNNED SILENCE settled over the great hall. All gazes rested upon Domhnall Mackay as he left the dais and stepped down into the space between the raised platform and the rows of tables lining the hall. There, he turned to face Connor once more, his face bullish.

The gesture was unmistakable.

Domhnall was challenging Connor for the rule of Farr.

In many ways, Keira was still learning about life at this stronghold and the nature of the folk residing within it. However, she didn't need to have grown up here to realize that Domhnall's act was a gross insult to Connor.

A chill rippled through the air, despite the roaring hearth at one end of the hall.

Keira's pulse quickened, her palms growing damp. Nonetheless, Connor's hold on her hand remained firm and dry. If Domhnall's behavior upset him, he didn't show it.

Instead, when she glanced up at his face, she saw that his handsome features were now set in hard lines. It was the same expression she'd seen when he'd faced her father at Camster broch. The face of a warrior.

Keira's skin prickled with danger.

"Think about what ye are doing, uncle," Connor said after a pause, his voice deceptively gentle and at odds with the austerity of his expression. "I know losing Adair and the bairn changed ye ... but this is one step too far."

Domhnall's mouth twisted. "Don't presume to tell me who I am. Ye know nothing of what I've lived through."

Connor's expression darkened. "If we fight, and I win, ye will die."

"Aye, lad." Domhnall flashed Connor a harsh smile before flipping his dirk. The movement was expert, practiced. Domhnall was nearly twice Connor's age, yet the years hadn't slowed his reflexes or sapped the strength from him. "And the same goes for ye."

"Connor," Morgan warned as Connor released Keira's hand and moved around the table. "He's not worth it. Banish him, and be done with it."

Domhnall snarled at that, before spitting on the floor before him. "After I deal with yer brother, ye are next."

Fury ignited in Morgan's green eyes. In an instant, his handsome face transformed into something feral. He rose to his feet, his right hand going to the hilt of his dirk at his hip. "Not if I gut ye first."

Next to him, Gritta also rose to her feet. The wolfhound's hackles bristled, and baring her teeth at Domhnall, she released a low growl from her throat.

Connor ignored the exchange between his brother and uncle.

Keira's gaze never left him as he stalked down from the dais and faced Domhnall. Steel scraped against leather when he drew his own dirk.

The two men circled each other. Domhnall flipped his dirk once more, a show of arrogant skill. In contrast, Connor didn't show off. He circled his opponent, his big body coiled, his gaze watchful.

Domhnall attacked first. He closed in on Connor in short, shuffling steps that brought him under the chieftain's guard.

But Connor reacted swiftly. His hand snapped up, grasping his uncle's wrist and preventing the dirk from gutting him. He then struck with his own blade. The tip of Connor's blade scored the leather vest Domhnall wore. A warning.

Domhnall twisted away and danced back a few steps. They circled each other once more, and then Domhnall attacked again, slashing at his nephew's face.

It was a deadly dance. They circled, gazes locked, before attacking, withdrawing, and then attacking again.

Domhnall drew first blood, with a sideways slice that caught Connor across his upper arm. The blade cut through the sleeve of his lèine. Connor let out a hiss of pain between clenched teeth and struck out at Domhnall, scoring a thin line across his bearded cheek.

"I'm going to enjoy slitting that bitch's throat once ye are dead," Domhnall snarled. "But not before I cut yer whelp out of her belly."

Nausea washed over Keira at this threat. Seeing the maddened light in the older man's eyes, she didn't doubt him for a moment. She knew that others here, Morgan and Kennan in particular, would defend her. However, she was too terrified about Connor's fate to dwell upon her own.

Domhnall had insulted Connor to enrage him, but his opponent remained cool, his movements as calculated as ever.

Anger twisted Domhnall's face, and he lunged forward. Connor leaped back—but not quite fast enough. His uncle's blade bit into his arm once more, and more blood bloomed on the pale linen of his lèine.

Lord, no. Keira's heart was in her throat now.

Pressing his advantage, Domhnall attacked again. Connor spun then, his big body moving with surprising grace, as he struck low, slashing his uncle across the front of a thigh.

Domhnall's curse rang out across the great hall. Around them, all those gathered for the evening's announcement had risen from their seats and formed a crowd encircling the two fighting men.

Blood ran down Domhnall's braies, soaking the thick leather. He staggered and went for Connor again, slashing in a frenzy this time.

Keira wrapped her arms about herself, clutching with each strike, each near miss. She couldn't bear this, and yet she couldn't look away.

Domhnall was out for blood. He didn't intend to merely injure his nephew, to incapacitate or humiliate him.

Looking on, Keira found it hard to believe that Domhnall, who'd seen Connor grow from a bairn to a man, could now be trying to kill him. And yet, she shouldn't have been surprised. She knew that some of the worst, the bitterest, feuds were between kin.

Domhnall lunged then, his curse ringing across the hall. He leaped high as he aimed a killing strike at Connor's throat.

Connor ducked beneath his opponent and deftly brought his dirk up under Domhnall's ribcage, burying it to the hilt.

Domhnall Mackay's agonized grunt followed.

He crumpled to his knees, even as he continued to strike out viciously with his blade.

Connor had just dealt him a mortal blow, but Domhnall wasn't going down yet. Breathing hard, Connor moved out of range. His gaze remained riveted upon his uncle, his face all hard angles, his eyes pitiless.

Domhnall's dirk clattered to the wooden planks, and he wheezed a curse, blood bubbling up onto his lips.

The entire hall went silent then. Everyone watched, as the man who'd just challenged the chieftain to a duel to the death slumped on his side.

The gurgle and rattle of his labored breathing was the only noise, a terrible sound that caused Keira's already roiling stomach to clench.

Connor's last strike was a killing one, but it wasn't a clean death.

Long moments passed, and still no one said a word.

Keira didn't pay any attention to the reactions of those around her. Instead, her focus remained upon the grisly tableau just a few feet away: Domhnall Mackay slowly drowning in his own blood, while Connor, chieftain of the Mackays of Farr, stood over him.

Crimson trickled down Connor's arm, dripping on the floor, but he paid his own injuries no mind.

When Domhnall's gurgling and raspy breathing finally ceased, and the man lay still upon the floor, Connor's gaze swept the hall—cold and fell. "Does anyone else care to challenge my authority here?"

Heart beating hard, Keira sank down into her seat.

Around her, Connor's kin were all pale and strained. Only Niel Mackay appeared unmoved by what he'd just witnessed.

He lounged back in his seat, observing Connor under shuttered lids.

Of course, that question had been directed at Niel. Keira knew the real reason why the clan-chief's son had come here. He'd been sent by his father to get the full story on Connor's decision to remain wed to his Gunn wife, and maybe to advise him to change his mind.

Had the ugly scene that had just unraveled before him altered Niel's perspective on things?

"I'd forgotten how good the Mackays of Farr are with daggers," Niel drawled finally. He then picked up the cup of ale before him and favored Connor with a toast.

There wasn't anything mocking in the gesture, although Connor's face was still stone-hewn as he stared back at him. He didn't reply, waiting instead for Niel to make his position clear.

"It's evident ye feel strongly about this marriage, Connor," Niel admitted after a pause. "And who am I to stand in the way of yer happiness?"

With that, Niel Mackay favored his friend with a wolfish smile and drained his cup of ale.

30

THE LOOKING GLASS

"YE WERE LUCKY," Cullodina observed as she peered
down upon the two wounds on Connor's left arm. "The
cuts are deep ... but the blade missed the large veins. I
should be able to sew them up."

Connor nodded his thanks, a muscle bunching in his
jaw. "I've suffered worse in battle."

It was true—Keira had seen the recent scars on his
torso.

Cullodina's face tensed. "Aye, but never from yer own
kin." Anger hardened her usually soft grey eyes.

Looking on, Keira shared the healer's outrage. She
couldn't believe that Domhnall had tried to kill Connor—
over her.

Servants were currently scrubbing away the blood
that stained the floor of the great hall. Meanwhile, his
uncle's body had been carried outside and would be
burned upon a pyre the following dawn outside the castle
walls. There would be no grave for Domhnall in the Farr
kirkyard; he hadn't earned his place alongside his
forebears.

Keira's gaze returned to the two nasty gashes upon
Connor's arm.

It sickened her to think just how much worse it could
have been.

Sitting at the healer's side, she assisted Cullodina as
she cleansed the cuts before deftly stitching them with
threads of catgut.

Keira was on edge and nervy in the aftermath of the
duel.

The entire keep had gone into shock, the hallways and stairwells eerily silent. The fight they'd all witnessed had been too vicious for even the most garrulous of servants to gossip about.

Eventually, Cullodina finished sewing Connor's wounds. She then packed up her healing unguents and bandages into her basket, promised to visit him the next day, and left the solar.

No sooner had the healer disappeared when Jaimee, Morgan, Kennan, and Cait entered. And although Keira was pleased to see them, and knew they'd all been worried about Connor, irritation flared within her all the same.

They hadn't had a moment alone since the duel with Domhnall.

Connor's handsome face was wan, as the battle fury that had consumed him during the fight ebbed. She couldn't imagine what he was feeling right now—after all, he'd just slain his uncle.

Even if it was a fight for his life, she knew her husband was more sensitive than he let on to the rest of the world.

Jaimee rushed to her brother's side, clutching his hand. Tears trickled down her cheeks, and her throat bobbed.

"Sorry ye had to see that, Jaimee," Connor said, his voice husky as he met his sister's eye. "I never thought Domhnall would react as he did."

"That stinking piece of shit," Morgan growled. He approached the bed, his wolfhound padding beside him, and placed a calming hand on his sister's shoulder. "If ye hadn't killed him, Connor, I would have."

Keira entered the women's solar and was relieved to find it empty. After such a tumultuous day, she needed a few moments alone. Connor was resting, for the draft Cullodina had given him for the pain had made him sleepy.

It grew late, and most of the keep had retired to their beds, but Keira wasn't tired.

The solar was a welcoming space. It smelled of the herbs she and Jaimee had collected. Cait's loom sat near the window, and servants had been in here, stoking the fire and lighting cressets. A golden light filtered over the chamber as Keira headed toward one of the high-backed chairs next to the hearth.

However, when she passed by Jaimee's looking glass upon the wall, she halted.

A tall, statuesque woman with thick oaken-colored hair stared back at her.

For a moment, it was like meeting the gaze of a stranger.

Keira had always believed herself ugly at worst, plain and best. Her sisters' comments had wounded her deeply over the years, yet as she looked back at her own reflection, she realized she'd been wrong to take their taunts to her breast.

Her sisters had been spiteful, her parents cruel, but she had allowed them to diminish her—had allowed their words to color and create her world. But Connor had helped her overcome that. His warmth and friendship in those early days of their relationship allowed her to recognize her true worth, and in return, others had responded kindly to her.

She would never let anyone denigrate her again.

She was no classic beauty, no 'Jewel of the Highlands', yet she liked the face that stared back at her. Aye, it was a trifle long, and she had her mother's sharp nose and her father's crooked mouth. But she liked her smooth skin, high cheekbones, and midnight-blue eyes.

Keira smiled at her reflection, warmth spreading through her as the woman in the looking glass returned the expression.

For the first time, she felt truly at ease in her own skin.

The thin column of dark smoke drifted into the early dawn. The morning was still; for once the strong winds that often raced in from the sea and buffeted the castle's thick stone walls had died. The sea was flat, gleaming like a polished shield-boss.

Connor went up onto the walls alone, his gaze sweeping over the rugged coastline till it settled upon the smoke.

His uncle's pyre burned.

Watching it, he felt something knot deep in his chest.

It was a dark day indeed when kin raised swords against kin. But Domhnall had left him with no choice.

No one would come between him and Keira. Not anymore.

But all the same, the sight of his uncle drowning in his own blood, the life draining from his eyes, would haunt Connor for a long while. He was glad his father wasn't alive to see such an event.

Drawing the fur mantle he wore about his shoulders close, he continued to watch the smoke rise into the rapidly lightening sky. The dull throb in his arm was a reminder of yesterday's events, a day he wasn't ever likely to forget.

It had started with the hope of reconciliation but had rapidly spiraled into something else entirely. Connor hadn't ever wanted to be one of those lairds that had to assert his physical dominance to establish respect. He hadn't wanted to cow his warriors, his kin.

But as he'd stood over his uncle and cast a baleful gaze around the great hall, he'd been ready to spill more blood.

What he felt for Keira scared him a little; it was a fiery passion, a connection that welded them together soul to soul.

Soft footfalls roused him from his brooding then.

Connor turned to see his wife approach. Like him, she wore a thick fur cloak about her shoulders, for it was chill upon the walls. Her thick brown hair framed her face and tumbled over her shoulders. Her eyes were dark upon her pale face.

"Morgan said I'd find ye up here," she greeted him softly, halting a few feet away. "Am I intruding?"

He shook his head. "Ye never intrude."

Connor reached for her, drawing her into the circle of his arms. He buried his face in her hair, breathing the scent of rosemary in deeply. Just the feel of her eased his tension and the guilt that had dug its claws into him.

Drawing back from his embrace, Keira angled her face up, her gaze spearing his. "Ye are sad," she murmured. "I see it in yer eyes."

His mouth quirked. "Aye ... Domhnall doesn't deserve my grief ... especially after what he did. But I find myself remembering the years when he wasn't so bitter. Before his wife died. He was a different man then."

Her gaze shadowed, and then she leaned into him once more, into the hollow of his shoulder, as they both turned their attention to the smoke column.

"I can't help feel responsible for all of this, Connor," she said finally, her voice subdued. "Ye wouldn't have fallen out with yer uncle if ye hadn't brought me back here."

"No," he admitted, his tone turning rueful "but I'd be miserable ... and in time I'd have become a bitter man like him." He tightened his clasp on her, welcoming the warmth of her strong, lush body against his. "I knew I couldn't bear to be parted from ye ... even if it took me a while to admit it to myself."

"I think yer uncle knew what was happening," she replied after a brief pause. "That was why he was so harsh with me ... he knew ye would eventually soften."

"He'd planned to challenge me for a while," Connor agreed. "I saw it in his eyes sometimes. He'd been biding his time."

"So, he wanted to be chieftain?"

"Aye ... taking orders from his nephew chafed him from the first. The situation with ye gave him the chance he'd been awaiting."

Her arms, which were now wrapped around his torso, tightened. "Speaking of troublesome individuals ... ye don't think Niel is going to cause ye any problems?"

Connor's brow furrowed. He'd left his friend breaking his fast with Morgan in the solar before coming up onto the walls alone.

"He might," Connor admitted. His belly tightened as he revealed this to Keira. He didn't want to worry her, but he didn't want there to be any secrets between them either. He'd always found it easy to confide in this woman, right from the beginning. It was exhausting keeping his inner-most thoughts and fears to himself; with Keira, he could speak plainly. "But I think he will leave things be for the moment."

Connor paused then, his throat thickening. "It's strange how things work out in the end," he said softly. "But meeting ye has changed me for the better. When we met, grief and a sense of unworthiness dogged my steps. I used to feel as if I would remain forever in my father's shadow ... but thanks to ye, I'm the leader I need to be."

His wife drew back then, taking his hands in hers and squeezing gently. She tipped her head back, lifting her chin to meet his eye. "Whatever may come in the future, know that I will always be at yer side, Connor." Her voice was soft, yet there was steel just beneath. Life had forged this woman, made her stronger than anyone he'd ever met.

She'd weathered much. Rhianna Ross had used her, exploited Keira's loneliness and yearning for a family of her own, to gain her own freedom. He wondered idly, where the woman who should have been his wife was now. Rhianna Ross was reputed to be a great beauty, yet Keira would always outshine any woman in his eyes.

She had something, a sensuality and strength, that had drawn him from the first.

This ordeal could have destroyed a weaker soul, yet the woman who stared up into his eyes was as tough as the wild lands that bred her. And soon, she would bear him a child.

Warmth spread over Connor, and a smile curved his lips, chasing away the guilt and sorrow that had cast a deep shadow over him this morning. "Aye, love," he murmured. He stepped to one side and slung a protective arm over her shoulders, steering her back to the stairs. He was done brooding. "Whatever may come, we shall face it together."

EPILOGUE

DOOM-CROW

Five months later ...

"WE SHOULD BE getting back." Keira glanced out across the sea, frowning. When she and Jaimee had set off on their walk along the cliff path toward the village of Swordly, the sky had been clear, save for a few fluffy white clouds scudding across the horizon.

Now though, the brisk sea-breeze had picked up, causing Keira to pull her woolen cloak close, and dark clouds were moving in from the north-east.

Jaimee halted, her gaze following Keira's. "Aye," she murmured. "It looks like we'll be cutting our walk short." Disappointment laced her voice. Jaimee wasn't happy unless she took a long walk every day. Most mornings, Keira liked to join her. Keira's belly was swelling noticeably now; she was around three moons away from giving birth. She found that the walks eased the discomfort that the weight of the growing bairn brought.

Not only that, but she and Jaimee never ran out of things to chat about on their walks.

"Come on." Jaimee pushed her unruly hair out of her eyes and swiveled around. "Connor will have my guts if we return looking like drowned rats." Her gaze flicked to Keira's belly. "We don't want ye getting a chill."

Keira brushed away her sister-by-marriage's concern with a wave of her hand and a smile. Pulling her cloak tighter still as another gust buffeted them, she turned, and together they set off south once more. Despite the approaching rain clouds, it was still a lovely morning to be outdoors.

Spring was indeed upon them.

The winter had been long and bitter. Even though she was the Lady of Farr, Keira hadn't escaped the biting chill. The cold and damp this year had been relentless, and Farr Castle's glowing hearths hadn't been able to keep it at bay. For weeks on end, Keira endured aching, numb fingers and toes. Itchy chilblains had risen upon her toes and had only just subsided with the warmer weather.

Crocuses and snowdrops lined the cliff-top path, and as they neared Farr village, Keira spied lambs running after their mothers on the green hills east of the castle. A smile curved her lips at the sight.

Spring was a time of new life, new possibilities. Her hand went to her belly then, and she felt a small yet determined kick against her palm. Keira's smile widened. The bairn would be a summer child; it was due in July.

They passed through the gates and entered the landward bailey, to find a crowd of warriors gathered around two men at sword practice. Rough voices and booming male laughter echoed off the stone ramparts, and as the crowd parted, Keira saw that the two men sparring were her husband and brother-by-marriage.

Not for the first time, she was struck by how similar the two men were physically. However, Connor was the bigger and broader of the two, his long blond hair glinting gold in what remained of the morning sun. Lithe and long-limbed, Morgan nimbly side-stepped his brother's strike and lunged forward with an attack of his own, a grin flowering across his face. Morgan's shoulder-length dark-blond hair curled damply with sweat this morning.

Both men were shirtless.

Keira stopped and watched the fight unfold. It was a fine sight indeed. As the parrying continued, the 'click-clack' of wooden swords clashing ringing through the air, she had eyes only for her husband.

The past weeks had been magical. Even the gnawing cold hadn't been able to shadow her happiness. The initial connection that she and Connor had forged in those early days returned stronger than ever.

Sometimes Keira felt so happy that her chest ached from the force of it.

The 'clip-clop' of hooves behind her drew Keira's attention then. Dragging her gaze from her husband, she turned to see Niel Mackay ride into the bailey, a party of warriors behind him.

Tensing, Keira's light-hearted mood faded.

This man was a doom-crow. His presence at Farr was an unsettling one. He'd visited a couple of times since Connor had slain Domhnall, and each time, he'd attempted to rally Connor's support for an early spring raid on the Gunns.

Connor had refused, citing his wife's pregnancy and poor weather as excuses. Niel hadn't been pleased, yet he'd grudgingly accepted. However, just a week earlier, they'd received word that Niel had eventually led his own bloody raid into Gunn lands.

Connor had been in a dark mood for days afterward. "Idiot," he'd muttered. "Does he want to bring the king's wrath down upon us?"

Observing Niel Mackay's arrogant face, Keira clenched her jaw. No doubt, the man was back to try and convince Connor to ride out on another raid with him.

Connor and Morgan halted their sparring. Pulling on a lèine and pushing his sweat-damp hair back from his face, Connor walked across to meet the clan-chief's son.

Niel swung down from his courser and strode to Connor, clasping arms with him.

"This is a surprise," Connor greeted him. His voice and expression were pleasant, although Keira picked up the guarded edge to him. "I thought we were going hawking *next* week?"

Niel's handsome features tightened, his blue gaze shadowing. "Aye, well ... things have changed. There won't be any hawking or hunting till we get back from Inverness."

Connor's brow furrowed. "Inverness?"

Niel's mouth pursed. "King James has called a council of the northern clans. I've just come from Balnakeil broch ... Robert Mackay will be one of many meeting us there."

A pause followed. Behind Connor, Morgan inclined his head. "*Us?*"

"Aye," Niel's gaze flicked to Morgan. "Da wants all his chieftains ... and their nearest kin ... present for the council."

"When is it?" Connor asked.

"A week from now," Niel replied. "I'm here to fetch ye."

Silence followed this news. Keira let out the breath she hadn't even realized she'd been holding. She didn't like the sound of this council, although Connor had warned her that such a meeting was coming. The king had cautioned the chiefs of the northern Highlands to stop their feuding, but none of them heeded him.

Moments passed, and then Connor nodded. "Very well ... we will make preparations to leave as soon as possible."

Niel smiled in response, although his sharp blue eyes didn't share the expression. Like Connor, he knew what this council meant. The king was vexed. Niel likely wanted safety in numbers.

"Go on inside," Connor waved to the stairs behind him. "Ye look like a man who could do with a tankard ... or two ... of ale."

Niel huffed a laugh. "Aye, will ye be joining me?"

Connor nodded. "Morgan will take ye up now ... I'll be there shortly."

Connor's gaze shifted to Keira then, and for the first time since entering the bailey, Niel looked at her as well. His attention flicked to her swollen belly, before an enigmatic smile lifted his mouth at the corners. "Ye are looking well, Lady Mackay."

Lady Mackay.

It was the first time Niel had addressed her so. Had he gotten used to the idea that one of his father's chieftains had wed a Gunn? Perhaps, with the king's council looming, he realized holding on to such things were pointless.

Keira inclined her head before favoring him with a nod. "Niel."

The clan-chief's men led the horses off to the stables, while some of Connor's men joined them. Morgan clapped Niel on the back and accompanied him toward the stairs. "Come on ... I could do with an ale myself. Ye can tell me what the king is planning."

"If I had any idea, I'd tell ye," Niel replied, a bitter edge to his voice now. "But Da doesn't share such details with me."

Watching Niel and Morgan go, Keira wondered at the relationship between the clan-chief and his son. At Samhuinn, she'd thought them as thick as thieves, yet Niel's comment now made her wonder if that wasn't the case.

Moments later, Keira and Connor stood alone in the landward bailey.

Spots of rain pattered the cobblestones. The bad weather she'd seen rolling in from the sea was almost upon them.

However, Connor paid it no mind. Instead, his gaze held hers as he took Keira's hands. "Ye know this is a trip I must make?"

She gave his hands an answering squeeze. She'd been worried he'd insist she remain at Farr Castle, and she could see now that he indeed intended to leave her behind. "Connor, I want to come with ye."

"But shouldn't ye begin yer lying-in around now?"

Keira snorted. "I'm with bairn ... not an invalid," she replied. "Cullodina assures me that bed-rest a month out from birth should be sufficient ... we have plenty of time yet." Her fingers tightened further around his. "I want to come with ye, Connor."

He heaved a sigh, and she realized he was weakening. Like her, he didn't want to be parted. "I don't want ye riding ... we shall bring a wagon for ye."

"Aye, I am happy to travel by wagon," she replied, "as long as I can accompany ye."

Their gazes fused, and then a moment later, Connor favored her with a soft smile that made Keira's breathing quicken. He still had no idea just how devastating his smiles could be. Connor Mackay's smiles could be kind, boyish, sensual, or wicked. And she'd enjoyed learning the nuances of them over the past few months.

"Ye aren't worried that there will be Gunns at the council then?" he asked, reaching out and pushing back a lock of hair that had escaped her braid and blown over her face. "News of our union will have spread throughout the Highlands by now."

Keira shook her head, smiling. "I've weathered the worst of it," she replied. "George Gunn will be too busy defending himself before the king to worry about the likes of me."

Connor laughed at that, just as a squall hit the bailey. Biting needles of rain pelted them. Placing a protective arm about Keira's shoulders, he led her up the steps, flanked by high crenellations that kept off the worst of the rain, and into the entrance hall beyond.

Inside the hall, they shook off their damp cloaks and turned to each other once more. "I will be happy to have ye with me, Keira." Connor drew her to him then, his arms encircling her thickened waist. "I must admit, I'm loath to be away from ye."

"I'm pleased to hear that, husband." She smiled up at him, losing herself in the intense depths of his green eyes. Connor's love, his protection, cloaked her. For a few moments, she forgot the rain, forgot the king's council in Inverness.

All was well, and all would continue to be—as long as they were together.

FROM THE AUTHOR

I hope you found this story as fun to read as I did to write!

This my first 'mistaken identity' or 'deception' story— and I loved it. I wanted a few twists on the theme, which often has the hero as the deceiver, rather than the heroine. I also wanted this to be a very character-driven story with a hero and heroine with lots of complexity and depth.

I had to give Connor and Keira their happy ending. These two were truly made for each other!

Get ready for Morgan and Maggie's passionate story. Up next!

Jayne x

HISTORICAL NOTES

Although HIGHLANDER DECEIVED is in many ways a highly character-driven, intimate story, as with all my novels, I base it around real historical figures and events.

The story starts in 1426, the year of the Battle of Harpsdale, where Connor loses his father. This was a Scottish clan battle fought at Achardale, about 8 miles (13 km) south of Thurso in the Highlands. The Clan Mackay had invaded Caithness from the west, and Harpsdale was where the local Clan Gunn chose to make a stand. Despite 'great slaughter' on both sides, the battle appears to have been inconclusive.

King James's council in Inverness did take place in 1427—but we are getting ahead of ourselves! More about that in Book 2!

Angus-Dow Mackay and his son, Niel, were real historical figures, as is George Gunn, the Gunn clan-chief. The clan battles in this period were becoming a serious problem for Scotland—as such, I thought it would be an exciting period to set a series in.

As for the locations mentioned in the novel, all of them (except for Camster broch) are real. Castle Varrich was the seat of the Mackays, and likely the home of Angus Mackay, whereas the Mackays of Farr did reside at Farr Castle (also known as Borve Castle). These days, only the ruined shell of Farr Castle remains. With a stunning position overlooking the sea, the castle was used in ancient times as an outpost for raiding other clans. It is said that a Norseman called Torquil may have built the castle.

The ruins of Farr Castle sit upon a precipitous promontory, joined to the mainland by a narrow neck.

There are remains of what would have been a high rampart with flanking ditches. The site could also be approached from the north-east by sea. Only footings and the courtyard wall remain, but the outline of a range of rectangular buildings, with thick stone walls, sits on the western end of the site. The promontory slopes down toward the seaward end, where there are circular and rectangular hollows, probably marking the site of the well and more foundations.

Another landmark mentioned in the novel are the 'Grey Cairns of Camster'. These are two of the oldest stone monuments in Scotland—a pair of Neolithic tombs originally built more than 5,000 years ago. The monument consists of a long cairn and a round cairn. The long cairn has two internal chambers and the round cairn a single chamber with three compartments. The cairns are hauntingly sited on a windswept moor, in the middle of the famous Caithness 'Flow Country'. This lonely location has likely aided the cairns' preservation, protecting them from the ravages of modern farming.

I hope you have enjoyed my notes, I truly enjoyed researching the history and landscape of this wild and beautiful corner of Scotland.

CHARACTER GLOSSARY

The Mackay clan
Angus-Dow Mackay (clan-chief)
Estelle Mackay (Mackay clan-chief's wife)
Niel Mackay (Mackay clan-chief's son)
Rory Mackay (former chieftain of Farr—deceased. Wed to Rose Mackay, also deceased)
Connor Mackay (current chieftain of Farr)
Morgan Mackay (Connor's brother)
Jaimee Mackay (Connor's sister)
Kennan Mackay (Connor, Morgan, and Jaimee's cousin)
Cait Mackay (Kennan's wife)
Domhnall Mackay (Connor's uncle)
Chrissa (servant at Farr Castle)

The Gunn clan
Maddoc Gunn (sheep farmer and wool merchant)
Moira Gunn (Maddoc's wife)
Keira Gunn (the youngest of Maddoc and Morag's six daughters)
George Gunn (clan-chief)
Alexander Gunn (Gunn clan-chief's eldest son)

The Ross clan
Graeme Ross (Ross chieftain)
Rhianna Ross (Graeme Ross's niece—eloped with a warrior named Callum)
Maggie Ross (Rhianna's elder sister—widowed)

Other characters
Mother Jean (Prioress of Iona nunnery)
Father Lachlan (chaplain at Farr Castle)
Cullodina (healer at Farr Castle)

ABOUT THE AUTHOR

Award-winning author Jayne Castel writes epic
Historical and Fantasy Romance. Her vibrant characters,
richly researched historical settings and action-packed
adventure romance transport readers to forgotten times
and imaginary worlds.

Jayne is the author of the Amazon bestselling BRIDES
OF SKYE series—a Medieval Scottish Romance trilogy
about three strong-willed sisters and the men who love
them. An exciting new series about three lost Roman
centurions, THE IMMORTAL HIGHLAND
CENTURIONS, is now available as well. In love with all
things Scottish, Jayne also writes romances set in Dark
Ages Scotland ... sexy Pict warriors anyone?

When she's not writing, Jayne is reading (and re-
reading) her favorite authors, cooking Italian feasts, and
taking her dog, Juno, for walks. She lives in New
Zealand's beautiful South Island.

Connect with Jayne online:
www.jaynecastel.com
Email: contact@jaynecastel.com

CPSIA information can be obtained
at www.ICGtesting.com
Printed in the USA
BVHW030856240821
615123BV00001B/36